THE
TEST

NOVEL BY

ROBERT CALLIS

THE TEST

iUniverse books may be ordered through booksellers or by contacting:

iUniverse
1663 Liberty Drive
Bloomington, IN 47403
www.iuniverse.com
844-349-9409

Because of the dynamic nature of the Internet, any web addresses or links contained in this book may have changed since publication and may no longer be valid. The views expressed in this work are solely those of the author and do not necessarily reflect the views of the publisher, and the publisher hereby disclaims any responsibility for them.

Any people depicted in stock imagery provided by Getty Images are models, and such images are being used for illustrative purposes only. Certain stock imagery © Getty Images.

ISBN: 978-1-6632-6681-1 (sc)
ISBN: 978-1-6632-6682-8 (e)

Library of Congress Control Number: 2024919031

Print information available on the last page.

iUniverse rev. date: 09/11/2024

DEDICATION

This book is dedicated to my wife, Nancy Lee Callis.

    She passed away on April 16, 2024.

    She was my inspiration to write and my biggest supporter.
She carefully proofread everything I wrote. She was my rock.

    I will miss her every day for the rest of my life.

FORWARD

As a father of three dramatically different sons, I have often wondered why they are so different and what parts of me they could possibly have hidden inside of them. This is a story of a man with three very different sons and his attempt to understand them.

CHAPTER ONE

Every morning since he graduated from law school at the University of Wyoming, the man had stopped for coffee at the Pioneer Café in Kemmerer, Wyoming. It was his birthplace, his current home, and the location of his law office. He shared his law office with his father, who had brought him in as a junior partner when he graduated from law school and passed the Wyoming Bar Exam.

Woodly "Woody" Harrison, drove his Ford pickup truck around Triangle Park that made up the heart of the small town of Kemmerer. He parked about a block away from the Pioneer Café and shut off the engine. He stepped out onto the paved road and after closing the driver's door to the truck, he stood still for a moment. He found himself unconsciously sweeping his surroundings with his eyes looking for possible threats. Old habits were hard to break, and this was one habit he planned to retain until the day he died.

He sniffed the air. The smell of coal burning was poignant in the air on this early spring morning in 1965. That was not unusual for a town that was founded in the late 1800's because of the vast deposits of soft coal that made up the substructure of the land he stood on. Kemmerer had been established as a coal mining town, and it still was one.

Oil and natural gas deposits had been discovered near where he stood and yet, most of it was undeveloped prairie.

Kemmerer was a high plains desert town. Nearly two thousand five hundred residents lived at an altitude of about seven thousand feet above sea level and the mainstays of the town had been coal mining and ranching since it was founded. Ranching consisted of either cattle or sheep.

Since Woody had graduated from law school at the University of Wyoming back in 1946, the only economic change had been the building of the coal fired power plant just outside of the city limits by Pacific Power.

Woody looked down at his watch. It was almost six o'clock on this cool spring morning. He was pretty sure his best friend Big Dave Olson was already in their favorite booth in the Pioneer Café, joshing with the waitress. They had been meeting for coffee every morning since Woody had returned to Kemmerer to work for his father in the spring of 1946.

Things had changed since then. Now he was an equal partner with his father in the law firm, and he was responsible for most of the new business the office generated. His father still had his old clients, but Woody had been active with newcomers to Kemmerer, and with the sons and daughters of the old clients of his father.

Thinking of his friend Big Dave caused Woody to flash back to the summer of 1941 and the events that had made the two young men friends for life. A shiver ran down Woody's back as he remembered that night on the slope of Commissary Ridge. The thought passed, and he stepped up onto the sidewalk and headed for the front door of the café.

As he entered the moist warmth of the café, Woody paused and scanned the room. About half the chairs and stools were occupied by working cowboys, sheepmen, and miners. Small traces of cigarette and cigar smoke floated through the air.

He turned and saw his friend Big Dave at their favorite booth. Big Dave was jawing with the waitress and a steaming hot cup of coffee was cradled in one of his massive hands. Big Dave was a throwback to the age of the Vikings. His blonde hair and bright penetrating blue eyes contrasted with his six-foot four-inch frame that contained two hundred fifty pounds of pure muscle. He was clean shaven and dressed in cowboy boots, faded jeans, and a worn denim shirt. A cream-colored Stetson cowboy hat crowned his head.

Woody was a complete contrast. He was short and chubby with a moustache and bushy eyebrows. Big Dave often joked that Woody was the spitting image of Teddy Roosevelt, former president of the United States.

Woody reached the booth and slid into the opposite side from Big Dave.

"Well, hells bells," said Big Dave. "Look what the damned cat drug in."

"Good mornin' to you too, David," responded Woody.

"David!" exclaimed Big Dave. "God damn it. Whenever you call me that I know it's sure as hell gonna cost me some money or some time and effort. What the hell is it this time?" he asked.

Before Woody could respond, the waitress, a lady in her forties with a face full of hard-earned wrinkles, had appeared at the table and slid a full cup of hot black coffee in front of the young attorney. Then she looked at the two men and spoke in a voice that reeked of a life of too many cigarettes. "What'll it be, gents?" she asked.

Big Dave and Woody both ordered breakfast from memory. The waitress had offered no menu, but neither of the two men needed one. Twenty years of practice meant they had memorized the menu, and their orders seldom changed. If one of them ordered something different than normal, they invited a load of loud criticism from the other.

The waitress quickly departed, and both men almost simultaneously raised their coffee cups to their mouths and took a long sip.

"How's the wife and kids?" asked Woody after he set his coffee cup down.

Big Dave had gotten married when he was just twenty-one in 1944. He and his wife Carol had two sons and two daughters. The sons, Thor, and Mike were eighteen and seventeen, respectively. Thor worked for his dad on their sheep ranch and Mike was about to graduate from high school. He would likely join his brother in the sheep operation.

"Carol is just as mean as ever, "said a smiling Big Dave. "She's always on me about something I bin doin' wrong."

"If that's what she's focused on, she's gotta be one busy woman," retorted Woody with a grin on his face. "How's the sheep business these days?"

That was all it took to get Big Dave riled up and pontificating about crooked big government, bad weather, the Bureau of Land Management, or Mismanagement as he referred to it.

Their breakfast finished, the two men paid their bills, left a respectable, but not too big a tip for the waitress and headed out of the restaurant. After they cleared the front door, they shook hands and headed for their vehicles.

Woody climbed into his pickup truck and started the engine. Before putting the truck in gear, he watched as Big Dave got ambushed on his way to his truck by some old timer. The old man was no doubt looking for work. Woody knew Dave was sympathetic, but he had two large sons to help him on the big sheep ranch. He was still talking to the old timer when Woody drove past them on the way to the law office.

CHAPTER TWO

Woody pulled into the small parking lot behind the law office he shared with his father. As he exited the truck, he grabbed his ever-present battered leather briefcase and headed across the rough stone lot for the back door to the law office. He glanced at his wristwatch. It was five minutes past seven in the morning. He knew his dad would show up at seven thirty right on the dot.

He unlocked the door, entered the office, and flicked on the light switches, causing the hallway to fill with bright light. He paused to check the thermostat. Satisfied, it was unchanged from when he had closed the office the night before, he entered his office and flicked on the lights. He took off his suitcoat and hung it on a wooden peg on the wall. Then he set his briefcase on the top of his old wooden desk and slipped onto his comfortable leather chair. The chair was considered an extravagance by his father, but Woody had decided he wanted a comfortable chair in which to sit while at work. He spent too damn much time in that chair, and he appreciated his choice every time he sat in it.

Once seated, he rolled his chair over to the nearest three-drawer wooden file cabinet and inserted a key in the lock. He replaced the key in his pocket and pulled the drawer open. He reached inside and pulled out five thick file folders. All five were for BLM leases for rancher clients, including one for Big Dave. The applications for renewal of the leases had to be filed by the end of July for the next year, and Woody liked to get them over and done with early. He was halfway through the first file for Wesley Jordan when he heard the back door slam shut. Minutes later his father, a man who was fifty-nine years old, but looked like he was pushing seventy, appeared in his office doorway. Benjamin Harrison was an older physical copy of his son except he was completely bald, and he had no mustache. He had tried for years, but every effort to grow a mustache had turned into crop failure.

"Gettin' an early start?" he asked.

"Workin' these damn sheep land leases," replied his son. "I swear the BLM makes these things longer every year."

"Job security for them," replied his father with a half grin on his face.

"Wouldn't need no BLM if them ranchers had filed on multiple land claims back when they homesteaded this valley," replied Woody.

"Like today, they was too dumb then, and they ain't improved much," replied his father. With that, the old lawyer turned on his heel, and disappeared down the hall to his spacious office.

Woody returned to his files and used a red pencil to make notations on the documents as he read them. He was working on the fourth lease when there was a knock on the door frame and his father's legal secretary Daphne was standing there with a handful of envelopes.

Daphne had been the legal secretary for his father's firm ever since Woody was old enough to remember. She had to be older than dirt, but she was damn good at what she did.

"Mail just arrived," she said. She stepped inside and placed a handful of envelopes on the side of Woody's desk. Her mission complete, she retreated out the door and disappeared down the hall in the direction of his father's office.

Woody used the mail as an excuse to take a break from his file work. He slid the small pile of envelopes in front of him and began to sort through them. There were seven envelopes. Five of them were sales pitches for law books, referrals, and consulting. He tossed all five into the nearby waste basket. One was a bill for his membership in the Wyoming Bar Association. The last envelope was of fine expensive paper that almost felt like linen. The return address was for the most prestigious law firm in Salt Lake City. He recognized the name as one of the top attorneys in Utah. Woody had run into him at the last Wyoming Bar Association convention in Cheyenne. The man, Nate Chandler, had been one of the keynote speakers at the convention and Woody had been introduced to him by his father at a social hour after Chandler's address to the convention.

Nate Chandler was the top probate attorney in the state of Utah and one of the best in the Rocky Mountain states. Woody looked at the envelope and turned it over in his hand as if he were searching for some reason Chandler would be sending mail to a nobody young attorney like him.

Woody took out his pocketknife and carefully slit the top of the sealed envelope. He replaced the knife in his pocket and slipped the one-page letter from the envelope. He unfolded it and an expensive-looking business card fell out onto the desktop. He ignored the card and began to read the letter.

Dear Mr. Harrison:

I hope this day finds you well. I remember you from last year when I spoke at the Wyoming Bar Association Convention in Cheyenne, Wyoming. I have known your father for years and have great respect for him. I contacted him on a very personal estate matter by telephone and he suggested you would be the best lawyer in Lincoln County, Wyoming for the task I have been presented with.

I have a very wealthy client who has a very unusual request. Part of his request is for absolute secrecy and confidentiality. In keeping with his wishes, I would like to establish a time and date when we could meet in Kemmerer so I could explain his request and your possible part in it. I assure you confidentiality on my part as well.

If this offer is something you would wish to undertake, please contact me at the telephone number on the business card I have enclosed.

Respectfully,
Nate Chandler

Woody reread the letter two times before he finally put it down on his desk. Then he rose from his chair and headed out the door of his office and down the hall. When he reached his father's office, he knocked on the door frame and stepped inside.

His father's office was three times the size of Woody's small cubicle. The office was paneled in walnut and his father's desk was polished pine. The desk was devoid of any paperwork, other than a single file folder. His father looked up at his son's intrusion into his office with a look of expectation, not puzzlement.

"I assume you got a letter from Nate Chandler," said his father with a smile on his face.

"I did," answered Woody. "What's this all about?"

"I don't know any details," replied his father. "I only know he needs help, and I think you are better equipped to provide that than I am."

"Better equipped to do what?" asked a perplexed Woody.

"He needs help finding a special man for a special job here in Lincoln County, and you have a better handle on the ranchers around here than I do," replied his father.

"So, what do I do?" asked Woody.

"Give the man a call. Be polite. And listen to what he has to say," said his father.

"Yes, sir," said Woody.

He turned and retreated to his office. He shut the door on his way in and took a seat at his desk. He picked up the expensive-looking business card and then reached for the telephone on his desk.

CHAPTER THREE

The following morning Woody arrived at the café almost half an hour early. When he took a seat at his usual table, the old before her time waitress appeared with an empty coffee mug and a pot of coffee. She set the mug down and poured it full of hot black liquid.

"Your alarm clock broke?" she asked with a slight smirk on her face.

"My alarm clock?" asked a puzzled Woody.

"You're half an hour early. Even Big Dave ain't here yet," she replied.

"Oh that," said Woody. "Got a big day and needed a head start," he responded.

The waitress smirked and disappeared down the aisle in the direction of the kitchen.

Woody sipped his hot coffee. Lots of things had changed in the past few years but thank God the café still made a damn good cup of coffee. A man's gotta have some things to depend on. He looked up and glanced at the interior of the café. This early in the morning, the place was half full. The empty tables and chairs looked as worn out and tired as they probably were after many years of use and abuse.

While he sipped hot coffee, Woody thought back over his recent phone conversation with the renowned attorney Nate Chandler.

When he called Chandler, the man had been tight lipped about why he needed an attorney in Kemmerer. He managed to evade or ignore most of Woody's questions. His response was that the legal ramifications of the proposal were "delicate." Woody had no idea what a famous Salt Lake attorney thought was delicate, but things that fell in that category in Kemmerer, Wyoming, were few and far between.

"What the hell? Did you fall asleep here in the café last night?" bellowed out Big Dave as he slid into the chair opposite Woody.

Woody grinned sheepishly. Once again, he had been taken by surprise by Big Dave. He was always amazed how light on his feet and how silently the man moved for someone who was six foot four and weighed in a tad above or below two hundred and forty pound in his stocking feet.

"Nope. I just got an early start today," replied Woody.

"Last time you got an early start is when old man Kuster caught you and his daughter rolling around in his hayloft," said Big Dave with a wide grin on his face.

"Shit," said Woody. "I thought you had finally forgotten all about that unfortunate incident."

"Partner, I ain't never gonna forget that particular incident," said Big Dave. "And you're gonna be hearin' about that till the day you die. I'd have given one hundred dollars cash money to have been there and seen that in person."

"Well, you weren't, thank God," said Woody. "I was damn lucky to get out of there without a load of buckshot in my ass. That old bastard actually shot at me with his shotgun."

"He didn't hit you 'cause he just meant to scare you off," said Big Dave. "He's had enough problems with judges and courtrooms to know better."

Woody took another drink of his coffee and then started studying the top of the old scarred wooden table between the two friends.

"Go ahead and spit it out," said Big Dave.

"Spit what out?" asked Woody.

"Whatever the hell has you so befuddled that you got here half an hour before me for the first time I can ever remember," said Big Dave.

"How did you know when I got here?" demanded Woody.

"The waitress told me when I walked in the door. Hells bells, Woody, she was just as shocked as I am," said Big Dave.

"Nosy bitch," muttered Woody.

"Nope. She's just bein' observant, and she's also concerned and lookin' out for you. She don't want to be losin' a good customer. Especially one who tips as good as you do," said a smiling Big Dave.

"You're probably right," responded Woody.

"Hell, I'm damn near always right," snorted Big Dave.

Woody looked up at Big Dave. Then both men broke up in laughter.

Big Dave had an astonishingly long record of being right on almost everything the two men had been involved in. Woody knew it. And Big Dave damn well knew it.

Big Dave took a long drink of coffee, set his cup down and placed both elbows on the table as he leaned forward.

"So, what the hell is goin' on that's got you so all fired out of sorts, Mr. attorney at law?" asked Big Dave.

"I got a letter a few days ago," said Woody.

"Hell, I get letters all the damn time," snorted Big Dave.

"But this letter was from a big-time attorney in Salt Lake," said Woody.

"Who?" asked Big Dave.

"Nate Chandler, of Chandler and Chandler," replied Woody.

"What the hell does a big-time attorney like Nate Chandler want with a no- account country lawyer like you?" asked Big Dave. "He ain't suing you, is he?"

"No, no, he's not suing me," replied Woody. "Just the opposite. He wants to hire me."

"Hire you? Hire you for what?" asked a surprised Big Dave.

"He wouldn't really say," said Woody. "I tried to get it out of him, but he refused to say anything over the telephone. He's driving up from Salt Lake to meet me at the law office at one o'clock today."

"Does your old man know about this?" asked Big Dave.

"He was contacted by Chandler, and Dad referred him to me. He told Chandler I was better connected to the local ranchers than he was," said Woody.

"Local ranchers? What the hell does Chandler have to do with any of the local ranchers around Kemmerer?" asked a puzzled looking Big Dave. "There ain't no big-time ranchers in all of Lincoln County that I know of."

"I wish I knew," replied Woody.

"You got no idea what this Chandler fella wants?" asked Big Dave.

"Not a clue," replied Woody.

Big Dave picked up his cup and took another long drink of coffee. He set the cup back on the old table and was quiet for a moment as he seemed to be running things over in his mind.

"Seems to me if it has to do with local ranchers that would likely include me," said Big Dave.

"Of course it would," replied Woody. "I have no idea why he needs me to negotiate with a local rancher, especially when it isn't a particular rancher."

"He didn't mention no names?" asked Big Dave.

"He did not. I doubt he even knows who any of the local boys are," said a puzzled looking Woody.

Big Dave took another drink of coffee. He set his cup down and looked directly at Woody.

"When this Chandler guy leaves, you give me a call at the ranch. I'll come in, and we'll have a drink while you explain what the hell you've gotten yourself into this time," said Big Dave. "Then we'll try to figure out a way to keep your lawyer ass out of trouble."

"Works for me," said Woody.

Big Dave waved down the waitress. "We'll have the usual for breakfast," he told her. "Eat hearty, Woodrow. Sounds like you're gonna need to be at full strength when this big city lawyer shows up this afternoon."

The waitress arrived with breakfast, and both men observed the first rule of western dining. No talking when hungry men are eating. When they finished, Woody paid the bill and left a good tip, and the two friends headed out the front door of the café.

They shook hands.

"Don't forget to call me," said Big Dave.

"Fat chance I'll forget to do that," replied Woody.

Woody headed for his truck and the office.

Big Dave got in his pickup truck and headed back to the ranch.

Seconds later, the sidewalk was silent again.

CHAPTER FOUR

Woody kept himself busy for the rest of the morning, but he wasn't sure what he actually accomplished. He'd be working on a document and then find himself wondering what the hell this big-time lawyer wanted done in Lincoln County that required a lawyer who knew all the local ranchers.

He tried coming up with ideas, but none of them made any sense unless there was something illegal involved, or someone was looking to buy ranch land in the Ham's Fork Valley. But that made no sense. All a person had to do was hire one of the two real estate brokers in town and let them do all the leg work. They knew the ranchers as well as he did. He tried to come up with some scenario where he had a special talent, and he still came up empty.

Disgusted with himself, he pulled out a working file for one of the firm's customers. He needed to draft a new will for a local rancher and make the changes the man had indicated in his father's notes.

Woody was almost finished with the new draft of the will when his father stepped into his office.

"What's up?' asked Woody apprehensively.

"Nothing special," replied his father. "Just thought I check and see if you were ready for our special guest from Salt Lake."

"Since I got no idea what in the hell he wants with someone like me, I have to tell you I am plumb clueless," replied Woody.

"Maybe in this case, that's the best idea you can have for getting ready for a man like Nate Chandler," said his father. "You had any lunch?"

"I ain't in no mood for food," replied Woody. "I got a feelin' I'm better off talking to this Chandler feller on an empty stomach."

His father laughed. "Maybe you're right. Let me know how it goes." With that, his father turned and slipped out of Woody's small office. Woody turned back to the will he was working on.

When he had finished his first draft, he laid the will draft on his desk. He had learned long ago it was better to wait a bit before reading a draft after he had just finished it. He was more likely to find errors or things that needed to be revised. He had no idea why that was. He supposed he saw on paper what he thought he had put there rather than what had actually happened.

He picked up another file and opened it on his desk. He had no sooner started to read the first line of the paper than there was a loud rapping on the door frame of his small office.

Woody looked up somewhat startled. There in his doorway was a man in a navy-blue suit with a starched white shirt and a bold red tie. The man was somewhere in his fifties, and he sported a bit of grey hair in his otherwise black mane. His pencil moustache remained dark black. He was a shade under six feet tall and slender. His highly polished cowboy boots probably cost more than Woody made in six months.

"Howdy," said the man. "I'm Nate Chandler. You must be Woody. Your father told me to just come on in. I hope I didn't interrupt something important. You looked pretty intense."

Woody jumped to his feet like he'd been hit with a hog shocker. He recovered and extended his hand. The two men shook hands, and Woody extended his hand to point to the wooden chair in front of his desk.

"Pleased to meet you," said an awed Woody. "Please have a seat."

"Thank you," replied Nate. "I'd actually probably be better off standing. I been sitting on my ass for the past two hours drivin' up here from Salt Lake. But my daddy always told me never pass up a chance to sit rather than stand," he said with a smile.

Chandler sat in the chair and reached into his suit coat inside pocket and produced a folded document. He did not glance at the document, and he did not open it as he set it on the top of Woody's desk.

"I'm pretty sure you are wonderin' what the hell a lawyer like me is doing in Kemmerer wantin' to talk to a young buck lawyer like you," said Chandler with a smile.

"I am," replied a nervous Woody.

"Like I told your father, I have a problem, and I need someone like you to help me out with it," said Chandler. "It goes without sayin' that what I'm about to tell you is confidential and must stay that way. No one, and that includes your father, is to know anything about what I am goin' to tell you. Is that understood?"

"Yes, sir," replied Woody as he tried to make himself relax in his chair.

Chandler got to his feet, walked over to the door to Woody's office and closed it. Then he returned to his seat.

Woody remained rooted where he sat. His mouth felt dry, and he wished he had a glass of water, but he didn't.

"I have a client with a problem and a plan. He needs help with the plan, and that's why I'm here today. Your father thinks you're the man who can help me," said Chandler.

"I understand," said Woody.

"I need to tell you a story about the client, so you understand why I'm here today," said Chandler. "Then we'll discuss your role in the plan. Is that clear?"

"Yes sir," replied Woody.

"My client shall remain nameless to you at all times. Is that clear?" asked Chandler.

"Yes, sir," responded Woody.

"All right then," said Chandler. "My client is well educated with a background in chemistry, married early in life and had three sons. The sons are each one year apart in age. When the oldest son was seven, the wife divorced my client. My client left the area and found employment in the West and then went on to work for a major company listed on the New York stock exchange. He invented several medical products for his employer. He did not share in the success of those products in the marketplace, and then he resigned from the company and began a new company with him as the sole owner. He was able to obtain financial backing due to his reputation and then was able to create more new medical products that he had patented in his own name. The new medical products were extremely successful, and my client became a very rich man," he said.

"Do you have any questions so far?" asked Chandler he noted that Woody was furiously taking notes on a legal pad.

"No, sir," replied Woody, his nerves now under control and his interest in Chandler's story growing.

"Well then, let me continue," said Chandler. "My client is now a rich man. He was divorced when his sons were five, six and seven years of age. His ex-wife did her best to prevent him from seeing or talking to his sons. She was very successful at blocking any contact between my client and his sons. He has not seen or spoken to any of the three boys for twelve years."

Woody looked up from his note taking.

"Really. He has not seen or talked with any of his sons for twelve years?" said Woody. He thought for a moment and then spoke. "That would make the sons seventeen, eighteen and nineteen years old," he said.

"Your math is correct," replied a smiling Chandler. "The oldest son is just finishing his first year of college, and the middle son is just finishing high school."

"I gather your client is not invited to his middle son's high school graduation," said a stone-faced Woody.

"You gather correctly," replied Chandler.

"I am confused as to how I fit into this story," said Woody with a truly puzzled look on his face.

"The reason is both simple and complex," replied Chandler. "My client wants to set up a kind of test for his sons."

"A test? What kind of a test?" asked a curious Woody.

"He wants a test to find out what kind of men his sons are becoming," replied Chandler.

Woody remained silent. He was clueless about the test.

Chandler paused for a bit. He shifted in his chair and then he spoke.

"He wants to set up a test to see what kind of sons he has. He also wants to have a chance to get to know them personally and he has decided a test is the best way to do it," said Chandler.

"I don't understand," said Woody. "What kind of a test are we talking about?"

Chandler grinned and seemed to enjoy the moment before he spoke. "This is where you come in, my young friend," he said.

"My client has purchased two adjacent ranches here in Lincoln County. Ownership of the land is in a trust. His name appears nowhere where anyone can discover his ownership short of a court order," said Chandler.

"What two ranches?" asked an astonished Woody.

"The information on the ranches is contained on the papers in front of you," replied Chandler. "My client has a fairly simple plan, but one that he requires absolute secrecy about his involvement."

"I see," said Woody when he plainly did not.

"My client needs a special man to be in charge of the new ranch for this coming summer, from June through August. A short-term foreman if you will," said Chandler.

"Why?" asked Woody.

"Bear with me for a bit as I explain his plan," said Chandler. "Each of the three sons will receive a registered letter informing them of their father's demise," said Chandler.

"His demise! You mean you client is dead?" said an astonished Woody.

"No, he is absolutely alive and well. This part of the plan is a sham on his part, but is still not against the law," said Chandler. "I have researched the law and Wyoming law allows it. That is why he bought the ranches here in Lincoln County."

Woody sat in his chair stunned.

"Let me continue," said a smiling Chandler.

Woody nodded his head in ascent.

"The three boys will be invited to a reading of a special provision of my client's will in my office in Salt Lake City. They will be required to attend in person for the reading and they may be represented by legal counsel and/or their mother," said Chandler. "The reading will be of an unusual covenant in the will. The three sons will be required to work for the months of June, July, and August this summer on the ranch as ranch hands. They must finish the three months successfully. Their success will be judged and determined by the man you select to be the ranch foreman for that period of this coming summer. If they complete the three months successfully, each son to do so will receive a check for five hundred thousand dollars," said Chandler.

"What if they refuse?" asked a puzzled Woody.

"If they refuse, they will receive a check for fifteen thousand dollars at the time of the meeting in Salt Lake City in my office," said Chandler.

"What if they start but quit during the three months?" asked Woody.

"They will get a check for fifteen thousand dollars and a plane ticket home," replied Chandler.

Woody sat in his chair, running the facts he had just heard though his confused brain.

"Any questions?" asked a smiling Chandler.

"Let me make sure I understand," said Woody. "You want me to find you a man to be the foreman of a newly formed ranch in Lincoln County for a period of just three months. Who will this man report to?"

"He will report to me through you," said Chandler. "No one else."

"He gets his orders from you only?" asked Woody.

"He reports to you and the orders will come from the client," said Chandler.

"How does the client know what's going on at the ranch?" asked Woody.

"That is confidential between me and the client," replied Chandler.

"What's the foreman's compensation for the three months work?" asked Woody.

"Good question, Woody. I have included his compensation in the papers on your desk as well as your compensation for providing my client with a capable ranch foreman for three months," said Chandler. "Do you have any questions?"

"I'm sure I will, but I'm unlikely to think of them until you are halfway back to Salt Lake," said Woody.

Chandler laughed. "I don't blame you for your confusion. Just think it through. Call me with questions and find my client the best ranch foreman you can."

Chandler rose to his feet and shook hands with a still bewildered Woody. He was out the door and gone from sight while Woody was still trying to understand everything he had just heard from the most famous attorney in Utah.

CHAPTER FIVE

Woody spent the next hour carefully reading every document in the file the Salt Lake City attorney had left with him. He carefully read them. Twice. Then he got out his legal pad and began to make notes. When he was finished, he read over his notes. He had made a list of things he needed to do. First on the list was to make another list of the best candidates for the foreman's job.

He came up with five names. After writing them down, he thought about each man and their qualifications. He sighed and got to his feet. He was stiff from sitting too much and concentrating too hard. He decided to try to clear his mind. He told the secretary he was going for a walk.

"Where to?" she inquired as Woody had never gone for a walk during the five years she had been employed in the law office.

"Nowhere in particular," replied Woody as he slipped out the front door of the law office, leaving the secretary with a genuinely puzzled look on her face.

Woody paused in front of the law office. The sun was leaning to the west. The air had a taste of spring, but it was laced with the tang of a fading winter. He headed for Triangle Park and when he reached it, he did something he had never done before in his life. He found a bench in the park and took a seat. He sat there thinking. There was occasional traffic on the Triangle, but he didn't seem to notice it. Three or four folks walked by him, and all said howdy or hello. Woody just nodded his head in return. Five seconds after they had disappeared out of sight, he could not even remember their names.

Then a single thought slammed into his brain. He looked up at the sky. Then he stood and checked out his surroundings. He walked briskly back to the law office. He had a job to do and now he knew exactly what it was.

● ● ●

Big Dave entered the café about ten minutes before his usual time, expecting to be well settled and into his morning coffee before Woody showed up. He came to an abrupt halt. Seated at their table by the front window of the café was his friend Woody. Woody was wearing a suit! That gave Big Dave pause. He looked down at himself, checking to make sure he had managed to wear some clean jeans and a presentable denim shirt. Satisfied with his initial inspection, he marched over to the table and slid into the chair opposite his lawyer friend.

"What in the Sam Hill has managed to get you up so damn early?' asked a puzzled Big Dave.

Woody just grinned and raised his half full cup of hot coffee. "Better late than never," he said with a smirk.

"A bit cocky this morning, are we?" asked Big Dave. "Why do I think this has something to do with your meetin' yesterday with the big-time lawyer from Salt Lake?"

"That's a pretty good guess, cause it's right on the money," replied a smiling Woody.

"Hmmm," muttered Big Dave. "Somethin' tells me you are smiling after a meetin' with some hot shot attorney from Salt Lake City and you being so happy to see me this mornin' can't be good news for me," he said.

"I guess that all depends on what you consider good news," responded a still smiling Woody.

"That ain't hard to figure. If it's good for me and mine, then it's good news. If it ain't, then it's gotta be bad news," said Big Dave.

"Can I ask you a personal question?" asked Woody as calmly as he could manage.

"Fire away," said Big Dave. "If I don't like the question, I don't plan on answering it."

"Have you ever considered working for some other ranch outfit?" asked Woody.

"Why the hell would I do that?" asked Big Dave indignantly. "I ain't spent all these years building up a ranch, just so I could go work for somebody else. I'm my own boss and that's the way I like it."

"I'm not talking about full time," said Woody. "I'm talking about for a short period of time."

"How short?" asked Big Dave guardedly.

"Three months," said Woody. "The months of June, July, and August."

"You mean this comin' June, July, and August?" asked Big Dave.

"Yes," responded Woody.

"I ain't given it no thought 'cause I ain't had no reason to," said Big Dave. "Are you offerin' me some kind of a job this summer?"

"Yes, I am," said Woody.

"First of all, I got a job. I got a ranch to run, and it keeps me plenty damn busy. I ain't got enough hours in a day to do my own work, let alone get work done for some other yahoo," snorted Big Dave.

Woody knew Big Dave as well as anyone did. He reached down and grabbed his coffee cup and took a long drink and then carefully set the cup down on the battered tabletop. He was careful not to say a word nor even make any kind of hand gesture. He just sat there quietly. He knew Big Dave's curiosity would get the best of him. All he had to do was wait, which wasn't easy with someone like Big Dave across the table from him.

Finally, Big Dave broke the silence and spoke. "You do know I got my own ranch to run. Why in the hell do you think I might be interested in working just three months for someone else?"

Woody waited for a couple of minutes before replying. He took another drink of his coffee and set the cup down.

"This is an unusual job, and it requires an unusual person to be successful at it. Of all the ranchers I know in Lincoln County, you are the only one I believe could do this job successfully," said Woody.

"I told you I got a busy summer ahead taking care of my own ranch," countered Big Dave.

"You got two sons old enough and capable enough to run your ranch for three months in the summer as long as they can contact you for advice and decisions," replied Woody.

Big Dave leaned back in his chair and rubbed his chin. Then he leaned forward.

"Maybe so and maybe not," said Big Dave. "Why should I take this job for just three months?"

"Money," said Woody. "A good deal of money."

Big Dave sat up straight like he'd been smacked in the ass. "Money? What kind of money?"

Woody smiled at his friend. He knew he'd hit a nerve. "How much did you clear on your ranch last year?" he asked.

"You know how much I made last year," said Big Dave. "You do my damn taxes."

Woody pulled out a small spiral notebook from his jacket pocket. He opened it and then flipped to a page. "You paid taxes on a little over twenty thousand dollars last year," he said.

"Yes, I did," replied Big Dave. "So, what kind of money are we talkin' about for three months work?"

"My client is willing to pay up to forty thousand dollars for three months work this summer being the foreman and ramrod of a new cattle ranch here in Lincoln County," said Woody.

"Jesus Christ!" exclaimed Big Dave. "Anybody paying money like that is doing something damned dangerous or damned illegal."

Woody waited a few minutes for Big Dave to calm down. Then he leaned forward across the table and spoke in a low voice.

"It ain't dangerous and it ain't illegal, but it does require someone with some special skills, and you are the only rancher I know who could pull this off," said Woody.

Big Dave looked confused. "Explain what the hell this job is really about?" he said.

"I'd tell you if I actually knew," said Woody. "I can only tell you what I have been told."

"Which is what?" demanded Big Dave.

"Some rich dude bought the Crooked L Ranch and the Terry Ranch and combined them as one outfit. He's keeping the Crooked L brand for the new spread. He bought them to use as a test for his three sons," said Woody.

"Test? What kind of test?" asked a puzzled Big Dave.

"He wants to see how they handle being a ranch hand for three months," replied Woody.

"What?" exclaimed Big Dave.

Woody put up both of his hands as if in surrender. "Let me explain the whole story as I know it," he said.

Fifteen minutes later, including interruptions from Big Dave with questions, Woody completed his story.

Big Dave sat back in his chair, a puzzled look on his face.

Woody took a sip of his now cold coffee. The waitress magically appeared and refilled both men's cups with hot coffee.

Big Dave used one large hand to slowly turn his coffee cup around a couple of times. Finally, he looked up at Woody and spoke.

"So, some rich dude wants to find out what his three sons are made out of," said Big Dave. "Is that about it?"

"Pretty much," said Woody.

"And he ain't even seen or talked to any of the three since they were small boys?" added Big Dave.

"That's true," responded Woody.

"And I'm supposed to treat them like they was just ordinary young cowpokes?" he added.

"Yep," said Woody.

"Do I get my orders from this mysterious yahoo?" asked Woody.

"Nope. You get your orders from this attorney in Salt Lake, and you make your reports to him through me as well," said Woody.

"You mean this big shot lawyer Nate Chandler?" asked Big Dave.

"Yep," said Woody.

"Do I have to make written reports?" asked Big Dave with a frown on his face.

"Nope. He wants you to report personally to me," said Woody. "All that information is in this file," he said as he produced a file from his briefcase on the floor.

Big Dave opened the file and took out several sheets of paper. He glanced over the papers and then looked up at Woody.

"How and when do I get paid these forty thousand dollars?" asked Big Dave.

"You get half up front and the other half at the end of August," said Woody. "It's all spelled out in that paper in the file."

"How long do I have to think about this?" asked Big Dave.

Woody glanced at his wristwatch. "Before you get up from this table I need your answer," he said.

"Just like a damn lawyer," snapped Big Dave.

Woody pulled a small sheet of folded paper out of his suit coat pocket. "I've got three names on this list. Yours is the first. If you say no, I go on to the next rancher on the list," he said.

"Who are the other two ranchers?" asked Big Dave.

"None of your damn business," retorted Woody.

"Is Will Henry on that there list?" asked Big Dave.

"Same answer. None of your damn business," replied Woody.

Neither man spoke for the next few minutes. Woody kept his mouth shut. He had learned from his father that when making a proposal, the first person who spoke after the proposal was made was going to agree.

Finally Big Dave made a show of taking a sip of coffee. He set his coffee cup down on the scarred table and looked intently at Woody.

"Can I see the agreement in writing?" asked Big Dave.

Woody produced a sheet of paper and a pen. "Glance over the terms. If you're good with them, sign, and date the paper at the bottom."

Big Dave grabbed the paper. He then carefully read each line. Finally, he took the pen and signed and dated the paper. He shoved the paper and pen back at Woody.

"How in the hell did you know I'd agree to this cockamamy deal?" he asked in exasperation.

"Forty thousand dollars is a hell of a lot of money. Even to a hard ass like you," said a smiling Woody as he folded the signed paper and slipped it into his coat pocket.

CHAPTER SIX

Woody was smiling when he walked back into the law office. He pulled the folded agreement Big Dave had signed out of his pocket and laid it flat on his desk. He carefully reread the agreement and Big Dave's signature. Then he reached for the telephone.

He dialed the number of Nate Chandler's law firm. When the receptionist answered, he identified himself and asked to be connected to Mr. Chandler. In less than a minute Chandler picked up the phone.

"I hope you have good news for me, Woody," said Chandler in an anxious voice.

"I do, Mr. Chandler." said Woody. "I have the best man in Lincoln County for the job, and he signed the agreement this morning."

"Great news, Woody," said Chandler. "I have an important meeting in about fifteen minutes and when I'm finished with it, I'll call you back with some more information and some more instructions."

"I'll wait for your call, Mr. Chandler," said Woody. He couldn't help smiling as he hung up the phone.

• • •

A week later Woody found himself standing outside his home in Kemmerer at six in the morning. He was dressed in a suit and his briefcase sat on the sidewalk at his feet. He was not happy.

When he finally got that call from Mr. Chandler, two hours later, he had found himself buried in detail, and taking notes as fast as possible. Just when he thought Chandler was finished, the polished Salt Lake attorney ended the conversation with a request that was more an order than a request.

Chandler had instructed him to accompany Big Dave to Salt Lake City for a meeting at the attorney's offices. It was then that Woody realized his role in this project was far from over. He'd get paid, but he was to remain as Chandler's direct contact to Big Dave until the project was completed. So much for an easy pay day, Woody thought remorsefully.

Woody's thoughts were interrupted by the roar of the engine of Big Dave's Chevy pickup truck as he pulled up in front of where Woody was standing.

"Get your ass in the truck, Woody. We're burnin' daylight," said a smiling Big Dave.

Woody climbed into the passenger seat and before he could close the door Big Dave had let out the clutch and the big pickup truck was roaring down the road, headed south.

Woody collected himself and managed to get as comfortable as possible as they headed south across the flats at about twenty miles an hour over the posted speed limit. The two men did not talk much until they reached the junction with the federal highway that ran west to Salt Lake City. Once on it and headed west, Big Dave produced a big thermos and handed it to Woody. There was an extra cup on the thermos and Woody poured himself a cup and set the thermos down on the floor.

"Where the hell are your manners?" snorted Big Dave.

Woody, looking puzzled, said, "What?"

"The coffee is for both of us, you moron. Pour me a cup," snarled Big Dave.

Embarrassed, Woody grabbed the thermos and filled the second cup with hot coffee. He handed the full cup to Big Dave who just frowned at him in response.

After a few more minutes, Big Dave handed Woody back his empty cup and then asked a question.

"You got any idea where the hell this Chandler fella's office is located?" he asked.

Woody pulled out his pocket notebook, flipped through a few pages and then announced the address to Big Dave.

"Do you know where that is?" asked Woody.

"Does a bear shit in the woods?" replied Big Dave. "Of course, I know where it is. You just sit your ass back in that seat and I'll have you down by his office in three shakes of a lamb's tail."

The trip took a bit longer than that.

Traffic got a lot heavier as they neared Salt Lake City and once they entered the downtown area the traffic was like molasses. Thick and slow.

After almost twenty minutes, Big Dave stopped the truck in front of a tall older office building. "This is the place," he said. Then he drove around the block and found a public parking place, pulled in, and parked his truck.

Ten minutes later the two men were in an elevator headed for the tenth floor of the twelve-story building. They emerged from the elevator into a spacious and modern lobby that was light and bright, unlike the typical dark, wooden paneled offices of most law offices Woody had ever been in.

An attractive red headed woman in her thirties greeted them from a large curved polished wood desk.

"How may I help you gentlemen?" she inquired.

"We have an appointment with Mr. Chandler at 1:30," responded Woody.

The redhead stared down at a large book in front of her and moved her finger to a certain line. Then she looked up, smiled, and said, "I see you are early for your meeting with Mr. Chandler. Please have a seat in the waiting area, and I'll let him know you both have arrived."

She pointed in the direction of three large modern-looking chairs around a small round teakwood table. Woody and Big Dave each took a seat and began to look around the room.

"Somebody spent a shit pot full of money settin' this place up," said Big Dave in a loud whisper.

"They spent money they squeezed out of their legal clients," Woody whispered back.

Big Dave grinned in response. Then he just sat back in his chair and slowly took in their surroundings, including the red-headed receptionist. They waited in silence for about fifteen minutes. Then the redhead looked up and said, "Mr. Chandler will see you gentlemen now."

She pointed towards a large wooden door that was at least eight feet high and built of heavily carved wood.

The door opened and Nate Chandler stepped out into the reception area.

"Good afternoon, Woody, Mr. Olson," he said extending his hand. The three men shook hands, and then Woody and Big Dave followed Chandler back to his office. The huge door swung silently on its hinges and then was secured snugly with a muffled thump as it closed behind them.

CHAPTER SEVEN

The Salt Lake lawyer's office was huge. The ceilings were at least twelve feet high, and the walls were filled with bookcases. Everything in the room, including the large stone-covered desk was painted white. The walls held large paintings, which Woody recognized as copies of Remington and Russell western art.

Chandler motioned towards the two large white leather chairs in front of his desk. "Please have a seat, gentlemen," he said. Then he slid behind the massive desk into a large white leather chair. Woody was sure the chair was set at least six inches higher than the chairs he and Big Dave were sitting on.

Big Dave looked around the room once he was seated. He noted a small conference table with four leather chairs located on the other side of the room. To his right he could see the walls of glass that gave a good view of the Wasatch Mountain Range bordering the north end of Salt Lake City. It was an impressive view, and Big Dave was sure it was intended to impress all of Nate Chandler's clients.

After a few minutes of small talk, Chandler looked at his two guests. "Do you need anything to drink? Water? Soda? Lemonade?"

Both Big Dave and Woody declined his offer.

Nate Chandler sat back in his big chair and tented his hands in front of him. "I'm pleased you accepted the offer to be the foreman of the ranch for this summer, Mr. Olson. You have a key role to play in this plan of my client."

"Pardon me for interrupting, Mr. Chandler, but what exactly is it that you want Big Dave to do for your client in his temporary role of ranch foreman this summer?" asked Woody.

"Good question, Woody," responded Chandler. He then stood up. "Let's adjourn to the table where we can go over the plan in detail," he said. He led them over to the small conference table and each man took a seat.

Woody now noticed a black three ring binder in front of each of three chairs. Chandler picked up his binder and opened it. "Please open your copy of this file, if you would," he directed.

Woody and Big Dave opened their binders. "This is an outline of my client's plan," said Chandler. "Please follow as I go over the outline and then we will discuss each section of the outline until both of you understand it and are comfortable with your role in the plan."

For the next three hours he went over every item in the plan and answered all their questions as they arose. When they finally finished going through the outline, Chander closed his notebook and looked at Big Dave.

"Can you do all this?" he asked.

"Can I do everything I read in this here outline?" said Big Dave. "Yeah, I think I can, but I'm not sure how well this will work or what might go wrong or go south on us."

"All you need to do is fulfill your part of the plan," replied Chandler. "Whether the plan works or not is a problem the client will have to deal with. It is not your concern. If you have problems or issues during the summer, you are to contact Woody, and he will get in touch with me. Then I will pass on this client's decision to Woody."

"Why not have me contact you direct?" asked Big Dave.

"Because I doubt you are going to have access to a phone in your work environment this summer, let alone have the necessary privacy to conduct an open conversation," replied Chandler. "This way is a little more awkward, but I think it will be more secure and satisfactory to my client."

Big Dave put up his hands. "Works for me," he said.

"Excellent," responded Chandler. He looked at his watch and rose to his feet. "That's all for today, gentlemen. Thank you for coming." He escorted Big Dave and Woody to the massive wood door, and it swung silently open as he turned the latch.

Ten minutes later Woody and Big Dave were getting into Big Dave's truck in the parking lot. Big Dave started the engine and then turned to face Woody. "I don't know about you, but all that bullshit made me hungry and thirsty. Are you ready for some dinner?"

"I haven't eaten since breakfast and my backbone is making an acquaintance of my belly button, so yes, I'm ready for some supper," replied Woody.

"That's the most sensible thing I've heard you say since the day I met you," said Big Dave. He put the truck in gear and headed out into the heavy Salt Lake City traffic.

Woody could tell that Big Dave was headed north, not south, and back to Interstate 80 and the road back to Kemmerer.

"Where the hell are you going?" he asked.

"Ogden," replied Big Dave.

"Ogden? Why the hell are we headed to Ogden?" asked Woody.

"Cause that's where the wool warehouse is and I got a half a sack of wool hides in the back of the pickup," replied Big Dave.

"I thought it was too early to shear sheep?" asked Woody.

"It is," replied Big Dave. "This is wool I got off sheep that died or got kilt during the winter. I shear the bodies and keep the wool and then sell it."

"Sounds a little grisly to me," said Woody.

"Waste not, want not," replied Big Dave.

They drove to the wool warehouse in Ogden, Utah, and Big Dave got out, grabbed the big sack of wool, and hauled it inside while Woody waited in the cab of the pickup truck. When Big Dave returned, he was folding a check into his shirt pocket.

After he climbed back into the cab of the truck and started the engine, Big Dave turned to Woody. "Mexican for dinner all right with you?" he asked.

"I'm so damn hungry some of your crappy Viking food would be fine with me," he retorted.

Big Dave just laughed and headed for a small Mexican restaurant he knew well.

CHAPTER EIGHT

Big Dave pulled up next to an old metal building that had seen better days. The metal structure had a curved half-moon roof. It looked like a World War II military building. The parking lot was gravel, and the tan-colored paint was peeling off the metal sides of the building. Light was cascading out of the few windows on the side of the building and the muted sound of music was filtering out of the place. The only splash of color was the bright red front door. Woody could see no sign of any kind to indicate what was inside.

The two men entered the building, Big Dave leading the way. The place was well lit and Mexican music was playing from three-foot-high speakers they could see on the walls on either side of the building. The room was warm and smelled of spices and fried meat. Almost every table seemed full of hungry diners.

They were greeted by a young Mexican woman dressed in a bright colored flowered dress. She led them to a picnic table by the side wall and handed them menus. Seconds later she returned with silverware rolled up in a paper napkin and two large plastic glasses filled with ice water.

Woody surveyed the inside of the building. The walls were painted bright yellow. The floor was old concrete, worn smooth by years of shoes, boots and tires passing over it. Picnic tables like the one they occupied lined each side of the building with a wide-open space between them. The back of the building was walled off with drywall painted bright white. There were two swinging doors, and a serving window cut into the wall. Waiters and waitresses were constantly coming in and out of the swinging doors carrying trays of steaming hot food.

Every picnic table in the place was occupied except one. Woody's examination of the place was interrupted by the sudden appearance of a waiter. He was a young Hispanic man dressed in a white shirt and tight black pants.

"What can I get for you gentlemen?" he asked in perfect English.

Before Woody could even take a hard look at the menu, Big Dave had ordered for both of them, and he did so in perfect Spanish.

"Gracias, Senor," said the waiter with a smile, and he disappeared as quickly as he had appeared.

"You speak Spanish!" said Woody incredulously.

"If you have sheep, you need sheep herders. Damn near all good sheep herders are either Basque or Mexican. You have to learn how to talk to them and using Spanish is a hell of a lot easier than trying to teach them English," said Big Dave.

Their order arrived and it was piping hot with steam rising from their large plates. Accompanying the food were two cold beers. The two hungry men dug into their food and other than the Mexican music playing from the mounted speakers, the only sound was made by two hungry mouths.

When they finished their meal, the waiter again appeared out of nowhere and handed them the bill. Big Dave pulled out his wallet and peeled off enough bills to cover the tab plus a generous tip.

"I assume this is not your first time here," said Woody.

"Nope, it's not. I been here plenty of times," replied Big Dave.

"I never saw a sign out front," said Woody. "Is this place legal?"

"Far as I know it is," replied Big Dave with a smile. "But if you was to stand up and shout out 'Immigration,' this place would clear out in seconds."

The two men rose from the picnic table and walked out of the noisy, warm building and out into the cooler night air. The sun had gone down while they were eating, and it was dark out. There was a half-moon, and it provided some light, but not much.

They climbed into Big Dave's truck, and he fired up the engine. He pulled out of the gravel parking lot and onto the highway. Traffic was still heavy, but not like it had been in Salt Lake.

They drove back on the same highway and managed to hit red traffic lights at two intersections in a row. At the second stop, Woody heard Big Dave swear under his breath.

He looked over at Big Dave, but the big rancher remained silent. The light changed and they drove on and then Big Dave swore loudly.

"God damned sonofabitch," he said, looking into his rear-view mirror.

"What's wrong?" asked a puzzled Woody.

"This dumb asshole behind me has his brights on and it's blindin' me when I look in the mirror," snarled Big Dave.

"He should get signaled by some oncoming traffic. They can't like his bright lights in their faces either," said Woody.

"You'd think so," said Big Dave.

They drove for two more miles and indeed two oncoming vehicles did flash their lights, but the car behind their truck kept its bright lights on.

They hit another red traffic light and Big Dave stopped, slipped the gearshift in neutral and pulled on the parking brake.

Then he opened the driver's side door and stepped out of the cab. He reached behind the seat and pulled out a big lug wrench.

"What're you doing?" asked a surprised Woody.

Big Dave didn't answer him. He walked back to the rear of the pickup truck, a big wrench in his right hand. The driver of the car behind him saw him coming and frantically began rolling up his driver's side window.

When Big Dave got to the front of the trailing car, he stepped in front of it and swung the wrench hitting the left front headlight. The headlight burst into an explosion of glass bits. Then he moved over and did the same thing to the right headlight.

Satisfied, he returned to the cab of his truck. He slid the wrench behind the seat and climbed into the cab. He released the hand brake and put the truck in gear. The light changed to green and Big Dave released the clutch, pressed the accelerator and the truck moved rapidly forward.

"That should slow that sonofabitch down," said Big Dave.

Woody just sat there with his mouth hanging open.

Nothing was said for about half an hour. Then Big Dave started talking about the agreement with the attorney Chandler and his mysterious client. Not another word was said about what had just happened at the traffic light in Ogden.

CHAPTER NINE

It was after nine when Big Dave dropped Woody off in front of his home in Kemmerer.

Woody stood inside his front door and hung up his hat and coat. He had gone over that evening's event in his mind several times. At first, he was surprised at the violence Big Dave had shown. Then he remembered the night back when he and Big Dave and their friends, all eighteen years of age, had avenged their good friend. Then he seemed to understand. Big Dave did just what he felt he had to do. Nothing more. Nothing less.

● ● ●

The next morning Woody arrived for work at the law office and began work on a contract agreement for a client. He was interrupted a few times with new projects sent to him by his father. He buried himself in his work and when he finally took a break, he stepped out into the foyer of the office and found everyone was gone. He looked up at the clock on the wall. It was almost six thirty in the evening. He had worked straight through lunch and now his stomach was rebelling. He returned to his office. Put his things away and headed out the door, being careful to relock it. Then he headed for the café with his stomach rumbling loudly.

Two weeks went by. Woody had lunch with Big Dave each Wednesday and each time Big Dave asked him if he had any news about the mysterious project. On the second Wednesday, Big Dave told Woody that he would be starting work at the new ranch the following Monday. He had both of his sons home from school and had set up a schedule for the next three months for them and posted it on the wall in his kitchen. His wife Connie was not happy about that, but she realized that it needed to be out in plain sight so neither son could miss it.

When Woody returned to the law office, Suzie, the receptionist, and all-around girl Friday handed him a phone call message. He read the message on the way to his office. By the time he approached his desk, he was reaching for the telephone. The message was from Nate Chandler. It was a simple message. "Call me as soon as possible."

After speaking with the Salt Lake City law firm receptionist, Woody was passed through to Nate's personal phone.

"Woody. Thank you for getting back to me so fast," said Nate.

"I just got back from lunch and saw your message," responded Woody.

"I need you to be in my office next Monday at no later than 10:00 A.M. Can you do that?" he asked.

"I can be there," replied Woody. "Do you want me to bring Big Dave?"

"No, this is a meeting for just you and me. We will hopefully be meeting with all three of our client's sons," said Nate.

"Meeting with all three sons? For what purpose?" asked Woody.

"They have been instructed to fly here to meet with me concerning a bequest from their father's estate that affects all of them," replied Nate.

"Bequest? But our client is still alive," answered a confused Woody.

"They don't know that, and our client doesn't want them to know he is still alive," said Nate. "A bequest can come from the living or the dead. They will assume he is dead, which is our client's intent," said Nate. "Perhaps you have forgotten this was the client's intent that I explained to you earlier."

"You're correct. I had forgotten," said Woody.

"Not a problem," said Nate.

"So, what's the purpose of the meeting?" asked Woody.

"Our client's specific instructions are to let them know of the contents of the bequest, and the choices open to them," replied Nate.

"Can you refresh my memory of what these choices are?" asked Woody.

"Certainly, and I apologize if I neglected to tell you about them before. Our client's bequest is made to all three of his sons. It offers them a choice. Choice one is to come to Wyoming and work on his ranch as ranch hands for three months this summer for the months of June, July, and August. If they satisfactorily complete their work assignments for the three months, each of them will receive five hundred thousand dollars," said Nate.

"And if they do not successfully complete the three months, what happens?" asked Woody.

"They get a check for fifteen thousand dollars each," replied Nate.

"What's the other choice?" asked Woody.

"They can refuse to go to Wyoming and work on the ranch for three months. In that case they get a check for fifteen thousand dollars and a plane ticket home," said Nate.

"What if they refuse to come to Salt Lake City and meet with you?' asked Woody.

"They get nothing," said Nate.

"Do they know all this?" asked Woody.

"They know if they come to Salt Lake City for the Monday meeting, they get fifteen thousand dollars at a minimum and if they do not, they get nothing," said Nate.

"Do they know about the summer of work?" asked Woody.

"No, they do not. That will be provided to them as a choice at our meeting on Monday," said Nate.

"Do you know if they are all coming on Monday?' asked Woody.

"I do not. Monday might just be a meeting between you and me if none of them show up. But that's not our problem. Our job is to host a meeting and make the offers to any of them who show up," said Nate.

"That works for me," responded Woody. "I'll see you on Monday morning."

"See you on Monday," responded Nate.

Woody hung up the phone and sat back in his chair. As he thought over the conversation he had just completed, he then sat forward grabbed his appointment book. He quickly checked Monday and found he had an older couple coming in for a meeting on drafting their wills. He found nothing else requiring his presence at the office on Monday. He picked up the phone and called the clients and quickly changed their appointment to the following Thursday.

After hanging up the phone with his clients, he then redialed the phone and tried to reach Big Dave. He was not home and Connie, his wife, answered. She took a message to have Big Dave call Woody back as soon as he got home.

Woody took a deep breath and then grabbed the next file on his pile of projects to get completed and went to work. The rest of the day flew by and soon it was time to close up the office and head home for supper.

CHAPTER TEN

Monday morning saw Woody up at five in the morning. He was showered, dressed, and seated at the café for an early breakfast an hour later. He wolfed down his breakfast and barely tasted it. He was anxious to get to Salt Lake and he felt as nervous as any time he could remember. He drove at least ten miles an hour over the speed limit including when he hit the federal highway west to Salt Lake. He arrived in front of the tall office building that housed Nate Chandler's law firm by nine o'clock. He knew that was too early. He parked in a nearby public lot and then found a small cafe two blocks away. He entered the shop and stood in a short line until he was able to order a coffee, which he took to a small table in the far corner of the shop. He nursed his coffee and watched the customers come and go. Hardly anyone went to a table. Almost all of the shop's clientele grabbed coffee to go and were out the door.

Woody kept glancing at the big clock on the wall behind the café's counter. Finally, it was fifteen minutes before ten o'clock and he rose from his seat, leaving his empty coffee mug on the table and headed out the door. He quickly walked the two blocks to the building housing Chandler's law firm. He took the elevator up to the tenth floor and stepped out into the law firm's large reception area. He went up to the same red-headed lady he had seen on his last visit. She smiled in recognition and before Woody could say anything, she directed him to a seat and picked up the phone.

Less than five minutes later, Nate Chandler appeared and he and Woody shook hands. Then Nate led him into his large private office.

Once both men were seated at the round table, Nate asked Woody if he wanted coffee. Woody smiled and said no. He was up to his eyeballs in coffee by then.

"OK then," said Nate. "'First of all, do you have any questions about this morning's meeting with the sons?"

"Are they coming?" asked Woody.

"All three of them indicated they will be here this morning," replied Nate.

"All three?" said Woody.

"All three," responded Nate.

"Are they represented by an attorney or their mother?" asked Woody.

"Surprisingly, they are representing themselves. I asked them about legal counsel, and they said they didn't need any. I asked them about their mother, and they said she wanted nothing to do with her ex-husband, dead or alive," said Nate.

"Did they have questions?" Woody asked.

"They had tons of questions. None of which I was willing to answer until they were here in front of us," replied Nate. He pointed to a short stack of white file folders on the table. "These are copies of the instructions for this summer for each of the sons. The instructions should answer ninety percent of their questions, but I think they will ask us some things we don't expect," said Nate.

"How do we answer them?" asked Woody.

"Let me handle the answers unless they ask something concerning the Kemmerer area that I am unfamiliar with, and then I will defer to you," said Nate.

"Works for me," replied Woody.

"Can you think of any other questions?" asked Nate.

Woody thought for a moment and then looked up at Nate. "Do they have to make their decisions today?" he asked.

"Yes, they do. If they choose to take the money and fly home, I cut them a check for $15,000 and they sign a release and they are done with the whole affair," replied Nate.

"What if they choose to spend the summer working as cowboys to get the big payday?" asked Woody.

"Any of the sons who choose to do that will get a packet of instructions. They will be required to return to my office two weeks from today. I will have a private plane fly them to the Kemmerer airport, and you and Big Dave will pick them up and transport them to the ranch. During the drive, Big Dave will give them instructions and when they arrive at the ranch, they will be introduced to everyone else. The next morning, they will begin a week of instruction from Big Dave," said Nate.

"May I ask what kind of instructions?" asked Woody.

Nate smiled and laughed out loud. "It will be cowboy boot camp for them. Big Dave will teach them how to dress, how to care for their horses, how to saddle and unsaddle their horses, and by the fifth day they should be able to do all that on their own. Then they will get a rude introduction to hard work," he said.

"Big Dave is a no bullshit guy," said Woody. "Part of this is likely to be pretty unpleasant."

"I'm sure it will be, and I am pretty sure that is something that my client, their father, is counting on. He seems pretty keen on finding out what kind of young men he has fathered," said Nate.

"Knowing Big Dave like I do, I don't think I'd want to be in their shoes for the next three months," said Woody.

"Neither would I," said Nate with a big grin on his face.

Nate looked at his watch. "It's almost time for our guests to arrive. Do you want anything to drink?" he asked.

"Nope. I'm fine," said Woody.

Nate's intercom buzzed. He punched a button and held the phone up to his ear. "Thank you. Send them in," he said.

Then he turned to Woody. "It's showtime."

CHAPTER ELEVEN

The office door opened, and the red-headed receptionist held it for the three young men who cautiously entered Nate's office. Woody studied each of them as they entered and took chairs around the small conference table in Nate's office.

Nate introduced himself and Woody and then asked each of the three young men to introduce themselves. The tallest son, who appeared a bit older than the other two introduced himself first. "I'm Steve Mann. I'm nineteen years old and will be a sophomore in college in the fall. I'm the oldest brother." Steve was every bit of six foot four inches in height and built like a football player. He had dark curly hair and dark brown eyes.

The second son then spoke. "I'm Lee Mann. I'm eighteen years old and will be a freshman in college in the fall." Lee was tall, boyish looking with blonde hair and blue eyes. He was about six foot three inches tall but had a slender build like a long-distance runner.

Then the third son spoke. "I'm Travis Mann. I just turned seventeen and I'll be a senior in high school in the fall." Travis was also six foot three inches tall, and he had dark very curly hair and brown eyes. He was slim but had a muscular edge to his body.

All three young men looked nervous and kept glancing around at their surroundings in the large well-appointed office.

"I know you are curious about the nature of this meeting, and I want to thank all three of you for taking time out of your regular schedules to fly out here to Utah for this meeting," said Nate. "I'm an attorney, and I represent the estate of your father Wayne Mann. Your father was a very interesting man and a very successful one. He has engaged me and my law firm to manage his last requests and his estate. One of his requests is a bit unusual, and that is why we are all sitting here together." Nate paused as if to study each of three young men sitting across from him. He reached to his side and picked up some grey colored folders. He handed a folder to each of the sons and one to Woody, as well.

"Before you open the folders I have just handed you, let me explain its' purpose. Your father has requested that I offer each of you a choice based on his last will and testament," said Nate.

He then opened his folder and handed each of the three sons a single printed piece of paper.

"On this paper are the three possible choices your father has left for you," said Nate. "If you choose to refuse his offer of three months of summer employment in Wyoming, you will receive a check for fifteen thousand dollars and use your ticket to fly back home.

"If you choose to work as a ranch hand for the summer at a ranch outside Kemmerer, Wyoming, you will receive a check for five hundred thousand dollars at the successful end of three months' work."

Nate then paused. "If you chose to work at the ranch and either quit or are fired for cause, you will receive a check for fifteen thousand dollars regardless of how many days you have worked of the original three months."

"Are there any questions?" he asked with a slight smile on his face. He was sure there would be. He knew he would have questions if he were in their shoes.

"The job is to work as ranch hands for three months at a ranch in Wyoming?" asked a surprised looking Steve.

"That is correct," replied Nate.

"But we don't know a damn thing about how to be a cowboy," said a dubious looking Lee.

"Your first week on the job will be in a cowboy boot camp. There the foreman will teach you the fundamentals, and you will learn more as the summer progresses. You will be working with experienced cowboys as well as the foreman I mentioned before," said Nate.

"What about work clothes and gear?" asked Travis.

"All of that is covered in the folder I just gave you," said Nate. "You will find a list of items and you are to provide your sizes for each item and mail it back to me."

An awkward silence fell over the table as three young men's minds were moving at warp speed to try to absorb what they had just heard.

"I know this is a lot to absorb, and Woody and I will leave you three alone in my office for a bit. I'm sure you have a lot to discuss. We will return in half an hour and each of you will need to inform me of whether you wish to accept your father's offer of a summer's work, or a check for $15,000 to accompany you on your trip home," said Nate.

With that, Nate stood up. Woody joined him, and the two men walked out of the ornate private office, closing the large wooden door behind them.

As soon as they exited the office, Nate led the way to a small, but well- appointed conference room just off the main reception area of the law firm's office. He and Woody took a seat in two of the large, padded leather chairs surrounding the conference table.

Nate leaned back in his chair and looked over at Woody. "Well, how do you think that went?" he asked.

"I'm not sure," said Woody. "I was watching the three boys for their reactions and saw what I thought was surprise, confusion, and disbelief on their faces when you explained their options."

Nate chuckled. "If I had been in their shoes, I probably would have had the same reaction. They came here not knowing what to expect, and I am almost certain I would have been as shocked as they appeared to be."

"How do you think they will choose?" asked Woody.

"I honestly don't know," replied Nate. "My best guess is they will take the opportunity to make $500,000 for three months of work, even though they have no idea what the work will entail. They are young and not very sophisticated in the ways of the world yet. But they could surprise me. What was your impression of the three boys?"

Woody paused and scratched his chin. He thought about the question and then he spoke. "I saw three pretty spoiled young men," he said. "They and hard work have never been in the same room. This summer is going to be a severe shock to their systems."

"Anything about any of them that stood out to you?" asked Nate.

"The older one, Steve, was paying close attention. He is likely the smartest and of course he's the oldest. The middle son, Lee, looked bored and disinterested except when you mentioned the $500,000 at the end of the summer," said Woody.

Nate laughed.

"The youngest, Travis, acted like a typical spoiled petulant teenager. I'll be surprised if he makes it through the summer. He strikes me as a mama's boy," added Woody.

"It's going to be an interesting summer," said Nate with a smile.

Woody and Nate talked about local politics in Salt Lake City. Then Nate glanced at his watch. "Time's up," he said. He rose from his chair as did Woody, and they left the room to return to Nate's office. Nate politely knocked on the door of his office and then opened it.

"Are you boys ready for us?" he asked.

"Yes, sir," said Steve, the oldest.

Nate and Woody entered the room and took their seats across from the three young men. Woody noted that the folders in front of Steve and Lee were open, but that the one in front of Travis was not.

Nate opened a small leather-bound notebook and placed it in front of him. He removed a ball point pen and then looked up at the three sons.

"I'll start with you as the oldest, Steve," he said. "What is your choice?"

"I'd like the chance to work on a ranch for the summer and collect five hundred thousand dollars," Steve said carefully.

"All right," said Nate as he made annotation in his notebook. "What about you, Lee?" he asked.

"I, too, would like to chance to earn half a million bucks by playing cowboy for three months," Lee said.

"You won't be playing cowboy. You'll be doing hard labor as a cowboy," said Nate in a stern voice.

"Whatever," said Lee, avoiding looking Nate in the eyes.

Nate made a notation in his notebook. When he finished, he looked up at Travis, the youngest. "What about you, Travis?" he asked.

"I plan on spending three months working with my brothers as a cowboy," said the youngest son.

Nate nodded and made a notation in his notebook. Then he closed the notebook and looked over at the three young men.

"A car is waiting at the entrance to the building to take all of you to your hotel. The same car will pick you up in the morning and take you to the airport. I'd advise you to carefully read all the pages in the folder you were given. If you have questions, call, or write to me with them and I will get back to you as quickly as possible," said Nate. "Any more questions?"

"No, sir," said Steve. The other two sons shook their heads from side to side.

Nate got to his feet, as did Woody and then the three brothers. He led them to the door, and he and Woody watched as the three disappeared out the door and then into the elevator.

Nate and Woody returned to his office.

"Do you have any questions, Woody?" asked Nate.

"What happens next?" asked Woody.

"Here is your folder," said Nate. "You can read all about it. Those three boys will arrive here on the first of June and Big Dave will pick them up at the airport and then drive them to the ranch in Kemmerer."

"What about clothes sizes and boots?" asked Woody.

"All of that is in their folders. They need to fill in all the pertinent information and mail it to me, and I will forward it to Big Dave with a copy to you," said Nate.

He looked at his watch. "Do you want to go out to dinner, my treat?" asked Nate.

"No, thank you," said Woody. "I need to head back to Kemmerer."

"Say hello to your father for me," said Nate.

"I will," replied Woody.

"One more thing," said Nate.

"Yes?" said Woody with a look of slight surprise on his face.

"How do you think they will do as summer cowboys?" asked Nate.

Woody paused before he formed an answer. "I think three months of cowboy school under Big Dave will be a lot harder than anything they have ever done in their lives," he responded.

"I completely agree," said a grinning Nate. "Keep me as informed as you can."

"I will," replied Woody.

The two men shook hands and Woody headed to the elevator. Fifteen minutes later, Woody was driving his truck and headed to the junction that led back to the state of Wyoming.

CHAPTER TWELVE

As he drove east, Woody tried to organize in his mind what trying to oversee what happened to the three young men over a three-month period on the ranch in Wyoming was going to entail. He smiled to himself as he imagined how surprised the three sons were going to be after their first week under Big Dave. From what he observed of them at the attorney's office, they were soft, pampered, and slightly over sheltered.

All of that would change in a heartbeat on their first morning with Big Dave. He decided he should ask Big Dave if he could be present for that first morning. After all, he was the local attorney for the project, and he was sure the boys expected some oversight.

He looked in the rearview mirror and smiled. Then he laughed out loud. It would be like being on board a ship anchored in Pearl Harbor on the morning of the Japanese surprise attack and being awakened by exploding bombs.

• • •

The three brothers had all found their seats on the big four engine TWA passenger plane. As they were getting comfortable in their seats, the engines coughed and roared to life, one by one. Then the captain came over the scratchy intercom and told all the passengers to be seated and fasten their safety belts. Minutes later they could feel the big plane start to move and then after a short taxi down the runway, the engines roared loudly and then the airliner jerked forward and began picking up speed until the wheels lifted off the ground and they were airborne, headed for Chicago's Midway Airport.

Travis and Lee were seated together, and Steve was seated across the aisle from them. "When do we have to be at this ranch in Wyoming?" asked Lee.

"The man said we have to be in Salt Lake City on the morning of June 1," replied Steve.

"So, we have to fly in the day before?" asked Lee.

"If these folks are picking us up the morning of the first of June, I'd say we got no choice but to fly in the day before," replied Steve.

"Do we get paid for the day of travel from Illinois?" asked Travis.

"We get paid for working June, July, and August. Not before and not after," responded Steve who was still studying the folder he had been given.

"That doesn't seem fair," said Travis. "We're spending one day traveling and not getting paid."

Steve shot a look of exasperation at his youngest brother. "We also aren't getting paid for the day we fly home, little brother. But if we're each getting half a million dollars for three months work, I don't see much room for complaining."

"Steve's right," said Lee. "If I'm gonna get paid half a million dollars to be a pretend cowboy for three months, I could care less about one day getting there and one day getting home."

Steve looked up from his folder at his two younger brothers. "I'm not so sure this is gonna be a summer of playing pretend cowboy. You two need to read all this stuff in this folder. What I'm reading sounds like pretty hard labor to me," he said.

"What?" said Travis. He reached for his folder tucked in the seat back in front of him. When he pulled it out, his brother Lee was already reading his.

For the next ten minutes there was silence as the three brothers read the contents of their folders, broken only by the occasional comment of "shit!"

By the time their plane landed at Midway Airport in Chicago, the three boys had been silent for almost an hour. They had all finished reading the contents of their folders. It was then a combination of reality and disbelief that hit all three boys. They had signed up for a form of indentured servitude for a period of three months.

Finally, Travis broke the silence as the plane taxied to the terminal.

"Hells bells, maybe we should have taken the fifteen grand and run like rabbits," he said.

"I was kinda' thinkin' the same thing," said Lee.

"You two are full of shit," said Steve. "There's no such thing as a free lunch. If I gotta work my ass off for three months and get half a million bucks, I got no problem with that. I'll shovel cow shit for three months for $500,000. You two do what you want. You can call the attorney and say no thanks and he'll send you $15,000, but I plan on being a dude cowboy for a summer and pocketing a big payday at the end of August."

"But we don't know what kind of work we'll have to do?" whined Travis.

"Who gives a shit," said Steve. "Do you two idiots have any idea how long you'd have to work in the real world to earn $500,000? Do the math, dummies. That's about the income for working for fifty years for some company at a job you're liable to hate."

"But the $500,000 isn't tax free," said Lee. "We still gotta pay taxes on the money."

Steve sighed. "If the $500,000 is an inheritance and it is, then there ain't no damn tax on it except inheritance tax and we can check, but I'm pretty sure the minimum inheritance before getting taxed is more than $500,000 if my accounting instructor was telling us the truth," he said.

His two younger brothers had no comeback to Steve's analysis. Lee planned to look it up for himself. Travis planned to ask his mother. She knew everything.

The plane taxied off the field and finally stopped at Gate E11. The rolling steps were moved up to the side of the plane and the attendant then opened the plane door as the passengers gathered their things and began to move to the front of the plane where the door was located.

The three boys were greeted by their anxious mother and her new boyfriend. She hugged each of them and as soon as they were in their car, she began peppering them with questions about their trip and what the attorney had to say at their meeting. When they told her about the $500,000, she was shocked into silence. But her boyfriend wasn't. "No shit!" he said.

CHAPTER THIRTEEN

The days flew by for Woody. He had a stack of paperwork he needed to get caught up on and in the two weeks that followed his visit with Nate Chandler and the three Mann brothers, he received a surprise. Nate had referred two of his clients from Salt Lake to Woody's father's firm as they had business issues in Wyoming and needed local counsel. His father went out of his way to let Woody know that taking this job with Nate had brought the firm some additional dividends.

Finally, it was the twenty-fifth of May, a week before the three Mann boys were to show up for three months of hard labor as cowboys working under Big Dave. Woody looked at the clock on his desk. It was ten minutes before two. He was expecting Big Dave to meet him there at two to go over the plans for the next three months.

Sure enough. At two on the dot, Big Dave walked into the law firm and was escorted back to Woody's office. The two friends shook hands and Big Dave took one of the two chairs in front of Woody's desk. He carried an old battered three-ring notebook, which he placed on the desk between them.

Big Dave looked hard at Woody.

"Are you all right, Woody," he asked.

"Sure, I'm fine," replied a somewhat nervous Woody.

"You sure as hell don't look fine," responded Big Dave. "You look like a nervous cat in the room full of rocking chairs."

"I guess I am a bit nervous," replied Woody. "I want this to go well, and I don't want to screw anything up and upset my old man."

"I generally got no good use for lawyers," said Big Dave. "But I see you as a bit different. I know you well. We're friends. I trust you. I can't say that about many folks I know."

"I appreciate your confidence in me. I plan on doing my best," said Woody.

"Ain't nothing more a man can ask for," responded Big Dave.

Then he rubbed his hands together and said, "What do we work on first?"

Woody pulled out his notebook and after scanning almost three pages of notes he looked up and said, "Let's start with the three boys clothing, boots, and gear. Where are we on that?" he asked.

Big Dave opened his battered notebook. He scanned the first page and then looked up at Woody. "I got the list of sizes they sent you and I bought work clothes, including underwear and socks."

"You bought them underwear and socks?" asked a surprised Woody.

"It was my wife Connie's idea," replied Big Dave. "She said don't assume a goddamn thing when it comes to tenderfeet kids. So, I didn't."

"All right, underwear and socks," said Woody making an entry into his notebook. "What else?"

"I got jeans, denim work shirts, Justin boots, goat roper baseball caps, and leather work gloves," said Big Dave.

Woody took notes and then he looked up at Big Dave. "What about chaps?" he asked.

"I checked at the ranch, and they got plenty of chaps of all sizes. "We'll size them boys up once they get here," replied Big Dave.

"Do you have a training schedule of some kind?" asked Woody.

"Yeah, I do," replied Big Dave. "We start out with their clothing and boots. Then we go to meet a real horse and explain the issues with horses. They learn what horseshoes are and why we use them. Then we go over the saddle and its parts and what's used for what. Then we do the same with the bridle, saddle blanket, hackamore, lariat, and saddlebags."

"When we get through that, I'll have them each learn how to use the hackamore and lead rope and lead the horse around the corral. Then we work on learnin' how to saddle the horse and get a bridle on him," said Big Dave.

Woody was writing notes in his book as fast as he could.

Big Dave paused for a bit until Woody stopped writing. Then he started in again. "I teach them how to properly feed and water the horse. Then how to unsaddle the horse, and then how to wipe it down after a day's use and then how to curry comb the animal. We do this until they all get it absolutely right."

"What then?" asked Woody who had kept up in his writing as Big Dave spoke.

"Then we teach them how to mount and ride a horse in the corral. When they master that, I have all three of them catch and saddle a horse and then we go for a little ride. I teach them to walk, canter, and gallop the horse and hopefully they all manage to stay on board the cayuse," said Big Dave.

Big Dave paused again, waiting for Woody to finish his notes.

"Then I try to teach them how to use a lariat. We start standing on the ground and move up to learning to use the lariat on horseback. Finally, we move to trying to rope horses, cattle, and calves that are moving," said Big Dave.

"We do this until they are at least minimally proficient," added Big Dave.

"How long do you think that will take?" asked Woody.

"I plan on them being minimally proficient after one week," said Big Dave.

"What happens after that first week?" asked Woody.

"I plan on pairing each of the three boys up with a veteran cowboy. The ranch has four pretty good hands, and I will rotate the boys each day with a different experienced hand," said Big Dave.

"Then what?" asked Woody.

"Then we have them go out with their veteran partners and do cowboy shit," said Big Dave. "There's a ton of work to do and it ranges from cowboy work to carpenter, plumber, and bullshit jobs that happen all the time on a ranch," said Big Dave.

"What kind of work schedule do you have planned for the boys?" asked Woody.

"Same as the real cowboys," replied Big Dave. "They work six days a week with Sunday off."

"Can they go into town with the real cowboys on Saturday night?" asked a curious Woody.

"Nope, not for the first couple of weeks," said Big Dave. "To my way of thinkin,' they'll be too damn tired and sore to do anything in that first few weeks except feel sorry for themselves and wonder why the hell they decided to try to play cowboy for three months in Wyoming."

Woody laughed. Big Dave joined in.

CHAPTER FOURTEEN

On the thirty-first of May, Woody was working in his office when the phone rang. He put down his pen and grabbed the receiver.

"Woody here," he said into the phone.

"It's Nate Chandler," came the reply over the phone.

"The plane just took off. Should be in Kemmerer in a little under an hour," he said.

"I'll be there," responded Woody. He put his work paper away in a drawer and got up and grabbed his suit coat off the old wooden coatrack he kept by the door. He stuck his head in the door of his father's office and let him know he was headed out to the Kemmerer airport.

"Good luck," said his father with a big grin on his face. "Try to keep them children alive."

Woody nodded and headed out the door. He climbed into the two-year-old white Chevrolet Suburban of his father's and fired up the engine. He rarely ever drove the vehicle, and he let the engine warm up a bit before he put the big Chevy in gear.

He drove to the nearest gas station and filled up the tank. Then he bought a pack of chewing gum, paid for the gas, and drove the big vehicle out of town. He headed up the road next to the Ham's Fork River. The Kemmerer airport was located on a bluff just north of town. It took him about twenty minutes to drive up to the site. He parked the Suburban and got out of the cab.

Calling this place an airport was a stretch of the imagination. It was a long flat pasture of grass with some lights on the sides and the ends of the runway. There was a small shed that held the light controls and some other gear that Woody had no idea about its function or lack thereof.

An old shack stood next to the grass runway. The shack was small, but served no real purpose he could understand. One reason why is it had no roof. The original roof had been blown away years ago in a typical winter storm.

So, Woody sat on a rough, unpainted bench with no back and waited. He took out the pack of gum, unwrapped a stick and stuck it in his mouth. He didn't usually chew gum, but he felt nervous and thought needing to chew something would keep him occupied.

He shouldn't be nervous about meeting and picking up the three young men. He had met them and did not feel particularly threatened by them. But he did feel nervous. Originally, he had felt he and Big Dave should pick them up at the Kemmerer airport, but then Big Dave changed his mind.

He thought back to what Big Dave had said. "I'm the unknown in this deal. My job is to be a hard ass boss, and I fully intend to fulfill that role. I think it would be better to introduce me to them boys at the ranch where everything will be new and different and somewhat threatening to them. I intend to be as threatening as I can make myself. If you pick them up at the airport, then the uncertainty and the mystery about this whole plan just gets stronger. I want them to be uncertain. I want them to be unsure. I want them boys scared of me."

So, here Woody sat on the old wooden bench. The only thing at the tiny Kemmerer airport that served any practical purpose was the small-locked shack containing the electronics that operated the landing lights.

As he sat on the small bench waiting, Woody saw movement on the far end of the runway. When he looked harder, he could see a herd of sheep moving slowly up the ridge onto the runway, eating their way as they came. Apparently, the mowed grass on the runway was the result of some seed and fertilizer spread there by somebody. The sheep found it irresistible and soon about a third of the grass runway was covered in white, wooly sheep. There were a few bucks and lots of ewes and there were plenty of spring lambs running around the older sheep like children of all kinds are bound to do.

Woody was watching the sheep when his ears picked up on a distant noise. He listened carefully and then looked up at the sky. In the distance to the west, he could make out the outline of a small single engine airplane.

Woody stood up and stretched. He started to walk toward the runway and then he paused, in mid stride. His mind had grasped the obvious. The sheep. The sheep were on almost half the runway. How was the damn plane gonna be able to land with all those sheep in the way?

There was no way one man on foot could clear all those sheep off the runway so the plane could safely land. Woody was stumped as to what he might do.

Then the plane flew over the runway. The pilot was no doubt orienting himself to the grass runway he had never seen before, let alone landed on it. The pilot saw all the sheep, and then he flew to the north of the runway and the plane turned and headed back towards where Woody stood. This time the plane was flying only about fifteen feet off the ground. The plane roared over the startled sheep, and the entire herd of woolly critters began running for their lives. By the time the pilot had turned the plane and returned to the south end of the field, there was not a single sheep to be seen. They had scattered like scared rabbits. The pilot flew over the field, then turned and approached from the north. He landed gently in an amazingly short distance and then taxied over to where Woody stood, seemingly bolted to the ground.

The pilot shut the engine off and then opened the side door hatch. The three Mann brothers exited the plane, each carrying a small pack. Then the pilot exited the plane and walked over to Woody.

He was tall, dark haired, and wearing a flight jacket and a ball cap with the logo of the Denver Broncos on it. He smiled and extended his hand to Woody. The two men shook hands.

"Here's your passengers," he said to Woody.

"You really handled that problem with them sheep damn well," said Woody.

"Ain't my first rodeo," said the smiling pilot. Then he turned to the three Mann brothers. "I leave you boys in good hands," he said. "Good luck playin' cowboy here in Wyoming."

With that he walked back to the plane, climbed into the cockpit, and started the engine. After a few minutes, he taxied back onto the runway to the south end. Once there he revved the engine and then the small plane shot down the runway and was airborne quickly. A minute later he was gone from the view of his three former passengers and Woody.

Woody shook hands with each of the three young men and then led them to the big white Suburban. When they got to the vehicle, all three young men stopped and stood and then turned slowly as they took in their surroundings.

"Where's the town?" Lee finally blurted out.

Woody grinned and pointed to the east and slightly down from where they stood. "It's down there," he said.

All three boys looked where he had pointed, amazement in their eyes.

"Who let all those sheep loose so they could run all over the runway?" asked Lee.

"No one did," replied Woody. "This is open range with no fences. Those sheep go wherever they can find something to eat."

All three boys looked at Woody like he had two heads. Then they seemed to shrug it off.

"Toss your gear in the back and climb in," said Woody. Once everyone was seated, he started the engine and made his way back down into Kemmerer. As they drove through the small-town Woody could see the boys were intently taking in everything they could see.

"How big is this town?" asked Travis.

"It's a tad short of three thousand people," said Woody.

"That's all?" said a puzzled Travis.

"Welcome to Wyoming," said Woody and as soon as he passed the city limits, he hit the gas, and the big Suburban was rolling across the prairie toward the boys' home for the next three months.

CHAPTER FIFTEEN

As Woody drove through the sagebrush covered plains, he was expecting a horde of questions from the three Mann boys. He was surprised by a blanketing silence instead. He looked in the rearview mirror. The two younger brothers, Travis, and Lee were in the back seat, and he noticed their eyes were wide open and so were their mouths.

He was pleased with the silence. The less he had to tell them the better. They needed to learn for themselves rather than get all their information second hand. Plus, he was looking forward to their first encounter with Big Dave Olson.

• • •

As they drove south of Kemmerer, Woody watched the familiar sights pass by. When he approached the ranch, he slowed down to about thirty miles an hour and said, "We're here."

All three of the boys had their eyes glued to the vehicle's windows as they stared at their new home for the next three months.

The ranch buildings were located only about a hundred yards from the highway. They could see the one-story ranch house which was painted white and stood out from the surrounding outbuildings that were painted a faded red. There were two large metal barn-like buildings and three smaller metal buildings, all located within forty yards of the ranch house. There were two corrals and fencing near the barns and horses milled around in one of the corrals. There were about half a dozen pickup trucks of various makes and ages parked next to one of the larger metal sheds.

Woody pulled the Suburban up next to an old Ford pickup truck on the end of the line of vehicles and put the vehicle in park. Then he turned the key and killed the engine. "Everybody out," he said. "You're looking at your new home."

The three young brothers exited the Suburban and stood there holding their packs. Woody got out of the vehicle and started toward the front door of the metal shed. He stopped when he realized the three boys had not moved and were not following him. They stood, rooted to the bare dirt beneath their feet, staring at the giant empty space all around them.

Woody grinned. "Come on. Let's go inside. Nothing you see out here is gonna change in the next year, let alone the next hour."

He led the way, and the three boys followed him into the building. Woody held the door open and when everyone was inside, he closed it.

The shed was larger than it looked from the outside. Along one wall were eight long metal beds. Four of them were made up with bedding and had a trunk at the front end and a metal military looking locker against the wall on each side of the beds.

At one end of the shed there were three toilets, three shower heads and four sinks. There were no doors nor any kind of privacy for any of the fixtures.

At the other end of the shed was a sizeable area with a television, a radio, two old care-worn tables with an assortment of motley-looking chairs. There was also an old refrigerator and a small cook top with two burners. An old, battered coffee pot was the sole occupant of the stove. The walls were metal and painted a dull grey. The floor was concrete. There were a few windows along the wall where the bunk beds were located, but no others.

On the wall next to the door was an old metal cabinet with drawers halfway up and then open the rest of the way up. In the cabinet were three lever action rifles. On the other side of the door was a line of wooden pegs, most of which supported jackets of various sizes and colors.

"Pick out a bunk that's not made up and put your packs on it. That will be your bunk for the next three months," said Woody.

Each of the boys picked out a bunk and placed their packs on it.

"What now?" asked Steve, the oldest.

"We wait," said Woody. "Big Dave will be here shortly. He planned to be here when you arrived, but something must have come up."

"Big Dave?" asked Steve. "Why is he called Big Dave?"

"That question will answer itself when he gets here, son," replied Woody with a half-hidden smile on his face.

Steve shrugged, and he and his brothers each pulled out a battered old chair and sat down to wait. They didn't wait long.

CHAPTER SIXTEEN

The three brothers were talking softly among themselves when the door flew open and banged against the metal wall of the shed.

A huge cowboy entered the room, filling the entire doorway. He was tall, about six foot four inches, and big, easily weighing two hundred fifty pounds of what looked to be pure muscle. He was clean shaven, had dirty blonde hair cut reasonably short, bright blue eyes, and huge hands. He looked like a Nordic god or a Viking warrior, except he was dressed like a cowboy in a stained grey Stetson cowboy hat, faded denim long sleeved shirt and jeans with a wide belt buckle, and worn brown cowboy boots. A pair of worn leather work gloves hung out from the rear pocket of his jeans.

He took one step inside the door. Looked over the room. Spotted the three open mouthed boys seated around the old wooden table and strode over to them. He turned to look at Woody.

"Is this them?" he asked Woody.

"Yes, sir," replied Woody. "This is them. Stand up, boys, and meet your boss for this summer."

The three boys stumbled out of their chairs, Travis knocking his chair over on its back in the process. Woody picked up the chair and set it upright.

"This is Steven, Leland, and Travis Mann, your new help for this summer," said Woody.

Big Dave just scowled and looked at each of the boys over like they were a calf for sale. He stopped when he got to Lee. "Leland? What the hell kind of sissy name is that?" he asked, but not waiting for an answer.

He paused for a second as he looked the three young men over carefully. "Well, don't just stand there gawkin,' boys," he said. "We got work to do. Follow me," he said.

Big Dave turned and headed back out the door.

The three brothers just stood there in stunned silence.

"Don't just stand there," said Woody. "Follow the man outside."

The three brothers were jolted into action, and they hurried out the door, bumping into each other in the process.

When they got outside, Big Dave was standing next to the bed of his big Ford pickup truck. "Get your young asses over here," he snarled at them.

They hurried over to stand in front of Big Dave. Then he reached into the bed of the truck and picked up a cardboard box with the name "Steve" written on it. He handed the box to Steve. Next box was labeled "Lee," and he handed it to Lee. The last box was labeled "Travis." As he handed the box to the youngest brother, he said, "What the hell is a name like Travis. Sounds like some stupid Confederate general in the Civil War who got his ass shot off by Sherman."

Then he headed back into the bunkhouse building and when he got to the door he turned. "Let's go. Don't just stand there holding them damn boxes. You're burnin' daylight."

Then he quickly moved inside the building. He moved lightly on his feet for a big man and his movements were graceful and smooth.

He led the three brothers to their bunks. Then he turned to face them.

"Stand by your bunk," he said. "Put your box on the floor in front of you. When I tell you, pull out the item I mentioned and make sure you have that item and the proper amount of that item. Is that clear?"

"Yes, sir," the three brothers responded like they were in boot camp as newly enlisted soldiers.

"Open the boxes," commanded Big Dave. The three boys each complied.

"Take out six blue denim long sleeved shirts. Count them to make sure there are six," commanded Big Dave.

The three brothers did as ordered, and then laid the shirts on their respective bunk beds.

"Next item. Take out four pairs of blue jeans plus one leather belt," commanded Big Dave.

Again, the three brothers complied with his order and then laid them on the bunk bed with the shirts.

This ritual continued until the boxes were empty and the bunks were covered with shirts, jeans, belts, t-shirts, underwear, socks, cowboy boots, and a baseball cap with the logo of Lee Jeans on it.

"Now, pack that shit away in your locker and your footlocker at the end of your bunk," said Big Dave.

"Don't we get cowboy hats?" asked Lee in a fairly timid voice.

"Are you a cowboy?" asked Big Dave.

"No sir," he replied.

"Then you answered your own damn question," responded Big Dave.

When the three had all put their new clothes and gear away, Big Dave spoke again.

"Open your foot lockers and take out two sheets, a blanket, a pillow, and a pillowcase," he ordered.

The three brothers immediately complied with his order.

"Now, do any of you greenhorns know how to make a bed?" asked Big Dave.

None of the boys responded as they were all seemingly intent on studying the piece of concrete floor in front of their shoes.

"I thought as much," snorted Big Dave.

He grabbed sheets and blanket from the footlocker in front of him which was Lee's. Then he quickly demonstrated how to make the bed. He added the pillowcase covered pillow.

"Any questions?" he asked.

Hearing none, he said, "Make your damn bunks and do it now!"

Lee looked up and said, "But you already made my bed."

"Nope," said Big Dave as he immediately stripped the bed and dumped sheets, blanket, pillow, and pillowcase on the floor.

The three began making their beds. When they were finished, Big Dave inspected their work. "Pathetic," he said. "Do it again."

It took three tries before he was satisfied. Then he gathered them together.

"You boys are lucky. You get the rest of today off. Supper is at six. Breakfast is at six in the morning. Don't be late or you'll spend the day hungry. You'll meet the rest of the crew at supper tonight. After breakfast, meet me in front of the big red barn at a quarter till seven. Don't be late. If you are, you'll live to regret it. Any questions?"

There were none.

Then Big Dave strode out the door, with Woody in his wake and according to Lee, the smell of sulfur in the air.

The three boys stared at the closed door. Then they stared at each other.

"What the hell just happened?" asked a bewildered Lee.

"I don't know, but I'm pretty sure it wasn't good," said Steve.

The three brothers then opened their luggage and unpacked it, placing items in their individual footlockers.

"What the hell is that?" said Steve, pointing to Travis's hand.

"It's my slingshot," he replied.

"You brought a slingshot?" asked his big brother incredulously.

"I thought it might come in handy," protested Travis.

"Where you expecting an attack by wild monkeys" asked Steve.

Then Steve and Lee broke out in laughter at their younger brother's expense,

CHAPTER SEVENTEEN

The boys trudged over to the dining hall at a quarter till six. There they met the four regular ranch hands and the cook.

Slim was just that. A tall, slim cowboy who moved gracefully just walking across the floor of the kitchen. He said he was from Montana and had been cowboyin' since he got kicked out of his home when he was sixteen. He had brown hair cut short and long sideburns. He was cleanshaven and smoked hand rolled cigarettes.

Rocky was well named. He looked like a small version of Popeye, the sailor man. He was muscular and stocky. He walked bow legged and had a droopy mustache that looked like a crop failure on anyone less formidable in appearance.

Preacher was a thin, ascetic looking cowboy who had dark hair, very dark eyes, and a perpetual scowl on his face. He was called preacher because his entire known vocabulary began with God damn it.

The fourth cowboy looked like one. He was about six foot four inches tall with a hard, muscular lean body. He was clean shaven with close cropped dark brown hair. His arms were covered with tattoos. Most of them of a military nature. He introduced himself as Weston, an army veteran. He looked to be in his early thirties.

The last member of the ranch team was the cook. He was short, older, and had a full beard. He was a tad stocky, but he appeared to be light on his feet. He moved smoothly. He never introduced himself, but the others just called him Cookie. As the men sat down to a long table and dug into pots and plates of food, it became obvious to the three brothers the Cookie knew how to cook. The food was plain, but tasty and there was plenty of it.

Big Dave sat at the head of the table. The four cowboys sat on the chairs on either side of him. The three sons sat together further down the table. For about fifteen minutes no one spoke, and the only noise was of men chewing and utensils scraping on plates. The only words spoken after that were "Pass the damn potatoes," or something similar.

When the cowboys had finished eating, they got up from their chairs, gathered up their plates and utensils and walked over to the divider between the dining area and the kitchen and stacked their dirty dishes and utensils in a sink. All of them refilled their coffee cups and returned to their seats.

After a few short embarrassing minutes, the three boys followed suit. It was then that the cowboys began to chat with Big Dave and among themselves. None of them spoke to the three boys. Cookie disappeared into the kitchen after he finished clearing off the pots and pans of leftover food from the long table.

The three boys just sat there staring at the table, unsure of what they were supposed to do.

That ended about fifteen minutes later, when Big Dave pushed his chair back from the table. He stood up and faced the cowboys and the three brothers.

"You boys be ready to go to work after breakfast tomorrow," he said. "Cookie serves breakfast at six in the morning. We start work at six-thirty. You miss breakfast you go hungry till lunch."

Then he turned and went out the door of the cook shack. The four cowboys chatted a bit amongst themselves, finished their coffee and then deposited the empty cups in the kitchen sink and headed out the door. Bewildered, the three sons did the same and soon all seven men were in the bunkhouse.

Some of the cowboys read old paperback books, Weston read a Guns and Ammo magazine. The radio in the bunkhouse was on and tuned into some country and western music radio station. The three boys just sat together and took it all in.

Preacher looked up from his book. "If the music ain't to your taste, just ignore it," he said. "The radio station goes off the air at nine at night."

"What do you do then?" asked a curious Travis.

"We sleep," replied Preacher. "What in the goddamn hell do you think we do? We don't sit around and have a circle jerk." With that he stuck his nose back in his paperback.

Nine o'clock came, the radio went silent, and within minutes every man was in bed and the lights in the bunkhouse were turned out.

As each of the boys discovered, the night was dark and damn quiet. As long as you didn't include items like snoring and farting.

CHAPTER EIGHTEEN

There was no bugle in the morning to wake everyone up. The three boys awoke to the noise of men mumbling, water running, boots scraping on the wooden floor of the bunkhouse, and the smells of hot water and soap.

"Rise and shine boys," said Preacher as he walked past their bunks wearing nothing but a towel. "Breakfast is at six, and it's already five-thirty."

The three brothers managed to tumble out of bed and after grabbing their small toilet kits, they headed to the shower in the restroom at the end of the building. They were showered, shaved (except for Travis whose blonde hair and youth made that chore still unnecessary), and quickly dressed in their newly issued ranch duds.

Breakfast was surprisingly good. There were pancakes, sausages, fried eggs, biscuits, coffee, and orange juice. Each of the three young men filled their plates from the platters Cookie had placed on the long table and the food disappeared like magic.

Big Dave finished his breakfast first and rose from the table. He looked over at the three brothers and spoke. "You three join me in front of the big barn when you're done chowin' down." Then he turned and disappeared out the door of the cook shack.

The three wolfed down the remainder of their breakfast and after returning the dishes to the kitchen counter, they headed out the door.

Arriving in front of the big barn, they found Big Dave standing there with a western saddle arranged on top of a large old wooden sawhorse.

Big Dave studied the three for a moment. Then he spoke. "This is lesson one in cowboy school. Your main and most important tool is your saddle. You need to understand it, use it properly, and take care of it. Do that and you are liable to extend your life expectancy considerably as a cowboy."

He had picked up a narrow wooden dowel that was about two feet long. He used it as a pointer as he began to explain the western saddle to the three young men.

Big Dave used the crude pointer to touch the bottom of the saddle. "Under here is the saddle tree. It's the structural foundation of the saddle. It's the base that the rest of the saddle is built on. The wood is usually white wood. It's lightweight and is both flexible and strong. It fits the horse well and is designed to distribute the weight in the saddle to benefit the horse and the rider."

He paused and looked carefully at the three brothers. "Any questions?" There were none. The boys were silent.

"Next is the gullet." Big Dave used the stick to point to the area of the saddle between the front and back. "Its purpose is to provide clearance for the horse's spine and withers. It allows the rider to feel comfortable in the saddle. The gullet's size depends on the size of the horse. A gullet for a mustang would be narrower than one for a quarter horse or a paint."

"Any questions?" he said.

Silence.

Again, Big Dave pointed with the stick to the back of the saddle. "This is the cantle. It's the back of the saddle, behind the cowboy's seat. It helps protect the rider when taking a horse fast over rough ground. Any questions?"

Silence.

"This area under and around the saddle is the skirt," he said. It provides the rider stability and helps keep the saddle and cowboy in place when riding. It also helps protect the saddle from wear and tear over time. Any questions?"

Silence.

Then Big Dave pointed the stick to the stirrups. "The fenders are two leather loops that attach to either side of the saddle. They provide a place to rest your feet while riding and help keep your legs in place. They can be adjusted for the cowboy's height or size. Any questions?"

Silence.

Big Dave used the stick to point to the stirrups. "Stirrups are usually made of metal or leather and come in sizes suited for the rider. They are usually placed at hip level of the rider for the right positioning. Getting this wrong can make for a damn uncomfortable ride. You want to adjust them so that the heel of your boot is slightly lower than the toe to help your balance. Any questions?"

Silence.

Big Dave placed the end of the stick on the saddle horn. "This is the horn. It's located at the front of the saddle. It's used to help secure the cowboy's grip on the saddle. It helps when riding at different speeds and in rough terrain. It's used as a handhold when mounting or unmounting the horse. It's also a good anchor for tying stuff such as reins or lariats. Any questions?"

Travis timidly raised his hand.

"Yes?" asked Big Dave.

"Why is called a horn?" asked Travis.

Big Dave smiled. "'Cause it sticks out like a horn," he said.

"Oh," said Travis.

Big Dave used the little pointer again. "This is the rigging." He went on to explain each piece and what its purpose was and how it was used. When he was finished, he looked at the three brothers and again said, "Any questions?"

Silence.

Big Dave let a small grim smile move his lips. Then he pointed at Steve with the little stick. "You're the oldest and a college boy. You come over here and explain each part of the saddle as I point to it," said Big Dave.

Steve looked like he had just tried to swallow a cat. He was speechless and felt frozen in place.

"What's wrong, Steve?" asked Big Dave. "Did I not do a good job of explaining the saddle to you?"

Steve was silent. Finally, he got his mouth to work, and he said softly, "I can't."

"What's that you said?" asked Big Dave. "I couldn't hear you. Speak up boy."

"I can't," Steve finally blurted out.

"Why not?' asked Big Dave.

"I didn't understand you," said Steve.

"You mean you didn't pay attention. Ain't that correct, Steve," said Big Dave.

Steve hung his head. "Yes, sir," he said.

"Well, that seems strange for a college boy, you bein' so damn smart and all," said Big Dave. Then he gave each of the three boys a hard look. "This ain't no joke, boys. You need to know your equipment and how it works and what it's for. And you need to know how to fix it in an emergency if it breaks and something important, like your life, is at stake. You want to be a cowboy; you need to think like one. You need to know all your tools and the saddle is the basis of your toolbox. Do you get me?"

"Yes, sir," came the mixed reply from the three brothers.

"I can't hear you," said Big Dave.

"YES, SIR!" came the joint reply, this time.

"Good," said Big Dave. "Now here's what we're gonna do next. One at a time. Each of you is gonna give the rest of us a lecture about the saddle, starting with you, Steve. And the rest of us are gonna listen. If you get stuck, I'll help you out, but each of you boys is gonna know the saddle backwards and forwards before we leave this here barn. I don't give a shit how long that takes. We're gonna do it until you get it right. Understand?"

"YES, SIR!" came the response from the three brothers.

The exercise went on for three hours. By the end, all three brothers knew and could explain the components of the western saddle and answer questions about what the components did. When they broke for lunch, all three brothers were tired. They felt like they had lifted weights for three hours, but all they had done was work hard with their brains.

They broke for lunch and headed for the cook shack. Big Dave followed the three youngsters, and he swore he saw some new bounce in their step as they made their way to lunch.

CHAPTER NINETEEN

When lunch was finished, Big Dave led the three youngsters back to the big barn. They arrived at the big sliding doors that opened when pushed back on the rails they rested on. Big Dave slid them open. Then he led them inside the barn.

It was dark with shadows in the barn, interspersed with beams of light from the windows and small shafts of sunlight that came through the small cracks in the siding and the roof.

As their eyes adjusted to the lack of sunlight, they saw Big Dave move to a stack of two bales of hay lying on top of each other. Big Dave walked behind the bales and motioned for the boys to move closer.

Then he reached down and produced an odd-looking concoction of ropes. He held it up in front of them. "This," he announced, "is a hackamore. It's a rope bridle used to move horses around and keep them under control. It consists of a headstall that goes on the horse's head and attaches to the noseband. He pointed to each part as he spoke. "You can see the reins are rope attached to the side of the noseband. There is no bit in the mouth of the horse. The hackamore works like a bridle when leading and handling the horse. It uses pressure on the horse's nose and face to control and direct the horse."

Big Dave then had each boy pick up the apparatus and familiarize themselves with its parts and how they worked in controlling the horse. Then he led them to a nearby stall. Inside the stall was a brown gelding. Big Dave had the three boys stand on hay bales on the side of the stall so they could see every detail of the gelding. Big Dave slid into the stall slowly while talking softly to the gelding. He slid alongside the horse and then stood with the gelding's head on his right side. He took the hackamore and slid it over the horse's head and then moved it until he had it where he wanted it. When he was finished, he took a lead rope and hooked it to the hackamore.

"Open the stall door," he said to the boys. Steve moved quickly to unlatch and open the stall door and then stepped aside. Big Dave slowly walked out with the lead rope in his hand. He led the gelding out of the stall and walked it down the length of the barn and then led it back. Then he tied the lead rope off to a rung of a nearby stall.

He had each of the boys lead the gelding around in the barn. Then Big Dave had one boy lead the horse into the stall and unhook the lead rope. The next boy went into the stall and hooked the lead rope to the hackamore and then led the horse out of the stall and took him for a short walk and finally returned to the stall. After all three boys had done this exercise successfully, Big Dave quizzed each of them on the hackamore. When he was satisfied, he went to the tack room and returned with a bridle.

Big Dave explained each part of the bridle and emphasized how important the location and use of the bit was to control the horse. He quizzed each of them on the parts and use of the bridle, and then he returned to the stall that held the gelding. He slipped into the stall, talked softly to the horse, and then slowly slipped off the hackamore. Holding his right arm around the gelding's neck, he then slipped on the bridle. He took the reins in his hand and then led the gelding out of the stall and around the interior of the big barn.

After he returned the gelding to the stall, he removed the bridle and then reinstalled the hackamore.

Big Dave exited the stall and then faced the three boys. "Any questions?" he asked.

This time there were several questions from each of the boys. Big Dave answered each one in turn, and then he handed the bridle to Steve. "Go into the stall and remove the hackamore. Then put the bridle on the horse."

Steve took the bridle, slipped into the stall, and moved up next to the horse's head. He spoke softly to the horse and stroked the gelding's neck as he did so. He was able to remove the hackamore on his first try, but his attempt to put the bridle on the gelding took him three tries. When he was finally successful, he led the horse out of the stall by the reins and led it around the interior of the big barn.

When he returned to the stall, Big Dave took the horse, removed the bridle, and reinstalled the hackamore. Then he led the gelding back into the stall. He turned and looked back at the three boys. "Who's next?" he asked with a faint smile on his face.

"That'd be me," said Lee. He had more trouble with the exercise than Steve had, but he finally mastered the bridle and proudly led the gelding around the inside of the barn.

"You're next," said Big Dave to a nervous Travis. The older two brothers stood by ready to enjoy their younger brother's discomfort and expected him to struggle with the exercise. To their surprise and to Big Dave's as well, Travis had no trouble removing the hackamore and then placing the bridle on the gelding. He did it on the first try. Even Big Dave was impressed.

After Big Dave removed the bridle from the gelding and latched the gate to the stall, he turned to the boys. "Go get cleaned up for supper. You boys did pretty well today. Tomorrow, you get to try the whole works," said Big Dave.

Travis put up his hand.

"You got a question?" asked Big Dave.

"What's the whole works?" asked Travis.

Big Dave laughed. "You get to try to saddle and bridle a horse on your own," he said.

The boys were silent as they walked to the bunkhouse. They didn't speak a word until they were inside the building and Big Dave was out of hearing range.

"Holy shit!" said Travis. He and his brothers were quickly discussing what was waiting for them the next day and they were both excited and scared.

All three of them felt ravenously hungry at supper that evening, and they each ate two helpings of beef stew. While the other four cowboys and Big Dave chatted, the three boys ate and said very little.

CHAPTER TWENTY

Six-thirty the next morning found the three brothers sitting on the top of the fence of the corral next to the big barn. They had made it to breakfast at six and after wolfing down pancakes and sausage, they had put their dishes on the counter and headed out to the barn. They were surprised when Big Dave opened the big barn door from the inside and stepped out leading a grey mare. He led the horse to the corral fence and tied off the lead rope to the corral.

The three brothers looked at each other. How had Big Dave managed to beat them to the big barn?

When he finished, he turned to the three brothers on the corral fence. "One of you go in the barn and come out with a full bucket of water. One of you get a small sack of oats. The last one of you go into the tack room and get me a curry comb."

The last one off the fence was Travis. He looked puzzled.

"What's the problem, son," said Big Dave.

"What's the tack room?" he asked quietly.

"It's that small room on the far side of the barn. It's where we keep the tack," said Big Dave.

"What's tack?" asked a puzzled Travis.

"All of the things used to make a horse useful," said Big Dave. "Saddles, hackamores, bridles, and lariats. That stuff is called tack."

"OK," said Travis and he dashed into the barn.

Soon all three boys had lined up next to the tied-up mare, their tools in front of them.

"First things first," said Big Dave. "When you water a horse, you tie him off to something. Then you get a bucket of water and put it in front of him. He'll drink till he has enough."

"Second, you feed the horse. You take this burlap sack of oats and slip it over her neck and slide her muzzle into the sack and tie the sack off behind her. When she eats all the oats, then remove the sack."

"Third, at the end of the workday, you take off the saddle, saddle blanket, and wipe the horse's back down. Then you take this curry comb, and you comb out her coat." He then demonstrated how to use the comb and had each of the three brothers try it out.

"The last thing you do is check the horse's shoes," said Big Dave. He showed the boys how to approach the horse, where to stand, and then how to lift one foot at a time and how to inspect the hoof and horseshoe.

"If you find a rock wedged in the hoof, you pry it out. If the shoe has lost a nail or is loose, you tell Preacher. He's our best blacksmith here at the ranch. He'll fix the horse's hoof or shoe," said Big Dave.

"Remember this," said Big Dave. "At the end of the workday, you tend to your horse before you tend to yourself. And I mean every day you ride that animal."

"You boys rest a minute. I'll be right back out," said Big Dave as he disappeared into the dark confines of the big barn. He returned with a coiled lariat in his hand. He spent the next hour showing the boys how to hold a lariat and how to properly tie a lariat. Then he dragged out a big wooden sawhorse with four small wheels and a wooden cutout of a large cow on the end. The cutout was complete with small wooden horns.

"This here is Cathy the Cow," said Big Dave with a grin. "You boys are gonna learn how to throw a rope on a cow by practicing on Cathy."

He showed the boys how to handle the rope, how to set a loop, how to twirl the rope loop, and then how to toss it. He taught them each step separately, and then he had them combine all the steps.

After the brothers got fairly proficient throwing a loop over a stationary Cathy, he then tied a short rope to the front end of Cathy the Cow. "I'm gonna pull old Cathy past you, and you need to be able to rope her while she's moving away from you," said Big Dave.

The initial results from the boys' efforts were nothing short of comical. Then Big Dave took each boy, one at a time and coached them on how to hold, how to twirl, and how to throw the rope. By the end of the day, they had all been able to rope Cathy several times.

"I know you boys are feelin' pretty damn good about ropin' old Cathy, but tomorrow we move on to learning to ride a horse. Once you master that job, then you will learn how to ride the horse, twirl the rope, throw it, and get the loop around the head of a real cow while both the cow and your horse are movin'."

All three boys looked at him like he had just said they were going for a ride to the moon and back. The best description of their facial expression would be terrified shock.

Big Dave had them work with the lariat for another half hour and then he sent them to the bunkhouse to rest before dinner. The boys appeared at the dinner table and gobbled down plenty of supper, but they had little to say and when dinner was over, they headed to the bunkhouse and by eight that evening all three of them were asleep in their bunks.

Tomorrow was going to be a much harder day. And they knew it.

CHAPTER TWENTY-ONE

Shortly after five the next morning, the boys were awakened by the noises made by the other four cowboys in the bunkhouse. They showered, shaved, and got dressed for a new workday. The boys arrived at the cook shack fifteen minutes early, only to find Big Dave and the other four cowboys and Cookie having coffee at the big table.

The three brothers grabbed coffee mugs and poured hot black coffee from a big coffee pot on the cookstove. All three added cream and sugar and Travis grabbed a small glass and filled it with orange juice from a pitcher.

After breakfast, the trio followed Big Dave out to the big barn. Once there, he went into the barn and returned with three lariats. All of the ropes were coiled, but they had obviously been used before as they showed some signs of wear and tear.

Big Dave took one lariat and uncoiled it and then he recoiled it to his satisfaction. Then he looked up at his small audience.

"Today we are gonna practice roping a moving target," he said.

The three brothers looked around and then he could see confusion in their faces. "What's wrong?" asked a grinning Big Dave.

"What are we supposed to rope?" asked a curious Travis.

"We need moving targets so each of you are gonna take turns being a moving target and see if your brothers can put a rope on you," said a still-smiling Big Dave.

He gave Steve a lariat and told him to uncoil it and then coil it to his liking. When that was done, he had Travis stand ten yards to the left of where the rest of the group stood.

"When Steve signals me he is ready, I'll say go and Travis will run past us," said Big Dave. "Travis, you run at a lope to start with, not at full speed."

"Yes, sir," said a nervous Travis.

When Steve gave Big Dave a nod, he yelled, "Go," and Travis took off at a lope and he ran past where Steve was standing. Steve twirled the rope over his head and then threw it. It fell harmlessly about three feet behind Travis as he ran past the others.

"Let's try it again," said Big Dave. "Steve, you need to be twirling the rope and when I yell go, throw it faster."

"Yes, sir," responded an embarrassed Steve.

It took three tries, but Steve finally managed to lasso his youngest brother. Big Dave had them repeat the exercise ten more times. Then he asked Travis to run as fast as he could. To Steve's amazement he lassoed Travis on his first try.

Big Dave noted his surprise. "You are developing your hand eye coordination and now it's adjusting automatically. Keep at it and you'll get better and better."

Sure enough, the more they practiced, the better Steve got at lassoing his younger brother. After two hours of Steve throwing a lasso, they finally changed and Steve became the runner, and Lee the roper. Lee had more trouble than Steve did, and it took longer, but he finally seemed to get the hang of it and when he finally roped his older brother, he let out a whoop.

Big Dave smiled to himself. They continued the exercise until Lee was fairly proficient at roping his older brother.

Then it was time to take a break for lunch. The boys were tired, but excited at learning and developing a new skill they had never tried before. After lunch, they returned to the big barn and then it was Travis' turn.

Big Dave was again a bit surprised as Travis only missed his first try at roping his brother Lee. After that he never missed. Even when Lee was running as fast as he could, Travis managed to lasso him.

When they broke for the day, the boys trudged off to the bunkhouse. They were tired, but excited at finding out they could learn a new skill like using a lasso.

After supper, they turned in early and slept hard. They were fast asleep when the other four cowboys were still out on the front porch of the bunkhouse, chatting and smoking hand-rolled cigarettes.

When the four trudged into the bunkhouse to call it a night, the three brothers were dead to the world.

CHAPTER TWENTY-TWO

Once again, the brothers were awakened by the noises of the four cowboys taking showers, shaving, and getting dressed for the day. They rolled out of their bunks and quickly showered, shaved, (except for Travis), and got dressed. They were at the cook house fifteen minutes early, and they had coffee and chatted with the four older cowboys and Big Dave.

After breakfast, Big Dave led them back to the big barn. When they got to the barn door, he turned to face them.

"Today, we find out if you've got what it takes to be a cowboy," he said. "Go in the barn and pick out a horse in a stall. Then go to the tack room and get a saddle blanket, a saddle, and a bridle. Bring all that out to the stall and then saddle and bridle your horse. When you get that done, lead the horse out of the barn and then come back out front to me. Is that clear?"

"Yes, sir," replied the three boys in a ragged chorus. They moved quickly inside the barn and spread out to pick out a mount for the day.

Big Dave sat on an old barrel next to the front of the barn and waited. He knew today would be a big test, and he was anxious to see how his young students would do.

It took a while, which was no surprise to Big Dave, but the three all came out front of the big barn leading a saddled horse.

Big Dave went to each horse and checked the cinches and bridles and after a few adjustments he seemed satisfied.

"Follow me," commanded Big Dave and he headed on foot to the large corral. When the four of them reached their destination, the boys could see there were half a dozen young calves milling around in the big corral.

Big Dave hoisted himself up on the top of the corral fence and sat there looking down at the boys holding their saddled horses.

"Now we see how much you have learned," he said. "One of you is going to mount his horse and when I open the gate, you are to ride into the corral. Then pick out a calf and ride over and lasso it. When you have roped the calf, you bring your horse to a halt and twist the lasso around the saddle horn and keep your horse still. The other two of you will then follow the lasso rope to the calf and free the calf. Is that clear?"

All three boys nodded their heads in agreement.

"Who's first?" asked Big Dave.

"I'll go first," said Steve.

"You other two boys tie off your horses and sit up on the corral fence and be ready to jump off and go free the calf," said Big Dave.

Steve mounted his horse, and then directed it to the corral gate. Big Dave opened the gate, and Steve rode into the corral. Big Dave closed the gate behind him and climbed up on the corral fence.

"Pick out a calf and rope him," commanded Big Dave.

The calves were milling around at one side of the corral, obviously nervous and not happy to have the horse and rider in their midst.

Steve picked out one calf who was standing on the far edge of the small herd and rode slowly toward it. As he got close, he took the lasso off the saddle horn and opened it and began twirling it above his baseball cap. The calf appeared frozen in place. As Steve and his horse got close, the calf suddenly dropped his head and bolted for the other side of the big corral. Steve spurred his horse and followed the calf, still twirling the lasso over his head. When he got close to his target, the calf suddenly made a ninety degree turn to the right and the horse under Steve struggled to adjust to the turn and then tore out after the fleeing calf. Steve got within ten feet of the calf and tossed the lasso. He missed and the rope lay in the dirt of the big corral.

Steve calmly pulled his lasso back to him, coiling it as he did so.

"It ain't as easy as it looks when the target is movin'" called out Big Dave.

Steve nodded his head in agreement.

"Try it again, Steve," said Big Dave.

It took six tries, but Steve finally dropped the lasso over the calf's head and then Steve's horse came to a stop and the calf fell on its side. The two brothers jumped into the corral and ran over, and one put a knee on the calf to hold it and the other removed the lasso.

Then Big Dave called all three of them over to where he sat on the corral fence. "It ain't easy, but it's like lots of things. You got to work at it, practice it, and then it becomes more natural, and it gets much easier. Let's try it again, Steve."

Steve picked out another calf and this time he was successful on his third attempt. Big Dave kept up the exercise until he was satisfied. Then he ran the other two brothers through the same drill.

When the exercise was over to Big Dave's satisfaction, it was late afternoon. They had skipped lunch. The boys were tired and hungry.

Big Dave called them together. "I know you're tired and hungry. So am I. But you boys ain't done yet. You need to take your horses back to the barn. Put them in their stalls. Unsaddle and remove their bridles. Then get them water and grain. Then wipe them down and use your curry combs. Then put the saddles, blankets, and bridles back in the tack room after making sure the blankets are clean and in good shape. You boys got all that?" he said.

"Yes, sir." came the tired and disjointed response.

"Just remember. You ain't done until your horses are cared for and your gear is properly put away. When you finish, meet me back out here," said Big Dave.

The three brothers nodded, and each grabbed the reins of his horse and began to lead them back into the big barn and to their respective stalls.

Big Dave could not help smiling to himself as he watched them walk to the big barn.

"They're tougher than I expected," he thought to himself.

CHAPTER TWENTY-THREE

The next morning was largely a repeat of the previous day. The boys rode in the big corral and roped calves. Big Dave had brought in a new group of calves to make sure the morning was as challenging as he could make it. The three boys did very well, especially Travis, who had a natural feel for being on horseback and throwing a rope with accuracy.

After lunch, which the three boys were careful to remind Big Dave about, so they didn't miss it for two days in a row, he led them on horseback to a spot about a half mile from the ranch buildings. It was a small hollow that pushed back into some low hills.

They rode until they came to the end of the hollow where they faced an almost sheer wall of granite and rock. Big Dave had them tie off their horses and follow him on foot. He approached the hollow and walked over to an old metal box set on the ground. He used a key to open a padlock on the box and then raised the dust covered lid and produced a roll of targets. He took the targets out of the box and told the boys to stay put. Then he walked to the end of the hollow and used a small hammer and nails from the box to place a target on a post placed in the ground at the end of the hollow.

Then he walked back to the waiting trio. He walked to his horse and removed a lever action Winchester rifle from its scabbard and returned to where the boys were waiting.

Big Dave held out the rifle and had each of the boys handle it and get a good look and feel for the weapon. Then he took it back from them.

"You boys bin learnin' about the tools a cowboy uses. This here rifle is one of them tools," said Big Dave.

He then demonstrated how the rifle worked. He loaded shells into the receiver and then took the rifle and pulled down on the lever.

"The bullets are stored in a tube under the barrel of the rifle," he said. "When you use the lever, you cause the rifle to move a bullet into the barrel and to cock the rifle." He then did just that. Then he raised the rifle to his shoulder and took aim at the distant target. Then he pulled the trigger, and the rifle fired. The noise was loud and hurt the boys' ears.

"All them movies you boys have seen as westerns show all them guys shootin' rifles from horseback. All that is pure crap. You shoot a rifle over the head of a horse while you are mounted, and he's gonna buck your ass off immediately. Horses don't like the sound of a rifle firing no more than you boys did," he said. "Especially when its right next to their ears."

Big Dave looked carefully at each of the boys. "You never, I repeat, never shoot from horseback. You get on the damn ground, take good aim, and hit whatever the hell you're aimin' at. And you tie off your horse before you fire, or he'll run off from the damn noise. You boys got that?" he asked.

All three boys nodded their heads. They had been listening intently, unable to take their eyes off the rifle Big Dave held in his hands.

"Good," he said. "Now we're gonna learn how to shoot this here rifle and do it right."

Big Dave explained that a rifle was used because it was a much better, more accurate, and longer-range weapon than a pistol. "I've used rifles to kill coyotes, rattlesnakes, and critters that serve no useful purpose on a ranch."

He then took the three brothers over to the small make-shift rifle range and demonstrated how to aim and shoot the rifle and then how to reload it. Then he had each of them load the rifle and shoot at a target. Each boy got his own target and when they were done with the shooting lesson, he gave each of the boys their targets.

"Keep these targets as a reminder of today. At the end of the summer, we'll do this again and you can compare these targets with the ones you make then," said Big Dave. "Most cowboys learn to be better shots, but some don't. For some shooting is as natural as taking a crap."

When they were finished, Big Dave returned the items to the metal box, relocked it, and returned his rifle to the scabbard. Then the four mounted their horses and followed Big Dave back to the ranch buildings.

When they reined in next to the big barn that served as a stable, Big Dave dismounted and tied his horse off to the top rung of the corral fence. The three boys did the same.

Big Dave turned to look at the boys. "Take care of the horses, including mine. See you at supper." With that, he turned and walked off towards his small cabin.

The boys had done some inquiring of the cook and had learned that Big Dave stayed at the small cabin and the big ranch house was for the owner whom neither the cook nor any of the four cowboys had ever seen, let alone met.

Steve grabbed the reins to both his horse and Big Dave's and led them into the big barn. His two brothers followed with their horses in tow.

At dinner that night, both Big Dave, Cookie, and the four regular cowboys sat back in slight awe as the three young men tore into their supper of beef stew like they hadn't eaten a bite of food in days.

After supper, Big Dave retired to his cabin, Cookie started his cleanup of the kitchen, and the four cowboys sat on the front porch of the bunkhouse and smoked hand rolled cigarettes or poked in a fresh piece of chewing tobacco, as they swapped tall tales of previous jobs. Some of what they said was probably actually true. The three brothers sat on the porch and listened for about thirty minutes. Then they headed inside and stripped off their clothes in record time and were sound asleep in less than twenty minutes.

CHAPTER TWENTY-FOUR

This morning the boys were at the cook shack slightly after six-thirty. They found Big Dave and the regular cowboys drinking coffee with Cookie around the big cook shack table.

Since everyone was up and in the cook shack, Cookie proceeded to make breakfast. This morning, he made scrambled eggs, fried potatoes, sausage, and big thick slices of toast, along with hot coffee and cold orange juice.

The boys dug into their breakfast and ate fast and hard. They were finished and took seconds. After breakfast, everyone sat around the long table, drinking coffee, and chatting. The boys were surprised. No one hurried to get out the door to get to work. They just sat there and talked and drank coffee.

Finally, the talk died down and Big Dave spoke. "Today is Saturday. Get the chores done and then get cleaned up and head to town for some fun. Except for you three boys. Under your agreement, you stay on the ranch for the first two weekends and that means no trip to town for you until the end of the third week. I expect you to practice your ropin' skills today and tomorrow. And I expect you to do all the chores on this list today and Sunday to give Slim, Rocky, Preacher, and Weston a break." Then he paused.

"Any questions?" he asked.

Travis raised his hand. "You mean we can't go into town for two more weeks?"

"Yup, that's exactly what I just said," remarked Big Dave with a slight grin on his face. He noted the disappointed look on the faces of the three brothers.

"Besides, only Steve here is old enough to legally buy a drink in town. You other two would just be sippin' lemonade or Coca-Cola. Ain't no fun in that," said Big Dave.

He looked around the table. Then he looked back at the three brothers. "Each of you will pair up with one of the boys and learn which chores you'll be doin' from now on. Travis goes with Weston. Steve goes with Rocky, and Lee goes with Slim. I can't pair none of you boys with Preacher cause he'd just teach you things that were bad for you."

Big Dave stood up from the table. "All right. Now that all that bullshit is over, get the hell outta here and get to work."

Big Dave slipped out the door and Cookie began to wash dishes. Preacher stayed to help him.

"Let's go boys," said Weston. "You heard the man. We got shit to do."

Travis followed Weston out of the cook shack, and they headed to the barn. Once there, they fed and watered all the horses in their stalls. Then Weston ordered Travis to use a pitchfork, clean out all stalls, and pile the stuff on an ancient wheelbarrow that still had a steel wheel and no rubber tire.

Steve followed Rocky outside, and they headed for the end of the small buildings on the ranch. There Steve discovered the small pig pen. There were half a dozen pigs waiting by a small feed bunker. They fed and watered the pigs and Rocky taught Steve to check the pigs out for any injuries or sign of disease or other problems.

Slim led Lee to a small building on stilts surrounded by a wire fence enclosure. A door to the building was open and had a sloped plank that led to the ground. About a dozen chickens were out and about and pecking on the ground for God knows what. They cleaned out the chicken coop, replaced and repaired the nesting boxes with fresh straw where it was needed, and cleaned out the straw laden floor.

"Are we supposed to collect the eggs?" asked Lee. Slim grinned at him. "Nope. That's Cookie's job. He collects the eggs. We just keep the place clean and make sure the feeder and water trough are full. He showed Lee how to check and then fill the gravity feeder and water trough.

When each crew had finished their chores, they headed for the bunkhouse to clean up and change clothes for their trip into town. The boys stood by their bunks, unsure of what they were supposed to do.

Slim stopped, after stepping out of the shower, clad only in a towel. "You boys get cleaned up. We're all heading into town. That includes you."

The boys quickly complied with his order. When everyone was cleaned up and changed, they met outside the bunkhouse. The four cowboys piled into two old pickup trucks and headed to the highway and then into Kemmerer. The three boys stood there, unsure of what to do. Big Dave appeared and stared at them with an amused look on his face.

"You boys ride with me. Two of you in the bed of the pickup and one up front with me," he said.

"I thought we couldn't go into town for two weeks?" said a puzzled Steve.

"You can't," said Big Dave. "You're just goin' in with me to pick up supplies, and then we head back here. You don't get to stay and hoot and holler with the rest of the cowboys."

"Oh," said Steve, obviously disappointed.

The three brothers climbed into the pickup truck and soon were in Kemmerer. They drove past Triangle Park and then parked in an empty slot in the now crowded parking lot of the grocery store. They piled out of the truck and followed Big Dave into the store. He had Steve and Lee each grab a wheeled cart and told them to follow him.

They made a small procession in the store with Big Dave taking items off the shelf and tossing them into a cart pushed by Lee and Steve, with Travis bringing up the rear. It being Saturday morning, the store was full of shoppers, mostly women pushing shopping carts. By the time they reached the end of the store, both carts were full. Big Dave paid the bill, and they pushed the carts out to where the truck was parked. The three boys transferred the sacks of food and supplies into the bed of the pickup truck, and then returned the empty carts to the front of the store.

Big Dave drove the truck back to the ranch and had the three boys unload the groceries and supplies into the cook shack under the direction of Cookie. When they were done, they gathered outside and waited.

Big Dave came out and stood before them. "What's your pleasure?" he asked. "Ropin' calves or shootin' at targets?"

The boys looked at each other and almost in unison said, "Ropin' calves."

"Good choice," said Big Dave and led the way to the barn.

"Damn good choice," he thought to himself.

CHAPTER TWENTY-FIVE

Sunday morning was sunny and quiet. The boys woke up and showered and dressed as quietly as they could. The older four cowboys were dead to the world in their bunks. At least two of them were snoring loudly. Apparently, their Saturday night on the town had been intense, and they needed time and sleep to recover.

They had breakfast with Cookie and Big Dave. Cookie made French toast with real maple syrup and fresh sweet rolls. The boys had two helpings along with several cups of hot coffee.

When they had finished their breakfast and were nursing a last cup of hot coffee, Big Dave peered over his coffee mug at them.

"You boys up for a little ride?" he asked calmly.

The three brothers looked at each other and then at Big Dave.

"You bet," said Steve. This was followed by vocal agreement from Lee and Travis.

"Get the chores done and meet me at the big barn," said Big Dave.

The three boys rose from their seats and were out the door of the cook shack in a heartbeat.

Half an hour later, they met Big Dave in front of the big barn. He had his horse, a pinto gelding, saddled and tied off to the corral fence.

"Get your horses and get them saddled. We're burnin' daylight," he said.

It took almost twenty minutes for the boys to saddle, bridle, and lead their horses out of the barn. When they were all in front of Big Dave, he smiled and said, "Mount up."

Big Dave swung into the saddle and the boys followed suit, although a bit more slowly and awkwardly. Satisfied all were safely mounted, he led the way out of the work yard and headed for the banks of the Ham's Fork River. The morning was crisp and cool. The boys were learning the temperature varied a great deal during the day. The change in temperature from low to high in a twenty-four-hour period was about forty-five degrees. Thirty-five degrees in the early morning could easily hit eighty degrees by noon. The boys wore long sleeve denim shirts and lined denim jackets as did Big Dave.

He led them across a wide pasture, and then they came to the banks of the Ham's Fork River. The river originated in the upper Ham's Fork Basin. It began as a spring coming out of a rock cliff face and quickly turned into a stream that widened and deepened. The water was icy cold, even in the middle of the summer. It originated as snow melt and thus the low temperature. Trout loved it and the river had several species of trout including rainbow and cutthroat. All of them were considered good eating.

They rode along the river heading north toward Kemmerer. On the other side of the river was a roadbed containing the tracks for the Union Pacific Railroad. Most of the trains passed by the ranch during the night and did so silently because there was no reason to blow a whistle to announce their passing.

Big Dave took them on a tour of the boundaries of the ranch and pointed out landmarks and locations of springs to them. Some sections of the river were bounded by trees and bushes. Some sections were barren except for tall prairie grasses. After about three hours, Big Dave turned back toward the river. When he reached a spot with a good sized sandy open area on a sloping riverbank, he brought the pinto to a halt.

He turned to face the boys. "Anyone hungry?" he asked.

Astonishment filled the faces of the three brothers. Then they realized he was asking them if they wanted to have something to eat. They all answered in the affirmative.

Big Dave swung out of the saddle and tied the pinto off to an old log. He turned to look at the still mounted boys. "You boys plan on eatin' in the saddle, or do you think we might have lunch like civilized cowboys?"

The three boys quickly got off their horses and tied them off to the old log as well. Big Dave opened the big saddlebags on the pinto and took out a large black cast iron frying pan. He took it and several small packages out and set all of them on a flat rock. Then he pointed to a spot on the sand. "One of you boys build a fire there," he said.

None of the boys moved. They seemed uncertain of what to do.

Big Dave noticed their hesitation. "Are you boys tellin' me you got no idea how to make a fire?" he asked.

Steve stepped forward. "I know how, but I don't have any matches," he said.

Big Dave reached into his jacket pocket and took out a small metal tube and tossed it to Steve who deftly caught it in midair.

"Matches in there. Never go anywhere in Wyoming without matches unless you're some kind of idiot who thinks flint and steel are better," he said.

Steve and his brothers made a small firepit in the sand and began gathering dead wood for the fire.

Big Dave looked over at them and said, "Ring that fire pit with rocks and make sure a couple of them are good thick flat ones."

The boys began their search for rocks while Big Dave put together a small fishing pole, snapping three pieces of fiberglass together and adding a reel with fishing line to it. He threaded the fishing line through the loops on the pole and tied a lead sinker on it and added a fishhook on the end. He pulled out a small packet of corn and put the hook through a big kernel of corn. He stepped up to the river and cast the sinker and hook upstream from where he stood on the bank.

The boys had gotten a fire started and added dry wood to keep it going. Big Dave glanced over at them. "Don't make it too big. We want a fire hot and small, and we want rocks close together to put the skillet on them," he admonished them.

In fifteen minutes, Big Dave had caught nine brookies. He gutted them, cut off the heads, and then washed them off in the river. He laid the fish out on a flat rock. Then he pulled a plastic bag out of the saddlebag. He opened it and one at a time he dumped the cleaned fish into it and shook the bag. He looked up to see the boys staring at him. He smiled.

"The bag has salt, pepper, and corn meal in it. I coat the fish with it by puttin' it in the bag and shakin' it," he said.

When all the fish were coated, he laid them out on the flat rock. He pulled out a small plastic bag and took out four big pieces of bacon.

He brought the frying pan and the bacon over to the fire. He put the bacon in the skillet and set it over the fire between two larger flat rocks with the handle toward him. The skillet quickly heated up and the bacon began to sizzle and cook. The aroma was delicious.

When Big Dave was satisfied, he took the bacon out of the skillet using his knife. He produced four small metal plates and set a piece of bacon on each plate. Then he collected the fish and set all of them in the frying pan on a small sea of bacon grease. He tended the cooking fish and occasionally turned them using his knife.

When he was satisfied, he took the skillet off the hot rocks and set it on the sandy ground. He used his knife to put fresh cooked trout on each of the four metal plates, joining the pieces of cooling cooked bacon.

He produced four small metal cups and a canteen of water. He filled each cup and handed it and a plate of fish and bacon to each of the three amazed brothers.

All four sat cross-legged on the sand with a plate of food and a cup of water. "Eat up," said Big Dave.

The three boys looked at each other. Then they looked at Big Dave with puzzlement on their faces.

Finally, Steve spoke for them. "But we got no silverware," he blurted out.

"If you were Indians, you'd use your fingers," said a smiling Big Dave. "But you're not, are you?" he said.

Then Big Dave rose to his feet and went to the tied-off pinto. He took a small cloth bundle from his saddle bag. Then he turned and walked back to the still-seated boys.

"Here," Big Dave said, as he unwrapped the bundle and tossed each of the brothers a brand-new folding knife just like the knife he had been using. "Never go out in the country unprepared," he said.

The boys quickly opened the blade of their new knives and used it to cut and fork their meal of fresh trout and bacon.

"This is delicious," said a surprised Travis.

"It really is," echoed Steve.

Lee's mouth was full of fish, so he just nodded his head in agreement.

The four ate in silence and when finished, Big Dave had them clean their plates in the river and used sand to clean the frying pan. Big Dave filled the clean frying pan with river water and used it to extinguish the fire. After everything was packed away in his saddlebags, he mounted the pinto. The boys followed suit, and the four horsemen then turned their horses and followed the river south in the direction of the ranch.

Once back at the ranch, the boys unsaddled their horses and put the tack away. They fed and watered their horses and curry combed them. Then they separated and did the rest of their daily chores.

At supper that evening, they were joined by their newly rested and sober fellow cowboys. The brothers were usually quiet at meals, but this time they excitedly talked about their impromptu fishing trip. The old cowboys just grinned and took their dishes to the cook shack counter before heading back to the bunkhouse.

Sunday was over.

CHAPTER TWENTY-SIX

After breakfast on the following Monday, Big Dave had the four cowboys, and the three brothers stay seated at the table.

"For you three boys, the cowboy school is over," said Big Dave. "Each of you will be paired with a real cowboy for work this week. At the end of the week, we'll decide how to proceed for the next week. You boys will do what the real cowboys do, except get to go to town on Saturday night. No time in town for you boys for the first two weeks."

Travis raised his hand. Big Dave smiled. "We ain't in school, Travis. You got somethin' to say just speak up."

"Does that mean we can go to town for Saturday night beginning next week?" he asked.

"Maybe," said Big Dave.

"I thought you said we had to stay here just for the first two weekends?" asked Travis.

"Maybe means what it says. If you boys have proved yourselves worth of enjoyin' Saturday night in Kemmerer, you'll get it. If you haven't, you won't," responded Big Dave.

"Who decides?" asked Lee.

"Who do you think decides?" thundered back Big Dave. "I'm the ramrod of this outfit, and I decide what does or doesn't happen. Is that perfectly clear to you?"

"Yes, sir," replied Lee meekly.

"Happy to clear that up for you," said Big Dave in an insincere tone of voice.

Then Big Dave paused. He looked over at the four cowboys, the cook, and the three young men.

"This Wednesday we're gonna brand calves. It's a big job and every one of you sons-of-bitches is gonna have a job that needs doin.' Is that clear?" he said.

Everyone at the table nodded their heads that they understood. Nobody was foolish enough to ask any questions. They knew Big Dave would cover every detail for them. All they had to do was listen.

"Today we're gonna work in groups," said Big Dave. "Slim, Rocky, and Preacher will drive the herd to the big pasture south of the ranch house. Steve and Lee will ride with them and help. You two boys will do what you are told to do, and that will include opening and closing a couple of gates as the herd is driven through them. When you're drivin' them cows, I want you to weed out the cows with no calves. All I want in that pasture are cow-calf units. Is that clear?"

A ragged chorus of yeses filled the air in the cook shack.

"Weston and Travis will check the fences on the big pasture and the gates and make any repairs needed. Then they'll do the same to the work pasture."

"Once them cow-calf units are in the pasture, I want you three cowboys to check them for any health issues or other problems. Now we may get all them cow-calf units driven here and separated today. Then again, we may not. If we don't, then we'll keep the herd as static as possible till the morning. That would mean three of you ridin' night herd for five hours and then three more 'til morning," said Big Dave.

"Any questions?" asked Big Dave.

There was silence. Then Travis timidly raised his hand.

"You got a question, son?" asked Big Dave.

"Yes sir," said Travis. "What's a work pasture?"

Big Dave chuckled. "It's a smaller pasture where we drive in the calves after separatin' them from their mamas. In that pasture we will rope, drop, and immobilize the calves and then brand them, vaccinate them, and dehorn them. Then we let them up and let them back into the big pasture where they can find their mamas," said Big Dave.

"Oh," responded a wide-eyed Travis.

"Tell him why it's called a work pasture," said Preacher with an evil grin on his face.

"We'll be workin' on about four hundred and twenty calves," said Big Dave. By the time we're done, that little pasture gonna be a mess of mud, shit, and blood. With that many calves, we'll be brandin' for most of two days."

"Anybody else got a question?" asked Big Dave.

He was greeted with silence and grins on the faces of the four cowboys.

"Once we got the cow-calf units in the big pasture, we let them rest and eat. Then the next day, which likely will be Wednesday, we'll start brandin' calves. Rocky, Slim, Preacher, and Weston know exactly what to do. You three boys ain't got a clue. But you'll learn damn fast. It's likely we'll start brandin' on Wednesday, and I'll explain everyone's jobs the night before at dinner."

Big Dave took a final look around the table. He liked what he saw.

"Let's get to work," he said. "We're burnin' daylight."

In less than three minutes, the cook shack was empty except for Cookie who was starting to wash dishes.

CHAPTER TWENTY-SEVEN

Less than twenty minutes later, Slim, Rocky, and Preacher were mounted and headed south of the ranch house. Steve and Lee followed in their dusty wake. Weston and Travis mounted their horses and headed for the fenced in pastures to check the fences as they had been ordered.

Big Dave stood on the porch of the cook shack and watched them all ride off, leaving small clouds of dust in their wake.

"Now the damn fun starts," mumbled Big Dave to himself.

Travis followed Weston as they made their way to the large, fenced pasture that was bordered on the west by the Ham's Fork River. After they opened the gate and passed through it, Weston dismounted, handed his reins to Travis. He closed the gate and then took the reins from Travis and remounted his horse. He rode next to Travis's mount and turned to face him.

"We take it slow, real slow," Weston said. "We look for loose staples, broke wires, and damaged posts. When we find a problem, we fix it. If the problem is big and needs stuff and tools, we ain't got, we flag it with one of these strips of red cloth. You got that?"

"Yes, sir," replied Travis.

"Son, I ain't no sir. I'm a cowboy, nothin' more. I spent five years in the damned army salutin' bozos who had officer tabs on their shoulders and not much else between their ears. I had enough of that army shit. You call me Wes. I'll call you Travis. That work for you?" asked Weston.

"Yes, sir, I mean yes, Wes," said a now smiling Travis.

They rode slowly alongside the fence bordering the big pasture. Weston led, and Travis followed about a horse length behind.

Meanwhile the three experienced cowboys led the way north, along the east shore of the Ham's Fork River, passing through at least two gates through fenced pastures. The two brothers followed. After about half an hour they reached the far end of the main grazing area of the ranch.

The day was warm under the cloudless sky. But like every day in Wyoming, there was a breeze. Unlike some high-wind days, this one was relatively mild and almost pleasant. The rolling hills around them were covered with green grass nurtured by the spring rains and snow runoff.

When the five riders reached the north end of the ranch, the three cowboys reined in their horses and maneuvered so they were side by side. The two boys moved their horses, so they were facing the cowboy trio.

Rocky was the unofficial leader of the cowboys, and he immediately took charge. He looked over at Slim and Preacher and then at the two young men.

"Let's gather the entire herd and move them to the first fence line. When we get there, we'll open the gate, let the cow-calf units through, and push the single cows back. Once we've got them separated, we'll move the cow-calf units in a herd to the next big, fenced pasture," Rocky said.

"Anyone got a problem with that?" he asked.

"Works for me," said Slim. Preacher just nodded his head in agreement.

"Steve, you'll work with Slim, and Lee, you'll work with me. You do exactly what we say. Nothin' more and nothin' less. You understand?" asked Rocky.

"Yes, sir," said both boys, almost in unison.

"Cut out that sir shit," said Rocky. "We're cowboys, not dude assholes."

Both boys nodded their heads meekly.

"Let's move some cows," said Rocky.

The five riders spread out and began to haze the cows away from the south fence line. Soon they had the herd of over eight hundred cattle moving south towards the banks of the Ham's Fork River.

The three cowboys did most of the real herding, using the two boys as flankers to keep the herd from turning and herding strays and stragglers back to the main herd as it moved south.

When they reached the main gate to the large pasture, Rocky had Lee on the ground manning the gate and Steve on horseback to help him if a single cow tried to get through. By the time they reached the gate with the herd and pushed the cow-calf units through, it was almost two in the afternoon.

Rocky gathered the riders together. "Good job, boys," he said. "We got all the cow-calf units through and settled in the big pasture. They got the river for water and unless Wes and your little brother screwed up, the fences around the pasture are secure and this herd ain't goin' nowhere without our say so."

Twenty minutes later, Wes and Travor rode up to where the five waited on horseback.

"Any trouble?" asked Rocky.

"Nope," replied Wes. "We found a few low spots and just one break. We fixed them and the pasture is tight all around. This herd ain't goin' nowhere less we move them."

"Good job, Wes," said Rocky. "Let's head up to the ranch and get some grub. My backbone and my belly are getting' too damn close for comfort."

The cowboys laughed, and Lee and Steve joined in.

Rocky led the way, and the seven cowboys rode south to the ranch for a much deserved and overdue lunch.

When they reached the ranch, Rocky directed Wes and the three boys to take the horses in the barn, unsaddle them, and get them fed and watered. He, Shorty, and Preacher headed for the cook shack.

By the time Wes and the boys had finished unsaddling and feeding the horses and then wiped them down and curry combed them, almost twenty minutes had passed. They hurried to the cook shack to find Cookie, Big Dave, Rocky, Slim, and Preacher waiting for them while drinking hot cups of coffee.

As Wes and the three brothers grabbed coffee cups and stood in line to get hot coffee, Cookie and Big Dave were pulling hot platters out of the ovens and placing them on the table. There was hot roast beef and gravy, mashed potatoes, beans, and freshly baked biscuits.

The platters of food were magically emptied in a matter of minutes, and there was absolutely no conversation. Just the sounds of good food being devoured by hungry cowboys.

"Eat hearty boys," said Big Dave. "Today was a walk in the park. The real work will start early tomorrow morning. Breakfast will be at five in the mornin.' Be saddled and at the pasture by no later than six."

"Six?" thought Travis. "The sun was barely up then."

CHAPTER TWENTY-EIGHT

The cowboys and the three boys were awakened at about 4:30 the next morning by Big Dave banging a big spoon on a tin pot. The racket was loud, and everyone was immediately out of bed.

"Roll outta them beds, you sonsabitches," yelled Big Dave. "You're burnin' daylight, and it's my daylight."

The next twenty minutes was a noisy combination of showers running, toilets flushing, and sinks receiving hot water. Along with the sounds of men cursing, laughing, and the occasional loud fart.

By five in the morning, four cowboys, the three brothers, Big Dave, and the cook were busy in the cook shack. The cowboys and boys drank hot coffee and wolfed down pancakes with syrup and scrambled eggs and small link sausages.

By five-thirty, the men were out saddling their horses in what little light the slowly rising sun cast out over the prairie ground of Wyoming.

When everyone was gathered at the branding pen in the corner of the fenced-in pasture, Big Dave stepped in front of them. Behind him they could see several cardboard boxes and a small propane fueled fire along with several long branding irons.

Satisfied everyone was present, Big Dave spoke to the group.

"All you boys know what to do, but this is for the three greenhorns," he said. "Slim, Rocky, Weston, and Preacher will separate the calves from the cows and drive them into this temporary enclosure we've made here. I'll man the gate. When all the calves have been pushed into the branding enclosure, the fun will begin.

"Slim and Rocky will be our ropers this morning. Weston and Preacher will switch off with them in the afternoon. The ropers will rope a calf and bring it down. Then the two-man team will follow the taut rope to the calf and dump it on its side if it's still standin.' The front man will put his knee on the front side of the calf and release the lariat. The rear man will get behind the calf and grab its upper leg. Then he sits on the ground and puts his boot on the calf's ass while he grabs the calf's upper rear leg and pulls it back towards him and holds it tight. Then I'll brand the calf. After I finish, the free cowboy will dehorn the calf and then vaccinate it. When he's finished, we release the calf and get ready for the next one. Every one of you boys got that?" Big Dave asked.

He was greeted with a serious, but slightly confused silence.

"I thought so," said Big Dave. "We're gonna give you boys a demonstration, and then we'll start brandin' these calves."

Rocky climbed on his horse and then loosened his lariat. He rode over to the milling herd of confused and frightened calves. He roped one calf around the neck. As the calf tried to run, Rocky's horse came to a hard halt and Rocky wrapped the lariat around the saddle horn. When the calf took out the slack in the rope, it jerked the calf to a halt. Rocky then moved his horse into the branding pen, pulling the reluctant calf behind him.

Then Slim and Weston moved swiftly with Slim in the lead. He had his gloved hand on the taut lariat and followed it to the downed calf. He knelt with his knee on the calf's shoulder. Weston slid on his butt behind the calf and grabbed its upper leg and pulled it back while slamming his boot into the calf's butt. The result was the calf was temporarily immobilized.

Big Dave appeared with a hot branding iron and carefully pressed it on the calf's exposed flank. The result was the stink and smell of burning hair and flesh and the panic yelps from the terrified calf.

At the same time Preacher appeared on his knees at the head of the calf where he dehorned the calf and then used a syringe to inject a vaccine into the calf.

When Big Dave was done, he returned to the propane fire and placed the branding iron into the hot blazing fire. Preacher got to his feet and returned to the stack of cardboard boxes for more supplies. Then Slim and Weston released the terrified calf and got to their feet. The calf scrambled to its feet and ran bawling around the branding enclosure.

Big Dave then stepped in front of the three shocked-looking boys. "That's how it's done, boys. Now you boys wait here by the gate and help us drive the calves into this pen and keep the cows out."

With that, Big Dave, Preacher, and Wes mounted their horses and joined Slim and Rocky in the large fenced-in pasture. The three boys watched from the gate leading to the smaller branding pen. The five mounted men expertly used their horses to separate calves from their mothers and drive them to the gate.

Steve manned the gate with Lee and Travis standing on either side of the gate to help haze calves through it. Steve kept opening and closing the gate to let calves in and keep the cows out. After almost an hour, all the calves were in the branding pen and their anxious mothers gathered at the gate and expressed their displeasure with forlorn noises.

Slim and Rocky entered the branding pen on horseback and remained in the saddle.

Big Dave, Wes, and Preacher got off their horses and tied them to the fence. Big Dave turned to face the three boys. "Now it's your turn. Weston will start with Travis as a team, and then Steve and Lee will be the next team. Any questions?"

"Do we brand all these calves?" asked an amazed looking Steve.

"Not possible," said Big Dave. "We have over four hundred calves, and we'll shoot to brand slightly over half of them today. Then we'll do the same thing tomorrow."

"Won't the calves get hungry and thirsty separated from their mothers?" asked Travis.

"There are troughs of water against that far fence, and we'll feed them hay at the end of today. They won't like it, but they'll be fine," said Big Dave.

"Any more questions?" asked Big Dave.

There were none.

"Let's brand calves. We're burnin' daylight," said Big Dave.

Slim and Rocky mounted their horses and loosened their lariats in their gloved hands. Big Dave stood by the propane fire, and Preacher stood by the boxes of supplies.

Rocky nudged his horse close to the milling herd of frightened calves and roped one around the neck. The calf ran until he reached the end of the lariat, and then he was suddenly jerked back and down on his side as the rope became taught. Wes ran out to the horse and then with one gloved hand on the taut lariat, he reached the downed calf and dropped on the calf's front shoulder, using his knee to pin the calf to the ground. Travis followed him down the length of rope until he reached the calf and then he got behind the calf and dropped to the ground on his butt and grabbed the calf's upper rear leg with his gloved hands. Then he remembered his instructions and jammed his right boot against the calf's butt. He felt the sensation as he pulled with his arm and pushed with his boot to immobilize the frightened calf.

Big Dave suddenly appeared with a hot branding iron and branded the flank of the helpless calf. He released the branding iron as smoke rose and then the stink of burned hair and flesh wafted into the noses of both Wes and Travis. At the same time Preacher was busy dehorning the calf with a clear colored gel and then using a syringe to inject a vaccine into the calf's body. When he was done, Preacher stood and raised his hands in the air.

With that signal, Wes and Travis released the calf and got to their feet. Once he was standing upright, Travis glanced to his left and saw his two brothers following a taught lariat to a downed calf and then the fun began.

Steve was first, and he quickly got his knee on the calf's shoulder. Lee had more trouble with his first try. He grabbed for the calf's upper hind leg and missed it. Twice.

"Damn it, Lee," yelled Steve. "Grab the leg and pull."

Lee was successful on his third try and then remembered to put his boot in the calf's ass and push hard. Steve then released the lariat. Big Dave branded the calf, and Preacher dehorned and vaccinated it. Steve and Lee scrambled to their feet. Lee turned to say something to Steve about what just happened when he saw Steve point behind Lee. Slim had roped another calf, and Steve led Lee to the taught rope and followed it to the downed calf.

This time Steve moved quickly and had his knee on the calf's shoulder. Lee dropped to his butt and this time grabbed the calf's upper leg on the first try and then found his boot tightly against the butt of the frenzied calf. In mere seconds, the calf was branded, dehorned, and vaccinated.

This routine continued for four hours. As soon as they had one calf branded, it was time to move on to the next calf bawling at the end of a taught lariat.

They broke briefly after four hours for a water break. The break lasted ten minutes. Steve looked at his watch. It was only ten in the morning.

"Back to work, cowboys," thundered Big Dave. "We're burnin' daylight."

Then they were back at it. They took a short half hour break at about one in the afternoon. Cookie was there to serve hot coffee, lemonade, and roast beef sandwiches. Big Dave and the four cowboys ate voraciously. The three boys could barely eat anything but drank lots of lemonade.

Then they were back to work branding calves.

CHAPTER TWENTY-NINE

The branding lasted until four-thirty that afternoon. Big Dave called an end to it by shutting off the propane fire.

"Let's get this crap cleaned up, boys," he said.

Travis, Lee, and Steve leaned against the back side of the cook's truck and stared out in front of them. The once grassy area of the branding pasture was a mess. Hardly a blade of grass was visible. The area was a sea of mud, blood, piss, shit, and hair. The boys looked like they had played ten quarters of tackle football. Their clothes were filthy, bloody, and their boots covered with mud and shit. Their leather gloves were stiff with everything they saw around them in the branding pen.

The four cowboys put out hay and water for the calves and then led their horses back to the barn. The three exhausted boys followed behind them like blind men looking for the light. They stumbled as they walked. Every joint in their bodies seemed to be loudly objecting at the same time.

Once the horses were unsaddled, fed, and watered, the tired cowboys and brothers headed for the bunkhouse. Cookie had put out baskets for them to dump their dirty clothes into. He took great pains to inform the three boys that this was a one-time event. They had to wash their own clothes, but branding time was an exception to the rule. They all stripped and then made their way to the welcome hot showers. The four cowboys finished first and once dressed, they headed over to the cook shack.

The three boys were much slower and staggered from the shower stall to their bunks after drying off. They dressed in clean clothes and then headed slowly to the cook shack, stumbling along like they were on the end of a three- day drunk.

Cookie had been busy. The cowboys and the three brothers filled their plates with big ribeye steaks, mashed potatoes, gravy, and heaps of hot beans. There were fresh baked biscuits and containers of fresh butter and strawberry jam. Two large pitchers of lemonade and a large pot of coffee were in the middle of the long table.

To the exhausted boys' surprise, their stomachs went from being disinterested in anything to suddenly being ravenously hungry. Once again, there was little talk and only the sound of hungry men eating and the scrape of silverware on plates as they did so. The cowboys drank several cups of hot coffee, while the three brothers downed multiple glasses of cold lemonade.

When every scrap of food had disappeared, the cowboys and the three boys placed their empty dishes on the counter for Cookie to wash up. Then they retired to several old, battered chairs on the small porch outside the cookshack.

Big Dave pulled out a long slim cigar and lit it. Three of the cowboys rolled their own cigarettes and lit them. The exception was Preacher. The boys just sat there with full stomachs and their energy tanks empty.

Big Dave let out a long stream of cigar smoke and leaned back in his chair. Then he turned to look at the three brothers.

"You boys did pretty well today. You should do better tomorrow since now you have some idea of what the hell you're supposed to do," he said.

The boys just nodded their heads. They were too tired to respond.

After a few minutes, the cowboys got to their feet and headed to the bunkhouse. The three brothers followed in their wake.

When they reached the bunkhouse and slipped inside, the boys sat on the end of their bunks. Wes looked over at them. "You boys look like you bin rode hard and put away wet," he said. The other three cowboys broke out in laughter.

The three young men just nodded their heads. They were too tired to try to come up with a response.

"Well now," said Wes. "It can't be all that bad. It's just cowboy work. That's all it is."

He was met with silence. Then he grinned and continued.

"I ever tell you boys about my uncle Bart?" he asked.

He got no answer.

"Well, then, that's shame on me," he said with a grin on his face. "Old Bart was a gold miner up in the Yukon about ten years ago. He wrote a letter to Monky Ward."

Travis looked up at him. "Who is Monky Ward?" he asked.

"I guess you tenderfeet know it as Montgomery Ward, the big catalog outfit out East," replied Wes.

"Why'd he write to Montgomery Ward?" asked Travis.

"He sent a letter askin' for a carton of toilet paper, and he enclosed ten dollars in cash in the letter," said Wes.

"What happened?" asked Travis.

"He got a letter back from Monky Ward," answered Wes.

"What did the letter say?" asked Travis.

"The letter said old Bart had to include the catalog number of the merchandise he wanted to buy before they could ship it to him," replied Wes.

"What'd he do?" asked Travis.

"He wrote Monky Ward another letter," said Wes.

"What did he write?" asked Travis.

"He wrote them that if he had the Monky Wards catalog, he wouldn't need the damn toilet paper," said Wes with a big grin on his face.

The other three cowboys howled with laughter, and Travis just sat there with a red face.

Wes patted him on the knee. "Don't feel bad, Travis. I done pulled that joke on lots of folks. Now you can use it on some greenhorn in the future."

Travis grinned, and he and his brothers joined in the laughter.

The three brothers got undressed and slid into their bunks. Minutes later they were sound asleep. Their tired bodies welcomed a night of rest and recuperation.

CHAPTER THIRTY

At about four-thirty that next morning Big Dave once again appeared in the middle of the bunkhouse with a wooden spoon and a metal pan. His form of alarm clock was both noisy and irritating.

"Rise and shine, boys. You're burnin' daylight. Get your bony asses out of them beds. We got work to do," yelled Big Dave.

There was a lot of cussin,' moaning, and complaining, but all seven of the inhabitants of the bunk house rolled out of their beds and headed for the toilet, sink, or shower.

By five in the morning, all seven hands were seated at the bunk house table along with Big Dave. Breakfast was eggs, bacon, fried potatoes, and coffee. Lots of hot coffee. The breakfast platters emptied like they'd been vacuumed up by some mysterious force. There was no dawdling around over coffee after eating. Everyone headed for the branding pen on their horses, depending on their job for the day.

Cookie began washing pots, pans, and dishes. When he was finished, he would start washing up the battered remains of the men's clothing from the branding work of the day before. Then he'd make up a lunch to take out to the branding pen. He was always amazed at the capacity of hungry men and boys to consume large amounts of food in a very short time.

As soon as the men arrived at the branding pen, they were confronted by hordes of anxious cows pressed up against the fence that separated them from their calves. The mooing noises grew more anxious with the arrival of the cowboys. The calves were all pressed up against the fence separating them from their mothers, and they seemed less than pleased with the arrival of eight cowboys.

Big Dave and Preacher set up the supply boxes and lit the propane fire for the branding irons. Rocky and Slim rode their horses into the pen and worked on their lariats. The three brothers just stood there against the fence with Wes as they waited for the first calf to be roped and the branding ordeal to begin again.

"I can't believe how sore I am," moaned Lee.

"We're all sore," said Steve. "Even the cowboys are sore."

"They sure don't look or act like they're sore," said Travis.

"Appearances can be deceiving," said Steve.

"I can't ever remember being this stiff and sore," said Lee.

"Me neither," said Travis.

"Quit complaining," said Steve. "It won't help."

"Maybe not, but it makes me feel a little better," said Lee.

"God, sometimes you can be such a baby," snorted Steve.

"I'm no baby," replied Lee tersely.

"Then quit acting like one," said Steve.

"You boys got all this energy to yak, you must be anxious to start wrestlin' calves," said a grinning Wes.

That remark silenced Lee and his brothers.

"You fellers ready?" asked Big Dave.

"Let 'er rip," replied Wes.

"Powder River," said Rocky.

"First off, let's do a bit of herdin' and separate them calves that been branded and send them out to their mamas," said Big Dave.

The boys were told to help drive the branded calves by herding them on foot, along with Preacher and Wes. Slim, and Rocky herded them on horseback, while Big Dave was the gate keeper, opening and closing it as each branded calf approached. The entire exercise took about an hour and some branded calves remained in the branding pen despite their best efforts. The newly released branded calves wasted no time in locating their mothers and reuniting with them. When they were done, Big Dave secured the gate and walked over to the branding iron fire. He checked the branding irons in the fire and then turned to the cowboys and the three brothers.

"Bring us a calf," said Big Dave.

Rocky and Slim moved their horses closer to the milling herd of calves and quickly Rocky had a calf roped and when the lariat went tight, the calf was flipped on its side to the beat-up ground of the pen.

Wes led Travis to the taut rope and followed it down to the struggling calf. He quickly got his knee on the calf's shoulder, and Travis practically slid on his butt in a position behind the calf. He grabbed the top hind leg and pulled it back while jamming his boot on the calf's butt. Big Dave appeared out of nowhere and applied the hot branding iron. The smell of burnt hair and flesh suddenly filled the air and everyone's nostrils. Day two of the branding session was on.

There was no dry patch of ground in the branding pen. And not a blade of grass was evident. The ground was a muddy, bloody mess, mixed with feces and urine. The smell was startling.

The boys worked in their familiar teams. Travis with Wes, and Steve with Lee. The first two calves were brought down and held in an awkward manner as the boys and Wes kinked up muscles finally began to loosen. Then things seemed to find a rhythm and the branding went smoothly. There were less calves in the pen and that made it easier for Slim and Rocky to isolate calves and rope them.

They branded calves for three hours and then took a break as Preacher had to open more boxes of dehorner cream and more bottles of vaccine. The break only lasted for fifteen minutes, but it was welcomed by the three boys and the four cowboys as well.

The three brothers leaned against Cookie's truck. They had been warned not to sit on the ground. They would immediately stiffen up according to Big Dave. They had no desire to sit on the ground anyway as it was a mess of mud, excrement, and blood. Their boots, jeans, and gloves were covered in it.

Finally, Preacher was ready and Big Dave turned to his crew. "Let's brand some goddamned calves," he said loudly.

Even after managing to stay standing upright, although leaning against the cook's truck, the boys' muscles had already started to stiffen. Plus, the effect of extremely hard physical labor the previous day and now adding more on the second day had tested their strength, endurance, and their mettle.

After three more calves being taken down and branded, Lee complained to Steve. "I can't do this anymore," he said. "My arms are tired, my hands are sore, my shoulders hurt, and my ass is covered with mud, blood, piss and shit."

"When this is over and we take a shower and put on clean clothes, you'll be fine," Steve assured him.

"I didn't sign on for this crap," said Lee. "I ain't cut out for this kind of work. This kind of stuff is fine for shitkickers like Rocky, Slim, Preacher and Wes. They're just dumb cowboys. This is all they're ever gonna be. I'm gonna be someone. This kind of work is beneath me."

Steve looked at his brother with amusement. "Sure, it's hard, dirty work," he said. "But we do this for three months and then get paid half a million bucks. Just ninety days and this will be just a bad memory," he said.

Then Steve looked around to make sure no one was within listening distance. Satisfied, he continued. "Three months is just ninety days. We have already worked ten of them. Only eighty days left," he said.

"Easy for you to say," said Lee. "You're older and stronger and you act like you're actually enjoying being a shit kicker. Not me. This ain't for me."

Steve thought for a bit and then turned to his brother. "Lee, think of it this way. Every day you work, you earn about $5,500. And it's likely tax free. I'm willing to bet you money you will never in the rest of your life be able to duplicate that."

Lee wanted to argue, but he knew Steve was right. He hissed through his teeth.

"Suck it up and damn soon it will all be a bad dream memory," said Steve.

"I'll try," said Lee.

"Let's go boys. We're burnin' daylight," said Big Dave.

Amid a host of groans and curses, the four cowboys and the three young brothers moved back into the branding pen.

Slim and Rocky mounted their horses and uncoiled their lariats. Then they rode into the mass of frightened calves and began to swing their ropes over their heads.

Slim was the first to drop his rope over the head of an unbranded calf and Wes and Travis were running toward the suddenly downed calf. Immediately Rocky had his rope on another calf and Steve ran toward the calf at the end of the lariat, closely followed by Lee.

Both teams quickly had their calves immobilized and the resulting branding, dehorning, and vaccinating began. The ground was barren, slick, and more than once, one of the boys or Wes had their boots slip on something slick and ended up on their butts prematurely.

As the hours passed, even Big Dave lost count of how many calves they had branded. To the boys, the work became almost mechanical. They did the same thing repeatedly until it became almost robotic for them. The monotony of the work was broken only by the danger inherent in it.

Twice Lee had lost a calf's leg causing Rocky to have to have his horse move to bring the calf back down to the ground. Then Lee slipped again and got kicked in the mouth by the hoof of a young calf.

Big Dave stopped branding and hurried over to the prone Lee, who was openly crying. He got Lee to sit up, checked his mouth, and then sent him over to Cookie. Cookie grabbed his first aid kit from the truck and had Lee sit on the open tailgate. Then he examined his mouth, cleaned the small wound with water and then applied antiseptic and a small band-aid to the wound.

"You're good to go," said Cookie. "I'll check it again at supper."

"You mean I have to go back to grabbing calves?" asked an astonished Lee.

"Son, you aren't hurt bad. It ain't more than a scratch. Keep it clean, and it'll be fine," said Cookie.

"Will I have a scar on my face?" asked a very worried Lee.

Cookie laughed. "I ain't no doc, son, but I can't figure how that little cut will leave a scar."

"Oh," said Lee. He was both relieved the wound wasn't worse and pissed he had to go back to wrestling with frantic calves.

Lee returned to the branding pen. Steve was waiting for him. Wes and Travis had helped brand three more calves while Cookie had been tending to Lee.

"Ready?" Steve asked Lee.

"Ready as I'm gonna be," said Lee.

"Good," said Steve. He motioned to Rocky, who nodded and immediately tossed his rope around the head of a nearby startled unbranded calf.

To the four experienced cowboys and the three young brothers, the rest of the day seemed almost mechanical. Although they were tired, the three brothers had learned a great deal about their simple job, and they became instinctive in performing it. Their muscles hurt and ached, but they still worked efficiently and although their movements felt mechanical, they were working more efficiently than they had the previous day.

Suddenly they were done. The last branded calf ran to the fence that separated him from his mother and stood there as she licked his face through the fence wire.

"That's it, boys. Let's pack it in," said Big Dave.

The three brothers helped Big Dave and the cowboys to collect their equipment and stow it in the truck. Cookie and his truck had disappeared some time ago, and they had not even noticed it.

Once the gear was collected and stowed and the propane fire extinguished, Slim and Rocky mounted their horses and headed for the barn. Big Dave drove the pickup truck loaded with gear and Preacher and Wes as passengers. The three boys trudged along the dirt road leading back to the ranch compound.

When they reached the bunkhouse, they stripped off their filthy and torn clothes, tossed them in Cookie's big laundry basket, and headed for the shower.

When they were getting dressed, Steve glanced at his watch. It was only three in the afternoon, but he felt like it was midnight. He and his brothers were so tired, just pulling on clean clothes was an effort. From the time they heard Big Dave call the job done until now, none of them had spoken a word. Even talking was too much effort for the three exhausted brothers.

As they slowly made their way to the cook shack, the smells of cooked meat, fresh bread, and other things they could not get their noses to identify wafted in the air. Suddenly all three of them felt ravenously hungry. They picked up the pace and soon were seated at the big table in the cook shack.

The other four cowboys and Big Dave had arrived before them. They were sitting at the table, drinking hot black coffee.

Cookie appeared from behind the counter and set platters of steaks, baked potatoes, beans, and hot biscuits on the long table in front of them.

Talk ceased and platters of food quickly made their way around the table as the five men and three boys filled their plates and then focused their energy on eating as much food as they could shovel into their hungry mouths.

CHAPTER THIRTY-ONE

When the platters were empty and the men had collected their dinnerware and set it on the counter for Cookie, they returned to their seats and drank more hot coffee. The boys settled for more lemonade.

Big Dave got up from the long table and refilled his coffee mug from the big coffee dispenser Cookie kept on the counter. Once the mug was full, Big Dave took a swig, nodded his head, and returned to his seat at the table.

"Good work today, fellas," said Big Dave. "You worked hard, and we got all the calves branded and vaccinated. Here's the plan for tomorrow. Slim and Rocky will herd the cows and calves back to the river pasture and Preacher and Lee and Steve will take down the temporary fence and store it. Travis and I will do a scout through the south end of the ranch to make sure we don't miss any cow calf pairs. See you boys at breakfast."

The four cowboys slipped out of their seats and refilled their coffee mugs. Then they moved out to the small porch in front of the cook shack, and each found a seat in an old wooden chair. The three brothers sat for a moment and then exited the cook shack and headed for the bunk house. Big Dave stayed seated, sipping his hot coffee.

Cookie was busy cleaning off plates and cooking utensils and then filled the big old iron sink full of hot water and soap to do the dishes and put them away.

"Hold up here, Cookie," said Big Dave.

Cookie paused and then looked up at Big Dave with a puzzled look on his face.

"I got a question for you, Cookie. Grab a mug and have a seat," said Big Dave.

Cookie quickly complied and after filling a mug with coffee, he took a seat at the table across from Big Dave.

"Did I do something wrong, Mr. Dave?" asked Cookie.

"Nope. You been doin' fine as far as I'm concerned," replied Big Dave. "You and them four cowboys were here when I took this job and so far, I got no complaints."

Big Dave shifted slightly in his seat and then took another swig of coffee.

"I got a question for you, and I'm plumb interested in your answer," said Big Dave.

"What is it?" asked a puzzled-looking Cookie.

"I'd like your hard ass honest opinion of them three boys," asked Big Dave.

"As boys?" asked a surprised Cookie.

"As would be cowboys," said Big Dave.

"They seem OK to me," said Cookie.

Big Dave paused as if trying to find a question that was eluding him.

"How 'bout you tell me about each one of them?" asked Big Dave.

Cookie scrunched up his face and looked down at the table. Then he looked up and spoke.

"I think the young kid, Travis, has the makin's of a real good cowboy. He's smart, quick to learn, and keeps his mouth shut unless he's asked something," said Cookie.

"What about Steve, the oldest?" asked Big Dave.

"He seems pretty steady. He ain't special, but he's careful and thinks before he speaks. He also ain't afraid of hard work based on what I saw over the past two days brandin' calves," said Cookie.

"And Lee?" asked Big Dave.

"Seems a lot more spoiled and selfish than the other two," said Cookie. "I can tell he ain't happy here and wants to pack up and go home to mommy," said Cookie. "He don't appear to have the makings of a good cowboy."

Big Dave stayed quiet and looked as though deep in thought. Then he looked up and spoke.

"I think you've noticed more than I thought you might. Can't say I can disagree with anything you said. I appreciate your bein' honest with me, Cookie. I really do," said Big Dave.

Big Dave handed Cookie his empty coffee cup and made his way back to his cabin. Once there, he poured himself a small glass of good whisky and pulled out the small spiral notebook he was using to document what went on at the cattle ranch during his limited three-month tenure there as the ramrod.

He sat at the small desk and began taking down some notes using an old wooden pencil like the ones he had used so long ago in Kemmerer High School.

CHAPTER THIRTY-TWO

The next morning broke early. It was sunny and hot. Everyone seemed to recover from the previous two days' hard work of branding calves, and no one was late to breakfast.

Cookie had prepared another feast of pancakes, sausage, fried eggs, Texas toast, and lots of hot black coffee.

Like every other morning at the ranch, conversation was loud and boisterous until the food was served. Then the talk stopped, and the eating started in earnest. No one stopped eating to start a conversation of any kind.

When breakfast was over and the table cleared of dishes, pans, and silverware, the men and the boys sat at the table in front of hot mugs of black coffee. They were waiting for Big Dave to issue his orders for the day.

There were no surprises. Big Dave gave them the same orders he had made the night before. The men finished their coffee and headed out of the cook house door to start on their chores for the day.

As the men filed out, Big Dave stayed seated and when Travis went to walk out, Big Dave held up his hand and motioned for the youngest of the boys to stay. Travis took the chair next to Big Dave and waited. When they were alone except for Cookie cleaning up in the kitchen, Big Dave finished the last of his coffee and put the mug down on the old table.

"Go to the bunkhouse and grab a lever action rifle from the gun closet and meet me in front of my cabin in ten minutes," said Big Dave.

"Yes, sir," responded Travis. He scooted out the door and did his best to keep from running to the bunkhouse instead of just walking. He was excited.

Big Dave smiled as he watched Travis make his way to the bunkhouse. "I think that kid was born one hundred years too late," he thought to himself. Then he walked to his cabin and collected the gear he would need for the day's work.

By the time Big Dave walked out on the front porch of the cabin, Travis was waiting for him. He was dressed in boots, jeans, and a denim shirt topped with a ball cap. He carried the lever action carbine in one hand and stood there like he was waiting for Santa to arrive on Christmas morning.

Big Dave did his best to hide his smile from the overly eager youngster. "Follow me," he said to Travis.

Big Dave led the way to his personal GMC pickup truck. Once there he had Travis stow his rifle on the rack mounted against the rear window of the pickup truck. Then he started the engine and drove the truck out the entrance to the ranch to the highway. Once there, he turned south instead of north towards Kemmerer.

He drove for about fifteen minutes, and then he pulled off the highway and across a culvert to a wire gate in the fence. Both men got out of the truck and Big Dave watched carefully as Travis expertly unsnapped the wires holding the bottom and top of the fence post that made up the end of the gate. Big Dave had Travis pull the fence gate back and then hold it while Big Dave drove the truck through the gate opening into an open field.

Big Dave waited in the truck while Travis secured the gate and then slid into the passenger seat. Big Dave drove slowly through the rolling and hilly pasture, pointing out things to Travis. He reminded Travis they were on a mission to look for any problems in the fence line, but also, they were looking for any possible cow-calf pairs they had missed and failed to brand the calf. The prairie surrounding them was turning dry, the color changing from green to light tan.

Big Dave drove up a small knoll and when he reached the top, he stopped the truck and took out a pair of binoculars from the seat of the truck. He scanned the area around them. He handed the binoculars to Travis and said, "Take a look around. See if your young eyes spot anything I missed."

Travis scanned the area and saw nothing but grass and sagebrush. "I don't see any animals," said Travis.

"Then it's likely we didn't miss any," said Big Dave. He happened to glance at the side mirror on his door, then turned to Travis and softly said, "Open the glove box and hand me the pistol in there."

Travis opened the glove box door and found a pistol in a leather holster. He carefully grasped the holster and handed it silently to Big Dave.

Big Dave took the pistol out of the holster and then he slowly and carefully opened the driver's side door and as he did, he pointed the pistol at the ground next to the truck.

Seconds passed. Then Travis heard a loud bang and then Big Dave snorting, "Got that little bastard!"

Big Dave pulled his hand with the gun back inside the cab of the truck. Then he put it back in the holster and handed it to Travis. He saw the puzzled look on Travis' face, and then Big Dave smiled.

"Was a goddamned gopher on my side of the truck. Hate those little bastards. They do no damn good and dig holes all over the damn place. A good friend of mine had a horse step in a gopher hole when chasing a calf and the horse fell and threw my friend into a rockpile," said Big Dave.

"Was he hurt?" asked Travis.

"He was dead, not hurt," said a grim-faced Big Dave. "Been shootin' gophers on sight ever since."

"Oh," said Travis, deciding any more details were probably not needed.

Big Dave put the truck in gear, and they slowly made their way down the knoll and then followed a faint two-track barely visible on the prairie. They drove slowly for about another fifteen minutes and then were confronted with hills to their right and left.

Big Dave stopped at the entrance between the two hills and then turned to his right and slowly drove up the slope of the hill on that side of the entrance.

As they climbed the hill, Travis could see the hills separated and created a small valley that featured a tiny pond created by a spring in a group of large rocks. When the truck reached the top of the hill, Big Dave stopped the truck and slipped out the driver's side door.

Travis opened his door and exited the truck as well. He joined Big Dave standing on the inside edge of the hill where he had a good view of the valley down below them.

The valley was not large, but long and narrow. The small pond was created by a spring coming up between two large rocks. There was plenty of green grass extending out from the spring and further out, the ground was mostly covered with sagebrush.

"Look at the other side of the spring," said Big Dave.

Travis looked and saw a large horse and a colt.

"The bay is a mare, and the chestnut is her colt," said Big Dave. "This little valley is a good spot for them. Plenty of feed and water and some shelter from the wind."

"Do they wander out of the valley?" asked Travis.

"Sometimes they do, but they don't go very far because of the spring," said Big Dave. "When the colt is bigger, they'll likely move further out of the valley, but not for a while."

As they watched, the mare grazed and the colt kept busy looking around, but not letting his mother out of his sight.

Then both men heard a sound like gentle thunder rolling through the small valley and up to the hilltop where they stood.

Big Dave became alert and scanned the far end of the valley. Soon, they could see a small herd of horses running into the valley, creating a dust cloud behind them.

Big Dave looked hard at the herd. "Here comes trouble," said Big Dave.

"Why?" asked Trevor.

"That herd is a pack of wild horses," said Big Dave. "See the big black stallion with the white feet in front of them?"

"Yes," replied Travis.

"He's gonna try to coax my mare into joinin' up with his herd and that's not good for me," said Big Dave.

Big Dave disappeared for a moment and Travis stood there transfixed as he watched the herd move through the valley and approach the location of the mare and colt.

"You watch that damn stallion, boy. He's gonna make his move," said Big Dave.

Sure enough, the stallion approached the now nervous mare, and the two horses touched their noses. After a bit of nuzzling and head tossing, the stallion turned and slowly began walking back toward the waiting herd.

The mare and the colt followed obediently like they were being led by a lead rope.

Travis was focused on the horses, and then heard a loud clicking. He turned to see Big Dave had the lever action rifle up to his shoulder and he was sighting in on the stallion. About five seconds later the air exploded with the sound of a rifle bullet being fired and the stallion suddenly tumbled head over heels and came to a jumbled stop on the ground.

As Travis waited, he watched for any movement from the stallion. There was none. The mare and colt just stood there dead in their tracks as if unsure of what to do next. The wild horse herd was in a semi-panic, and they were milling around as if trying to decide what to do.

"Watch for the lead mare," said Big Dave in a quiet voice.

Travis watched and sure enough, a large grey mare was moving toward the mare and colt and soon was nose to nose with them. After nuzzling the bay, the grey mare turned and began to walk back toward the still milling herd of wild horses.

"Enough of this shit," said Big Dave. He fired a second round and the grey mare shot forward like she was fired out of a cannon. She raced out toward the other end of the small valley and the wild horse herd quickly followed her.

The mare and colt stood there uncertainly, and then the mare turned back. toward the water hole and the colt followed.

Big Dave looked over at Travis. "The mare was trying to take over where the stallion left off. I put a round through her tail to let her know she was making a big mistake. She got the message and vamoosed," he said.

"So, the mare was going to take over for the now dead stallion?" asked Travis.

"The stallion was dead, so the lead mare was now in charge of the herd," said Big Dave. "She was smart enough to know it was time to get the hell out of Dodge."

Travis sat silent. But his face betrayed a question.

"Something wrong?" asked Big Dave.

"Shouldn't we bury the dead horse?" asked Travis tentatively.

Big Dave laughed. "No," he said. "We don't bury dead wild mustangs. His lying dead out there is a warning to any other adventurous wild horse herd. It won't take two weeks for all the critters out there to remove almost all traces of that dead mustang."

"How so?" asked Travis.

"The scavengers will take care of him," said Big Dave.

"Scavengers?" asked Travis.

"Coyotes, eagles, crows, magpies, bears, and lots of others, right down to ants and bugs," replied Big Dave. "Come by here in two weeks and you'll be lucky to see some hair and bones."

Travis sat back in his seat. He was satisfied, but still puzzled.

"Let's finish checking out the range," said Big Dave. "We still got some places to check." He slid back into the cab of the truck and Travis quickly followed him.

As Big Dave drove the truck away from the top of the knoll, Travis looked back down at the valley. The mare and colt were grazing beside the spring-fed pond as if nothing out of the ordinary had just happened.

CHAPTER THIRTY-THREE

By the time Big Dave's pickup truck rolled into the ranch yard, it was almost supper time. Big Dave parked the truck in front of his cabin and told Travis he'd join him at the cook shack in a bit.

When Travis reached the cook shack, he found his two brothers and all four of the cowboys lounging around on the small front porch.

"Where the hell have you been, little brother," asked Lee. "Me and Steve worked our butts off pulling fence posts and rolling up fence wire while you were joy riding around God knows where."

Travis tried to keep a straight face, but he failed miserably. He was simply bursting to tell someone, anyone, about what he had been a part of on the south end of the ranch.

"I saw Big Dave kill a wild horse stallion," came flying out of his mouth involuntarily.

Both older brothers had their mouths drop open in surprise.

"What happened?" asked Steve.

Travis went into detail as he gave his brothers a blow-by-blow description of what he had witnessed and heard.

Travis expected questions, but there were none. His brothers just stood there with shocked looks on their faces.

• • •

The pattern of eating, sleeping, and working hard outdoors continued until Saturday morning.

The four cowboys, the three boys, and Big Dave finished breakfast and then cleaned up their plates and silverware for Cookie to wash. Big Dave drew another cup of hot coffee and motioned for everyone to stay seated at the big dining table.

When he was satisfied, he had everyone's attention, Big Dave put down his coffee cup and looked around the table at the four veteran cowboys, the three young greenhorns, and his cook.

"Get your chores done this morning, and then you are free for the rest of the day and Sunday." He looked around the table. The four cowboys and the cook looked pleased. The three greenhorn brothers looked puzzled.

"That includes you three boys," added a grinning Big Dave. "I'll take you into town in my truck."

The four cowboys stood and exited the cook shack, and Cookie returned to the kitchen. That left Big Dave alone at the table with the three young brothers.

"Here are the rules," he said. "Number one. You are all underage. The legal age to drink alcohol in Wyoming is twenty-one. I will deliver you to Kemmerer, and you're on your own until I head back to the ranch at six o'clock this evening. I will drop you off in town. I expect you to be there waiting for me at six on the nose. Is that clear?"

All three brothers responded, almost in unison, "Yes, sir."

"Git to your chores, and I'll see you at my truck at eleven this morning. Got it?" he asked.

"Yes, sir," all three responded clearly.

Big Dave smiled as the three young men immediately got out of their seats and shot out the door of the cook shack.

When Big Dave walked out to his truck at eleven o'clock, the three brothers were all standing there by the side of the pickup. He noted they were all well- scrubbed and wearing clean clothes.

Big Dave climbed into the truck. He was promptly joined by Steve in the cab. Lee and Travis had scrambled into the bed of the truck and sat with their backs to the cab.

Big Dave started the engine. He put the truck in gear and drove off the ranch and onto the highway heading to Kemmerer. The drive took almost half an hour. The day was bright and sunny and fairly warm. The warm air had a fresh smell all its own, and it wasn't unpleasant. When Big Dave reached Triangle Park, he didn't stop and that got him a puzzled look from Steve sitting next to him. He caught Steve looking back at the park and grinned to himself. He pulled into the hardware store parking lot and stopped in a parking slot.

"I thought you were going to let us off at the park?" said Steve carefully.

"I said I would pick you boys up there at six this afternoon," said Big Dave. "This is where I let you out. I got things to do here."

Everyone got out of the truck, and then Big Dave reached behind the truck seat and pulled out a small red and white cooler. He handed the cooler to Steve.

"I don't want you young bucks gettin' into trouble trying to buy beer when you're underage. I also understand you're gonna try. Use this cooler instead." Then he pointed to a spot away from Triangle Park. "Over there is an old, abandoned livery barn. Been empty for years. When I was your age, my friends and I used to meet there on Saturdays and drink beer one of us had managed to buy or smuggle in. It's a safe place to get together and drink a few beers and relax. You boys enjoy yourselves, but you also behave and stay out of trouble. If something bad should happen, you come get me. I'll likely be at the lawyer's office on the other side of the park. Any questions?" he asked.

He was met with smiles and silence.

"All right then. You boys get lost. I got work to do," said Big Dave.

Steve picked up the cooler and led the way out of the store's parking lot and headed for the old, abandoned livery barn. His two brothers followed like they were on a tow rope.

Big Dave watched them walk away. He was unable to keep a big smile off his weather-beaten face.

CHAPTER THIRTY-FOUR

The boys were silent as they walked along an old sidewalk that was cracked in places and suffered from long ago frost heaves in other parts of the concrete walkway. Steve led the way, carrying the small cooler like it was weightless. After a walk of about four blocks, they turned a corner and there was the old livery stable.

It was in very poor condition. Parts of the roof were missing. Entire boards of siding were gone. But the structure still stood straight up and down. The fierce Wyoming winters and the daily strong winds had failed to affect the strong timbers that made up the skeleton of the old building. The sliding big door in front of the old building was gone, with only a few barely painted boards left to mark its passing.

Steve stepped inside and the two brothers followed. Nothing of any value or use remained inside the building. The stalls were still there, but there was no evidence of the hay that had once been used to line the stalls. The feed bunkers were empty except for the occasional deposit left behind by various mice. There were a few old wooden boxes and small barrels strewn about on the floor, but that was about the extent of the furnishings that remained.

"Grab something to sit on," said Steve. The three boys managed to collect some still intact wooden crates to use as seats. They pulled the crates into a semicircle and then sat down. Steve sat and placed the cooler in front of him.

Sunlight seeped through the gaps in the roof and the siding of the old stable and painted eerie imagines on the dirt floor. As the boys sat on their makeshift chairs, they were struck by the silence and the relative coolness of the interior of the old building.

Steve broke the spell by reaching down and opening the small cooler. A big smile spread over his face as he looked in at the contents. He turned the cooler so his two brothers could see what he saw.

Inside the cooler, buried in ice cubes, was a six-pack of Coors beer with an old beer can opener lying on top. Steve pulled out the six-pack and separated the cans. Then he put three cans back in the ice and closed the cooler. He took a can and used the opener to cut a small triangular hole in the top of the can. He did the sameto all three cans and then he passed two cans to his brothers' waiting hands.

"What the hell is Coors Beer?" asked a puzzled looking Travis.

"I never heard of it," said Lee.

"I have," said Steve. "It's made in Colorado and not available in most of the US."

"Why not?" asked Travis.

"I'm not sure. I think it has something to do with how it's brewed, and it affects how long it stays good to drink," replied Steve.

Lee took a drink of his beer. Then he looked up at his brothers. "Damn. It's pretty good stuff," he said. "Give it a try."

Steve and Travis did, and both were impressed by how the cold beer tasted.

"This is good stuff," said Steve. He was about to say something more, but his eyes caught movement by the open entrance to the old stable.

"Well, well. What the hell have we got here?" said a big, rough looking man dressed in less than clean jeans and a ratty looking t-shirt. He was followed into the old stable by three other men. They were smaller, leaner, and no older than the three brothers. The big man looked older and certainly meaner.

"What are you three assholes doin' in our place," he said in a loud voice with more than a reasonable amount of menace in it.

Steve looked the four strangers over carefully, and then he replied in an even voice.

"We're off work and relaxing," he said.

"You're trespassin' on my property," said the big man.

Steve studied the big man. He was about an inch shorter than Steve, but he was a good forty to fifty pounds heavier. He had muscled arms, but he had a sizable gut on him. He had obviously not had a razor in his hand for some time, and his resulting beard was ragged and scraggly looking.

He was dressed like a bum, but he was big, ugly, and acted and looked like trouble to Steve.

"I don't think so," replied Steve. "Our boss told us this place had been abandoned for years. He used it with his friends back when he was our age."

"Who's your boss?" demanded the big man.

"Big Dave Olson," replied Steve with an even voice. "Maybe you've heard of him."

"I have," replied the big man. "But that don't cut no ice with me. He ain't here. You are. And you ain't welcome here."

Steve was about to speak when the big man interrupted him. He had seen the cooler and then the beer cans in the three brothers' hands.

"How the hell did you young whelps get beer?" he demanded. "You three sure as hell ain't twenty-one."

"Big Dave gave them to us," replied Steve calmly.

The big man stared at Steve as if sizing him up. Then he spoke. "Ain't got no use for no Big Dave. You three are trespassing. Get your asses out of my building and leave the cooler behind. You're lucky I'm lettin' you take those beers you're drinkin' with you."

Steve was about to reply when Lee piped up.

Lee stood and faced the big man and his three companions. "Look. We don't want any trouble. If this is your place and we're not welcome here, we'll just leave," he said in a pleading voice.

"Then get up and get out," snarled the big man.

"Yes, sir," said an obviously frightened Lee.

Then Travis stood. He reached down and picked up the cooler by the handle. Then he stepped forward and held the cooler by his side.

"I'm sorry for us trespassing on your place, sir," he said. "You're welcome to the cooler and the rest of the beer."

"That's more like it," said the big man as he began to relax his posture.

Then something very unexpected happened.

With the cooler in his right hand, Travis suddenly swung the cooler behind him and then brought it over his shoulder and slammed it into the big man's head. The impact knocked the big man down to his knees. Then Travis clasped both his hands together and delivered a powerful uppercut blow to the big man face. The impact broke the big man's nose and blood splattered everywhere. It also knocked him on his back. He lay on the hard-packed dirt floor now specked with his blood, as well as splattered on his clothes.

The big man's three companions stood shocked in place. They couldn't believe what had just happened in front of their eyes.

Then Travis spoke. "You three drug store cowboys drag your friend out of here, or you'll wind up on the floor of this stable next to him. Do it now!" he commanded them.

His command broke the spell that had overcome the big man's three companions. They stepped forward and grabbed the big man by the arms and legs and drug him out of the old stable and were soon out of sight.

Steve and Lee managed to get over their initial shock and then stepped forward and clapped their little brother on his back.

"Where the hell did you learn to do that?" asked Steve.

Travis smiled. "I read it in a book," he said.

"A book? What book?" asked Steve.

"It was a history book," said Travis. "Before we came out here, I went to the library and took out some books on Wyoming. One of them was about outlaws and told the story about an old outlaw in Wyoming named Butch Cassidy."

"Butch Cassidy? Who was he?" asked Steve.

"He was a famous outlaw. He and his partner, a guy named the Sundance Kid, had a gang called the Hole in the Wall gang. Apparently one day one of the gang challenged

Butch to a knife fight to see who should lead the gang. The guy was bigger than Butch and much stronger," said Travis.

"What happened?" asked a curious Steve.

"He told the guy they had to set rules for a knife fight. The guy threw up his hands and yelled there were no rules in a knife fight. While he did this, Butch kicked him in his nuts and then when he went to his knees, Butch clasped his hands together and blasted him in the face and put him down. I used the cooler instead, but the principle of the idea came from the book," said a modest Travis.

Steve laughed. When he stopped laughing, no one spoke, and the ensuing silence created an awkward feeling in the old stable. Then Lee broke the silence.

"Now what?" asked a nervous Lee.

"Now we drink our beers and enjoy ourselves," said Travis.

"What if they come back?" asked a still unsettled Lee.

"Then we'll deal with it when they do," said a calm Travis.

"Works for me," said Steve as he raised the can of beer to his mouth and took a long swig.

The three brothers relaxed on their makeshift chairs and finished off their beers. They talked about their experiences in Wyoming and their impressions of everything from the ranch, the food, the work, and their fellow cowboys. During this time, they didn't see or hear any sign of the four departed bums Travis had run out of the old stable.

"One thing here has been good in my opinion," said Steve.

"What's that?" said Lee. "I can't think of anything good I've seen so far."

"The food. Cookie knows what he's doing," replied Steve.

"I agree with that," chimed in Travis.

"Also, all this hard work is making me stronger," said Steve. "I can feel it when I'm doing physical work."

"That damned branding session for two days damn near killed me," said Lee. "You two may be enjoying this indentured servitude, but I'm sick of it."

"I'd rather be back home, but I feel all right with it so far," said Steve. "I liked the feeling I got branding those calves. It was hard, physical work and I liked being able to handle those calves. The more I did it, the better I got at it."

"I kinda like it," admitted Travis.

"You two must be getting dumber," said Lee. "This whole deal sucks as far as I am concerned. I can't wait to get the hell out of here. How the hell can you like wrestling calves and sitting on a pile of mud, blood, and cow shit?"

"Good lord, Lee," said Steve. "It's just a little hard physical labor. It ain't gonna kill us."

"That's your opinion," said Lee. "I ain't cut out to be nobody's slave."

"You're not a slave, Lee," said Steve. "You're getting paid for every bit of hard work you do and then some. I doubt anyone is ever gonna offer us a payday for hard work like this one. I got no real complaints."

"Me either," said Travis.

"You're both nuts," said Lee. "I'm ready to chuck the whole thing."

"You're gonna throw away a chance to earn half a million bucks?" asked Steve.

"I don't give a crap if it was five million," said Lee. "I got better things to do with my life than hard work and being treated like a field hand."

Travis laughed. "You have no idea what being treated like a field hand is, Lee. You're just as spoiled as me and Steve."

Lee had no retort. He just glared at his younger brother.

When they finished their beers and their conversation, they went on a walking tour of Kemmerer. All three of them were surprised to be greeted with smiles and hellos when they met people on the street and along Triangle Park.

● ● ●

After he finished picking up the supplies he had on his list at the hardware store, Big Dave stowed his purchases behind the seat in the cab of his pickup truck. Then he drove past the center of town and parked in front of the law office. He entered the front door and was soon greeted by his friend Woody. The two friends each stopped and grabbed a cup of coffee from the coffee pot in the small break room and then retired to Woody's office.

"How's the baby-sittin' job goin'?" asked Woody.

Big Dave took a long swig of his hot coffee and then looked up at Woody. "It's been God damned interesting," he responded.

"Interesting is a big and complex word. Care to interpret it for me," said Woody.

"Them boys may be brothers, but each of them is as different as a wolf to a sheep to a bull moose," replied Big Dave.

"Hells bells, all kids are different," said Woody. "The idea that kids are small clones of their parents is pure nonsense."

"I got no idea what their mom and dad were like, but these boys sometimes come across as perfect strangers to each other," said Big Dave.

"Does that mean you've been having trouble with any of them?" asked Woody.

"Not real trouble. Them three is scared to death of me," said Big Dave with a chuckle.

"Tell me what you've learned about them," said Woody.

Big Dave paused. Then he took another big swig of coffee and put the mug down on Woody's desk.

"The oldest one, Steve, is pretty smart. He's a strong kid and he can do almost any hard work I throw at him. He don't complain, and he don't say a lot. He rarely talks unless he has a question about the job at hand. He's hard to read, but I think he knows he's here to put in his effort and get his work done right and on time. I got no real complaint about him."

"What about the others?" asked Woody.

"The kid, Travis, is a big surprise," said Big Dave.

"How so?" asked Woody.

"At first, I thought he might be a problem. and I needed to keep an eye on him," said Big Dave. "I thought he'd be a mama's boy."

"Is he?" asked Woody.

"Not at all. Turns out he's damn smart, and he may be one of the most natural cowboys I have ever seen. He asks good questions, he learns fast, and he has what I might call real natural ability to ride, rope, and handle stock. That kid would make a good cowboy on any ranch in Wyoming. He does stuff easily the first time while the other two are still struggling to get things right," replied Big Dave.

"What about the middle kid?" asked Woody.

Big Dave took another long drink of coffee, set the mug down, and looked down at his feet. Then he looked up at Woody.

"I ain't sure about that one," said Big Dave. "He's big enough and strong enough to do the work, but he ain't interested in learning the right way to do anything. I think it's because he sees himself above doing hard manual work and he resents being here and having to take orders and get sweaty and dirty. I'd bet good money that kid is a mama's boy. He don't like hard work. He don't like me. He don't like being here. I'll be surprised if he lasts the full three months of this summer."

"So, it's safe to say you're not fond of Lee," said a grinning Woody.

"I think that kid is as worthless as tits on a boar hog," replied Big Dave. He makes it clear every day that he don't want to be here."

Woody took a drink of his coffee and then set the mug on the desk. "I'll write up what you've told me and send it as a progress report to our friend in Salt Lake. Anything you want to add to what you've told me?" he asked.

"Nope. I took some notes about how the calf branding went and what each of them did," said Big Dave. He pulled out his notebook and took out about three pages of handwritten notes and passed them over to Woody. "They did better than I expected. Especially Steve and Trevor," said Big Dave.

Woody quickly scanned the notes for a few minutes. When he was finished, he put the notes in a file and looked up at Steve. "Your handwriting is a lot better than I remember," he said.

"I took my time. You're lookin' at the second effort, not the first one," said Big Dave. "You hear anything from the lawyer feller in Salt Lake?"

"Nope, not a word. I assume he's waiting for my report which I'll finish writing up now that I have your notes to include with it," said Woody.

The two friends finished their coffee and spent a few more minutes talking about a little local gossip. Big Dave invited Woody to come out to the ranch the next week to see the boys in action.

"What do you have them doing next week?" asked Woody.

"We start hayin' next week. It'll last most of the week. The ranch has a good crop of wild hay thanks to being next to the Ham's Fork River. Come out any day and plan on stayin' for lunch. Cookie does a damn fine job in that kitchen. I ain't careful I'm liable to lose my girlish figure," said Big Dave.

Woody roared with laughter.

Then Big Dave got to his feet, shook hands with Woody and he was out the door.

When Big Dave pulled up in his truck next to the park at six o'clock that evening, the three brothers were sitting on the ground waiting for him. They quickly climbed into the truck.

"How'd your day go?" Big Dave asked Steve.

"Interesting. Very interesting," said Steve with a slight smile on his face.

"Did you have any trouble?" asked Big Dave.

"No sir, no trouble at all," replied a smiling Steve.

Big Dave nodded his head like he understood what Steve really meant and put the truck in gear and headed back to the ranch. Kemmerer was a small town. Big Dave had already heard about what had happened in the old stable. Of course, the version he heard had originated with the four yahoos who had fled the stable so instead of three greenhorns, their attackers were a dozen grizzled cowboys.

Big Dave smiled and kept his eyes on the road. He felt proud of his three young men. Even spoiled Lee.

CHAPTER THIRTY-FIVE

Sunday morning the boys slept in until almost eight o'clock. Then they were up, showered, dressed, and headed to the cook shack.

When they entered the building, they were greeted with the sight of Cookie, sitting on a stool, reading a book. Only Rocky and Big Dave were seated at the table. They had obviously just finished eating. Their empty plates were shoved to the middle of the long table, and they were both enjoying another cup of hot coffee.

"Where's everyone at?" asked a puzzled Travis.

"You're lookin' at 'em," retorted Big Dave with a chuckle.

"Everybody?" repeated a bewildered Travis.

"Everybody who didn't get stinkin' drunk last night," said Big Dave.

Both he and Rocky laughed.

"Them other three cowboys musta wrestled with some bad whiskey," said Big Dave.

"Yeah, and the whisky won," added a grinning Rocky.

"Them other three so-called cowboys ain't found their way outta their bunks yet this mornin'," said Big Dave.

Steve looked around the almost empty table. "Where's breakfast?" he asked.

"On Sunday, I don't fix anything in advance," said Cookie. "But I can make most anything you want pretty quick."

"Pancakes," said Steve and Travis, in unison.

"Comin' up," said Cookie.

"What about you, Lee?" asked Big Dave.

"Can I get some eggs, scrambled and some bacon?" asked a tentative Lee.

"I'm on it," said Cookie and he disappeared back into the kitchen.

"Heard you boys had a little trouble at the old stable yesterday," said Big Dave as he raised his coffee cup to take another swig.

"How did you hear that?" asked a surprised Steve. "We didn't say a word about it to anyone."

"You didn't have to," said Big Dave. "Them four yahoos young Travis ran out of the stable were blabbing all over the Star Bar how they got beat up by half a dozen big strangers in the old livery barn."

"They did?" asked a surprised Travis.

"Kemmerer is a small town. Word travels fast around here. Especially when it involves any kind of violence," said Big Dave with a smirk.

"How did you know it was us?" asked a puzzled Steve.

"How many old, abandoned livery barns do you think there are in Kemmerer?" asked a smiling Big Dave.

"Oh," said Steve and then wisely decided to keep quiet.

"Anyone gonna tell me what really happened?" asked Big Dave.

Silence fell over the cook shack. All three boys were staring down at their boot tops.

"According to this one idiot, some huge giant who was almost seven feet tall used a baseball bat on the biggest one of the four yahoos and beat the shit out of him. Then his gang chased all four of them out of the stable and threatened them with decapitation if they came back," said Big Dave.

"What's decapitation?" asked a puzzled-looking Lee.

Big Dave, Rocky, and Cookie all roared with laughter.

"That's a load of crap," said Travis. "I sucker punched that big oaf with the ice chest. Then I hit him in the nose with my two hands joined together in a big fist. That was the entire fight."

"You did tell them to drag the idiot out of the stable, or you'd do the same to the rest of them," added his big brother Steve, who had a smile of his own on his face.

"That's true," admitted Travis.

"Travis told us he learned about that trick when he was reading a book about Butch Cassidy," added a now talkative Lee.

"Maybe we should start callin' you Butch, instead of Travis," said a grinning Big Dave.

Now everyone was laughing.

Cookie reappeared from the kitchen and delivered plates of hot food to each of the three boys. Big Dave and Rocky finished their coffee and headed out the door. On the way out, Big Dave hesitated and turned to face the boys.

"Get your chores done, and then you're free for the rest of the day," he said and then slipped out the door.

After the three brothers finished their breakfast, they split up and headed out to do their assigned daily chores. When they were finished, they returned to the bunk house and Lee and Steve decided to try their luck fishing for trout in the Ham's Fork River. They got tackle from a closet in the bunkhouse and then headed out toward the river.

Travis waited until they were gone. Then he headed over to Big Dave's cabin. When Big Dave answered his knock on the door, Travis stood there for a minute, as though he was trying to remember why he was there.

"You need somethin,' Travis," asked Big Dave.

"Yes, sir," said Travis. "Could you take me to the range and help me with my shooting?" he asked.

"Be glad to," replied Big Dave.

Fifteen minutes later they were on horseback headed to the ravine on the ranch they used for a shooting range. Big Dave carefully showed Travis the mechanics of the revolver and the lever action rifle. Then showed him how to sight and shoot them.

As he watched Travis shoot the rifle, a smile came to Big Dave's face. "The boy's a natural shooter," he thought to himself. Travis handled the Colt revolver and the Winchester rifle equally well.

When they were done, Big Dave and Travis policed up their brass, and slipped it into an old canvas bag. Then they returned to the ranch and put up the two horses.

Steve and Lee returned with some cutthroat trout. They gutted and cleaned the fish and presented them to Cookie. They all enjoyed fried fish for dinner.

CHAPTER THIRTY-SIX

After they finished breakfast Monday morning, Big Dave had everyone stay at the table in the cook shack.

"The wild hay is ready to cut," said Big Dave. "Here is the plan for the week. Rocky will drive the tractor and cut the hay with the sickle mower. Slim will drive the other tractor and pull the hay rake behind Rocky."

Travis put his hand up.

"You got a question, Travis?" asked Big Dave.

"Yes, sir," said Travis. "What's a hay rake and what does it do?"

Big Dave, the four cowboys, and Cookie all laughed.

"Good question, Travis," said Big Dave. He explained that after Rocky cut the wild hay down with the sickle mower, Slim used the hay rake to lift the cut wild hay and place it in long rows like furrows, so it could dry properly. He added that they would grease, oil, and examine both the sickle mower and the hay rake before they began. Preacher and Weston would help them service the equipment and help keep the tractors fueled.

"I expect the hay cuttin' to take about two days," said Big Dave.

"What do we do?" asked a curious Steve.

"You boys do all the chores, and you help Preacher and Weston check out the hay wagon to make sure it's ready to go. Preacher and Weston will pull out the baler and make sure it's ready to go as well. If Rocky and Slim need anything, it's your job to go get it pronto," said Big Dave.

"Is that clear to everyone?" asked Big Dave.

A chorus of "yeps, yeahs, and yes, sir" filled the air.

"Let's get movin," said Big Dave. "We're burnin' daylight."

Ten seconds later, the cook shack was empty except for Cookie and a lot of dirty dishes. Cookie sighed. Then he began to gather pots, pans, dishes, mugs, and silverware and started to put hot water and soap in the big metal sink.

The first two days went smoothly. By five in the afternoon on Tuesday, all the wild hay along the river on the ranch was cut and rolled up into long grass furrows that wound along next to the bank of the Ham's Fork River.

With the exception of a few mechanical issues, the entire enterprise went rather smoothly, and Big Dave was pleased when they all sat down for dinner on Tuesday evening.

After dinner was finished and the long table cleared, he motioned for everyone to stay seated.

"Tomorrow, we start baling wild hay," said Big Dave. "We'll wait until about ten in the morning to make sure any possible dew on the hay is gone. Then we start bailing."

Big Dave looked over at the three brothers. "You boys are new to this so let me explain how we're gonna do this job, so you understand. If you don't understand, then ask me questions when I've finished explaining. That all right with you three?" he asked.

"Yes, sir," the three responded, almost in perfect unison.

"Rocky drives the tractor. The tractor pulls the baler. Attached to the baler is a flat hay wagon. Slim will be on the hay wagon with a baling hook like this one," said Big Dave. He held up a large metal hook with an oblong handle to it. Slim will drag the bales back to the rear of the hay wagon and start to stack them with Preacher's help," said Big Dave.

When the hay wagon is full of wild hay bales, Rocky will stop the tractor. Slim or Preacher will jump down and unhook the hay wagon from the baler. Then Rocky will pull the tractor and baler forward.

Wes will drive the second tractor with an empty hay wagon up and he and Preacher will attach it to the baler. Then Preacher and Slim get on the new hay wagon and Rocky starts to bale again. Meanwhile Wes will hook up the loaded hay wagon to his tractor and haul it back to the area by the big barn where we store the bales. When he gets there, you three, along with Wes will unload the bales and stack them in the fenced area where we keep the hay. When you finish unloading and stacking the bales of hay, Wes will return to the hayfield. We repeat that until we have all the hay baled and stacked. It should take us about three days. Any questions?" asked Big Dave.

There were none.

"Let's make hay, boys," said Big Dave and everyone filed out of the cook shack and headed to their respective work areas.

Cookie watched them depart. Then he began his clean up routine with a smile on his face.

CHAPTER THIRTY-SEVEN

The three brothers followed Wes to the area by the big barn that had been set up as a fenced-in area to store the baled hay. They helped Wes hitch an empty hay wagon to his tractor. Then they leaned back against the wooden fence and waited. All three were a bit nervous about the next phase of puttin' up hay.

After a short rest, they were interrupted by the arrival of Big Dave in his pickup truck.

Big Dave got out of his truck and walked over to where the three brothers were leaning against the fence. As he walked past them, he looked over each of them up and down like he was searching for something. He stopped, turned, and looked directly at the three brothers.

"It appears to me that somethin' is missin'," he said.

The three brothers looked at each other in confusion. They had no idea what Big Dave was talking about.

Then Big Dave went to the passenger door of his truck and pulled it open. He then carefully removed three cardboard boxes and carried them over to where the boys were standing. He looked at the top of the first box and then moved his gaze to the three brothers.

"The top box is for Steve, the second box is for Lee, and the last box is for Travis," said Big Dave in an easy voice.

The three boys just stood there looking at Big Dave. They acted like they had no idea what they were supposed to do or say.

"Come get your presents, boys," said Big Dave. "Or should I say cowboys."

Steve stepped forward and got his box, then Lee and Travis did the same.

"Open 'em up. They're presents, not boxes of snakes," said Big Dave with a smirk on his face.

The boys opened their boxes and removed silver grey Stetson cowboy hats. They each held the hat in one hand and the box in their other. They were surprised and unsure of how they were supposed to act, so they almost froze in place.

"Try 'em on. They go on your heads. But get rid of them ball caps first. A man can only wear one hat at a time," he said.

The three brothers threw down the boxes and took off their caps and tossed them on the ground. Then they each tried on their new cowboy hats.

"Step over to the truck and check out your new hats in the side mirror," suggested Big Dave.

The brothers quickly complied, with Steve going first and Lee waiting behind him. Travis just went to the other side of the truck and used the mirror on that side.

When all three were satisfied with how the cowboy hats sat on their heads, Steve spoke up.

"What's this all about?" he said.

"You boys earned them hats," said Big Dave. "You ain't greenhorns no more. Now, you're Wyoming cowboys."

Steve and Travis started to voice their thanks, but they were interrupted by Lee.

"Does the cost of these hats come out of our pay?" asked Lee.

"Nope. They don't. These hats are a gift from me to you boys. You've worked hard, and you earned the right to wear them," replied Big Dave.

Then all three brothers thanked him profusely.

"Clean up them boxes and toss them and them old ball caps in the trash," said Big Dave. "It's about time for you boys to start some real hard work." With that he climbed into his pickup truck and drove off.

They had about ten minutes to enjoy their new cowboy hats before they heard the sound of the tractor driven by Wes. He soon appeared with a hay rack wagon piled high with large one hundred twenty-pound bales of wild hay.

They followed Wes and his tractor and hay wagon to the small fenced in area next to the big barn. Once he pulled to a stop, Wes shut off the tractor engine and jumped down to the ground.

He then addressed the three brothers, who had formed a small semi-circle around him. "I'll get up on the wagon and toss down a bale at a time. You three will carry or drag the bales and start stacking them on the ground and then on top of each other."

Wes then showed them where to stack the bales and once they got started, he would occasionally shout directions to them and showed them how to tie the bales into each other at the ends to make the haystack more secure.

It was hard dirty work and as soon as the last bale was off the hay wagon, Wes was up on the tractor and pulling out of the hay lot and back to the wild hay fields next to the river. By the time the three brothers had finished getting all the bales stacked correctly, they were hot, sweaty, and covered with dirt and bits of wild hay.

They soon fell into a routine. Wes would pull his tractor and loaded hay wagon next to the haystack and then start tossing the bales off the wagon. As soon as all the bales were off, he would climb back on the tractor and head back to the wild hay fields for another load. The boys would then work together to drag, lift, and toss the bales of wild hay into a solid foundation of long squares of hay. They usually had a break time of fifteen to twenty minutes between loads. They used that time to rest and to drink plenty of cold water from a big stone barrel with a spigot that Cookie had provided. Next to the barrel was a second barrel they could use when they managed to empty the first barrel.

The work was hard, hot, and dirty. The bales only got heavier as the day wore on. A little after noon Cookie appeared with a pickup truck, and he served the three brothers and Wes a hot midday meal from the tailgate of his truck. The boys and Wes sat on bales of hay as they had their lunch. When they were finished, Cookie collected their dishes and the uneaten food and placed them in the bed of the pickup truck. He then closed the tailgate, slid into the cab of the truck, and drove out of the hay pen and headed out to the wild hay fields where Slim, Rocky, Preacher, and Big Dave were working.

The lunch break lasted about thirty minutes and then it was time to go back to lugging, lifting, and stacking heavy bales of wild hay.

"Now I know why there are no more cowboys left in Wyoming," said Steve as they headed back to work.

"Why?" asked a puzzled Lee.

"They all died from over work branding calves and putting up wild hay," said Steve with a grin.

"Not funny," complained Lee, but both Steve and Travis had big smiles on their faces.

Then Travis got a puzzled look on his face. He got up and walked over to the growing stack of large wild hay bales. He poked at the nearest bale and then he walked back to where the brothers were sitting.

"I don't get it?" said Travis.

"You don't get what?" asked his brother Steve.

"They cut the wild hay. Then they rake it into windrows. Then they run a baler over the windrows and create these big bales. One of the hands uses a hay hook to grab the bale as it is coming out the chute of the baler. He drags it to the back of the flat hay wagon and there he and another cowboy stack it. When the hay wagon is full, they attach a new wagon and Wes drives the loaded hay wagon here. Then we unload the wild hay bales and stack them in this fenced in yard out here in the open," said Travis.

"I don't understand your question," said Steve.

"Why go to all that trouble and then just leave the hay bales out here in the pen in the open. There's no roof, and no cover for the bales. Why not store them under a roof or in a building like a hay barn?" asked Travis.

Steve waited for his younger brother to finish. Then he smiled.

"Have you noticed that there is a big difference in the temperature out here compared to back home in Illinois?" he asked his younger brother.

Travis considered the question. Then he responded. "Yep, I have," he said. "The same temperature in Illinois and Wyoming feels different."

"Why is that?" asked Steve.

"I'm not sure," said a puzzled Travis.

"The difference is humidity," said Steve. "Wyoming air is dry. Illinois air is humid with liquid."

"So?" asked Travis.

"I read where the difference in how it feels between the two states is about twelve degrees. So, if it's thirty degrees in both states in the winter, it feels like thirty in Illinois, but it feels like forty-two in Wyoming," said Steve. "In the summer Wyoming is cooler than Illinois."

"Because of the humidity?" asked Travis.

"Yep," replied his brother.

"What has all that got to do with no covering these wild hay bales?" asked Travis.

"Because of the lack of humidity here, they don't need to cover the bales. They stay dry and don't rot like they would in Illinois," replied Steve.

"Ah, now I get it," said Travis.

"On your feet, boys," said Lee. "I hear the tractor coming. Wes is headed here with another load of hay."

Five minutes later, Wes drove into the hay pen pulling a full wagon load of baled wild hay.

It was time to go to work again.

CHAPTER THIRTY-EIGHT

During the next three days, the three brothers' time was divided between resting in the shade and drinking lots of cold water and then sweating profusely as they wrested the heavy hay bales into position on the growing mound of baled wild hay.

About three o'clock on the third day, the boys were resting in the shade. Their jeans and shirts were soaked with sweat and covered with dirt and bits of wild hay.

"I'm sick of this shit," said Lee.

"It's just hard work, Lee," countered his older brother Steve. "It makes all of us tired, but it ain't gonna kill us."

"It may be hard, but it's a heck of a lot easier than branding calves," added Travis.

"I second that thought," added Steve.

"God didn't put me on this earth to work like some ignorant hired hand," retorted Lee.

"Maybe you'd rather be branding calves," snickered Travis.

"Shut the hell up," said Lee. "You're too young and dumb to know what you want."

"He wants what we all want," said Steve. "We want to work our three months and then collect our five hundred thousand dollars and go home to Illinois."

"Steve's right," said Travis. "I want to get the money, but I've learned a few things this summer."

"Like what?" snarled Lee. "How dumb you are?"

"Nope. I know I'm not dumb. I learned I like hard physical work. It makes me feel like I've done something when a job is finished. It doesn't matter if it's branding calves or putting up wild hay. I like the feeling of accomplishment and knowing I am up to doing something that is hard for a lot of folks," said Travis.

"You're an idiot," said Lee.

"Maybe so," said Travis. "But I like the feeling I get of getting something done. Just like I enjoy the feeling of throwing a rope on a calf or fixing fence. I like riding horses. I like working where when you look out and all you can see is the horizon. No people, no cars, no houses, and no smog."

"You can have all this shit," said Lee. "It's not for me."

"I hate to interrupt this intellectual discussion," said Steve. "But I hear a tractor coming."

The three boys got to their feet and flexed their tired bodies.

When Wes pulled up to the hay lot and stopped, the three brothers could see the grin on his face from thirty feet away. Then they looked at the hay wagon. There were only ten bales of wild hay on it.

"Where's the rest of the hay?" asked a puzzled Steve.

"This is it," said a grinning Wes. "Unload this, and we're officially finished with this hay crop."

Fifteen minutes later, the hay wagon was empty of hay and carried only three grinning young men as Wes drove them back to the ranch yard. Once there, they jumped off the hay wagon, headed to the bunk house, and had a hot shower.

Two hours later, the three boys, the four cowboys, Big Dave and Cookie were all seated at the cook house table and digging into huge sirloin steaks, fried potatoes, and glasses of ice-cold lemonade. A special surprise was ice cold watermelon.

Other than a few snorts and farts, the bunkhouse was silent by nine o'clock that evening.

CHAPTER THIRTY-NINE

That Saturday morning came bright and early. Breakfast was over quickly and soon all the chores were finished. The ranch's four cowboys quickly showered, shaved, and dressed in their best clothes for their weekly outing in Kemmerer. They piled into two pickup trucks and quickly disappeared into the distance. A long plume of dust marked their passing before it dissipated into the warm air.

When Big Dave pulled his pickup to stop in front of the bunkhouse, the three brothers were leaning against the wall of the old building. They were dressed alike in jeans, work shirts, and cowboy boots. The biggest difference was the new cowboy hats on their heads.

Big Dave looked out through the windshield of the truck. The three boys looked different than they did when they had arrived two months ago. They were now more muscular, darker with sun dappled tans, and the now well-worn clothes looked natural on them. He smiled. They looked like cowboys.

The boys piled on the truck. Steve in the front seat and Travis and Lee in the truck's bed. Big Dave put the truck in gear and soon they were on the highway headed north to Kemmerer.

Steve looked at the floor of the truck. Then he looked up at Big Dave.

"No cooler?" he asked.

"It's in the back," said a smiling Big Dave.

"Cool," responded Steve and he leaned back in his seat.

• • •

When they reached Kemmerer, Big Dave drove slowly past Triangle Park and watched as the three boys scanned the park for young females more thoroughly than a hunter seeking game. He smiled.

Big Dave parked in the grocery store parking lot, and he and Steve exited the pickup truck. Lee and Travis climbed out of the truck bed as Big Dave reached into the bed and pulled out the small red and white cooler. He handed the cooler to Steve.

"Make sure all three of you are at the edge of the park at six o'clock," he said. All three brothers nodded their heads and then Steve grabbed the handle of the cooler and led the way as the trio headed toward the old livery barn. Big Dave stood there, watching them go. Then he smiled again and turned to head into the store with his list of groceries Cookie had made out for him.

The brothers soon entered the old livery barn. The big front door was still lying on the ground and the barn was still missing siding and parts of the roof. The inside of the barn was partially lit by all the holes in the roof and the siding, and the invading sunlight gave the interior a surreal look. The three young men quickly found old barrels or boxes to use as chairs and pulled them into a rough semi-circle in the middle of the old barn.

Once the seating was arranged to their satisfaction, Steve placed the cooler on the hard packed dirt floor next to him and opened it. He stared inside and a big smile appeared on his face.

"I think we got promoted," said Steve.

"Promoted? What are you talking about?" asked Lee.

Steve tipped the cooler to its side and gave his two brothers a good look at the contents.

"Wow, it's a twelve pack," said Lee.

"You're right," said Travis. "We did get promoted."

There was less ice, but Steve didn't think that was a problem. He was pretty sure the beer would be all gone before the ice had melted and disappeared. He pulled out three cans. He tossed two of them to his brothers and then found the church key in the bottom of the cooler and opened his can. Then he tossed the opener to Lee, who used it and then tossed it to Travis.

All three brothers took a long swig of cold beer and then sat back and enjoyed the taste and the coldness of the beer, and the quiet atmosphere of the old livery barn.

They each finished their first beer and Steve passed out a second beer to his two younger brothers and then took one for himself. He used the church key and then passed it to his brothers. Then he retrieved it and returned it to the cooler.

The three brothers were halfway through their second beer and were discussing what they thought of their unusual summer jobs. The boys were each in separate camps when it came to their opinions about their so-called forced labor jobs. Lee hated all of it. He hated the work. He hated the sweat and dirt. He hated the lack of freedom. He hated having to take orders about almost everything. He was still nursing the idea of quitting and going home to a normal life, but when he mentioned that option, Steve laughed at him and called him spoiled and stupid.

"You are one clueless son-of-a-bitch, Lee," said Steve. "I am not nuts about spending my summer as a cowboy, but there are worse places I could be, and I know it. To me the whole deal is about the money at the end of the summer. When this is over at the end of August, I hope I never see or smell a cow again. But I have some good ideas about how to invest the five hundred grand and set myself up to make even more money. I say just suck it up. We only have a month to go. Working hard for two months and then giving up and going home with only fifteen grand isn't just dumb, it's stupid."

Travis had remained silent while he listened to his two older brothers. He was delighted with the chance to go home at the end of August with five hundred thousand dollars. But there was more to this summer job for him. He discovered he liked playing cowboy. And he had discovered he was good at it. But he was smart enough to keep his thoughts to himself. He was not interested in getting razzed constantly by Lee or Steve about actually enjoying this summer job of hard work. So, he kept his mouth shut.

Steve turned to Travis. "You ain't had much to say, Travis. How do you feel about this so-called summer job we are workin' at?" he said.

"It's all right," said Travis. "I can take it or leave it."

Steve was about to ask him another question when Lee stood up and put his finger to his lips as if to signal his brothers to remain silent. "Listen," he hissed at them.

Faintly at first, and then louder with each passing minute, the three brothers heard voices talking. The voices were getting closer to the old stable and from the sound of the voices, they belonged to females.

The three brothers remained silent. Lee standing and Steve and Travis sitting on two old barrels. Then shadows crept into the sunlight on the barren stable floor behind the old open door. The shadows moved and morphed into two young teenage girls. One blonde, one dark haired. The girls walked into the old stable still chatting with each other. The blonde had on a small backpack. Then the blonde noticed the three boys, and she seemed to freeze in mid-stride. She grabbed her dark-haired friend by the arm, and both girls came to a sudden and surprised stop.

The blonde managed to finally speak. "Who are you?" she croaked out.

"Well, we ain't the cops. We ain't the army. We ain't a troop of boy scouts. We're just three hired ranch hands enjoying a cold beer on a hot summer day in July in Wyoming," said Steve with a smile on his face.

"Oh," was all the blonde could manage to spit out.

"We're also harmless," said Steve. "We're just hidin' out here in this old stable having a few cold beers because none of us are twenty-one or older. We'd appreciate it if you kept our little secret from anyone else."

The blonde broke into a half smile. The two girls looked the three brothers over, apparently liked what they saw and seemed to relax.

"You mentioned cold beer," said the blonde. "You got any to spare?"

"Maybe," replied Steve. "What you got in the backpack?"

"Items we rescued from my mom's kitchen," replied the blonde.

"What kind of items?" asked Lee.

The blonde turned her attention to Lee. "Cookies. Hot out of my mom's oven," she said. "We were just going to hide out here in the old stable and enjoy them. We thought the place would be empty."

"You two ladies got names?" asked Steve.

"I'm Ann," replied the blonde. "This is my friend Fanny," she said, putting her arm around her dark-haired friend.

"So, you came here to eat stolen cookies?" asked Lee.

"You could say that" replied Ann.

"Cookies may be good, but one usually brings some kind of liquid refreshment to wash the cookies down with," offered Lee.

"I got that covered," said a feisty Ann. She reached into the pack and pulled out a quart of Jim Beam whiskey.

"You drink that stuff right out of the bottle?" asked Steve.

"Of course not," said Ann. "We ain't barbarians." She reached in the pack and pulled out two small old glass jelly jars.

Steve smiled. "How about you two grab something to sit on and if you'll share your cookies and whiskey, we'll share our cold beer."

"Sounds like a deal to me," said Ann.

A few minutes later the boys had scrounged up two more old barrels to sit on and placed an old wooden box in the middle of the hastily made semi-circle. The old box was soon covered with cookies, cans of cold beer, and the whiskey bottle.

Steve and Lee began explaining who they were and what they were doing in Lincoln County that summer. The girls lived in Kemmerer and would be starting their senior year in high school that fall.

"So, you're just here for the summer?" asked Ann.

"Yes, just for the summer," replied Steve.

"So where do you live?" she asked.

"We all live in Illinois," said Steve.

"Oh, so you're from back East," said Ann.

Steve looked puzzled. "No, no, we're not from back East. We're from Illinois."

"That's east of the Mississippi River, right," said Ann.

"Yes, it is," replied Steve.

"That's the East to us," said Ann. "This is Wyoming. This is the West."

"Oh," said a still puzzled Steve.

"Hell, it doesn't matter, we're just glad to meet you," said a smiling Ann.

All five of the young people burst out in laughter.

Travis kept his mouth shut. He did notice that in all the byplay and interchange of information, no mention was made of the boys' father, his ranch, or the money the three of them were working to earn.

The girls stayed for about two hours and chatted with all three boys. Then they left, but not before they had left hastily written notes on paper with their names, addresses, and phone numbers with Lee and Steve.

Once the girls had disappeared from view, Travis started laughing.

"What's so funny?" asked a puzzled looking Lee.

"You two," retorted Travis. "I can't believe my two older, more sophisticated, better educated brothers were sitting in this old shed, acting like lovesick puppies to two high school girls from a small town like Kemmerer."

Both Steve and Lee wanted to come back with something smart to say but were too embarrassed by the accuracy of their younger brother's observations. They kept their mouths shut and concentrated on drinking their remaining beers.

CHAPTER FORTY

At six that evening all three brothers were sitting on the grass in Triangle Park when Big Dave pulled up in his pickup truck and parked next to the curb. Steve climbed into the cab and Lee and Travis hopped into the bed of the truck. When he was sure everyone was safely seated, Big Dave put the truck in gear and headed back to the ranch.

On the trip home, Travis kept teasing Lee about being so awkward with a couple of small-town girls and laughing every time he made a point. Which was often.

Sunday was a quiet day. Steve went fishing. Lee just laid on his bunk. Travis got Big Dave to take him out to the home-made rifle range and spent two hours shooting revolvers and rifles with him. Even Sunday dinner was quiet. Good, but quiet.

All four cowboys, the three brothers, and Big Dave were at breakfast in the cook shack early Monday morning. When breakfast was over and everyone was putting their dirty plates and silverware in a bin on the counter for Cookie, Lee asked Big Dave if they could stay for a moment and talk.

"Sure," said Big Dave. "Not a problem."

After everyone was gone, only Big Dave and Lee remained. Cookie was in the back of the shack doing dishes and out of earshot.

"What's up?" asked Big Dave.

"I want out," said Lee.

"What do you mean you want out?" asked Big Dave.

"I want to go home. I'm sick of this place. I'm sick of being your slave. I'm sick of you bossing us around. I'm sick of working like a dog. I want to go home," said Lee.

Big Dave nodded his head. Then he sat back in his chair. He grabbed his coffee mug and took a long swig of black coffee. Then he placed the mug down on the table and looked Lee in the eye.

"Is there a reason you want to quit now?" asked Big Dave quietly.

"I just gave you my reasons. I'm sick of this place. I'm fed up with you. I'm sick of working like hired help. I want to go back home, and I want to do it now," said Lee.

Big Dave took another sip of coffee. Then he looked straight at Lee. His light blue eyes were hard. There was no humor or friendliness in them.

"I assume you realize that by doing this you forfeit your opportunity to earn half a million dollars, and you go back to your mama with just a check for $15,000," said Big Dave.

"Yes, I do," said Lee. "I don't give a shit about the money. I hate this place."

"All right then," said Big Dave. "I need to make some phone calls and arrange for a plane ride back to Illinois. It will take some time. As soon as I have the arrangements made, I'll tell you."

"What do I do for the rest of today?" asked Lee nervously. His earlier bravado had faded quickly. His real fear of Big Dave had now manifested itself.

"Well, out here in Wyoming when a hand tells you he quits, he's done. You stay in the bunkhouse today, come here for meals and I'll let you know as soon as I have made travel arrangements for you to go home," said Big Dave.

Lee paused and then breathed a big sigh of relief.

Big Dave got to his feet, left the empty coffee mug on the counter for Cookie, and then went out the door of the cookshack.

Lee sat at the table. Now that he had blurted out his plan to Big Dave, he was unsure of what to do next. He looked up and over the counter. He could see Cookie washing dishes. He got up and headed back to the bunkhouse.

CHAPTER FORTY-ONE

Big Dave went out to the corral where the four cowboys and Steve and Travis were leaning on the fence, chatting with each other. Big Dave gave each of their work assignments for the day and then turned to go.

"Where's Lee?" asked Steve.

Big Dave stopped in his tracks and turned around. He faced Steve as well as the others, whose eyes were full of curiosity about what was going on.

"Lee has decided he wants to go back home to Illinois. I plan to make sure he gets there," said Big Dave. Then he turned and walked away.

The two brothers stood rock still. They were both stunned by Lee's decision.

The four cowboys had knowing looks on their faces.

"I ain't a bit surprised," said Slim. "That kid never did a damn thing he looked comfortable doin'," he said.

"He's just a mama's boy," said Preacher. "Worthless as tits on a boar hog."

"I kinda liked him," said Wes. "He seemed to try hard, but he just wasn't very good at cowboyin'."

Steve bristled at the criticism he heard from the veteran cowboys, but he calmed down when Travis put his hand on his shoulder to reassure him.

Travis looked his older brother in the eye. "He made his choice. He has the right to make a choice. We all do. I choose to stay. So do you. He just chose different."

Steve waited until the four cowboys had walked out of hearing range. Then he spoke softly to his youngest brother.

"Why would he do it now? He had two thirds of the time under his belt. He was just thirty days away from a big payday. It makes no sense," said Steve.

"He's a big boy. If he's made a mistake, he'll live to regret it," said Travis.

"I'm gonna go talk to him. This is a mistake. I'll pound some sense into him," said an intense Steve.

"You do what you want. Lee is not a child. He's made his decision. I plan to do my best to respect his choice," said Travis.

"It's a stupid choice," blurted out an exasperated Steve.

"Maybe so, but it's his choice to make, not yours," said Travis.

Steve snorted and turned and headed to the bunkhouse at a fast walk. Travis stayed behind and headed for his daily chores in the barn.

When Steve walked into the bunkhouse, Lee was standing by his bunk, sorting out his work clothes. He turned to face Steve as he heard him approach.

"What the hell are you thinking?" blurted out a frustrated and concerned Steve.

"I'm doing what I should have done two months ago," said Lee. "This shit is not for me. I'm too good to be shoveling shit for some uneducated boob like Big Dave. I've had it, and I'm going home to a real life for me."

"You're tossing half a million dollars out the window. Do you realize that? So, what if you don't like the work or you can't stand Big Dave? A half a million bucks is nothing to sneeze at. Have you thought about that?" asked an exasperated Steve.

Lee looked away from his older brother. He didn't like having his decision challenged, even by his brother. Then he looked back at Steve.

"It's what I want. I'm going home. Now leave me alone and go back to shoveling shit for that big hillbilly," said Lee.

Steve stood there for a moment, staring at his younger brother who now refused to look him in the eyes. Then he turned and stormed out of the bunkhouse. His brother was a fool and Steve knew his mother would defend Lee no matter what he did. He had tried to change Lee's mind. He'd failed. He headed back to the barn to start his chores for the day. He smiled to himself as he remembered that shoveling shit was not on the agenda for today.

When he got back to the barn, he saw that Travis had saddled two horses and gathered the tools and gear they would need to ride the fence that morning. Travis did not ask any questions. He just climbed onto the saddle of his horse. Steve did the same, and the two brothers headed out to ride their designated section of fencing for the day.

When they found their first fencing repair job, the brothers stepped down from their horses and tied the two mares off to the fence. Then they got their gear and began to expertly repair the fence. When they were finished, they put away their tools and gear and each of them grabbed a canteen off their saddles and took a long swig of water.

Travis screwed the top back on his canteen and tied it off to his saddle. Then he turned and looked at his older brother.

"You have any luck with Lee?" he asked.

"About as much luck as turning that there dried cowpie into a hot pizza," said Steve.

"You did that well?" asked a smiling Travis.

"His mind is made up. I tried. I failed. Both of us know he'll be pissed as hell in two months when we each have a pot of money, and he's spent his fifteen thousand," said Steve.

"That's just Lee. He's emotional and does and says dumb things," said Travis.

"I believe the term you are lookin' for is stupid," said Steve. "Our brother is short-sighted and stupid."

"It's his choice," said Travis.

"It certainly is, and I plan to remind him of that every time I hear him bitch about a lack of money," said Steve.

The two brothers saddled up and began riding slowly along the long fence line that seemed to flow out to the horizon.

CHAPTER FORTY-TWO

At breakfast the next morning, Big Dave waited until everyone was finished and before they had gathered up their dishes for Cookie. He called Cookie to come out of the kitchen and join them at the table.

When everyone was seated, Big Dave looked around the table. Satisfied, everyone was there, he spoke.

"Lee has quit his job here," said Big Dave. "He'll be leavin' today. My friend Woody, the attorney, will be here this morning to give him a ride to the airport in Salt Lake. If any of you want to say goodbye to Lee, take a bit of time to do it now. When you're done, head out to your chores that I assigned you for today."

Then Big Dave got up out of his seat, slapped his cowboy hat on his head, and headed out the door of the cookshack.

Nobody moved or said a word for a minute. Then Preacher got to his feet, looked at Lee, made a face of disgust, snorted, and walked out.

Then Slim, Rocky, and Wes all stopped to shake Lee's hand, and they followed Preacher out the door. Cookie got to his feet. He looked over at Lee. Then he spoke.

"I'm disappointed in you, son," he said. Then he returned to the kitchen.

Both Steve and Travis stood and hugged their brother.

"Good luck," said Travis and he turned to leave.

"You always were a dumb shit," said Steve. "I guess I kinda knew you would always run home to mommy when things didn't go your way." Then he followed Travis out of the cookshack.

Lee stood still for a couple of minutes and then walked out the door and headed for the bunkhouse.

When he reached the bunkhouse, he paused at the door and looked back at the ranch. He could see the four cowboys now mounted and riding out to work on their assigned chores. He could see his younger brother on a horse, holding the reins for a second saddled horse as Steve walked up to him. Then Steve mounted his horse, and he and Travis rode around the big barn and out of sight. Lee sighed and felt something in the pit of his stomach that didn't feel right. He dismissed it as Cookie's lousy breakfast and went inside.

Lee got out his duffle bag and carefully folded and placed his personal clothes and items in it. He removed his work clothes and left them in a pile on the floor next to his cowboy boots. He dressed and then made sure he hadn't missed anything he wanted to take home. He left all of his work clothes in a pile on his bunk. He noticed his cowboy hat hanging on a peg on the wall. He stared at the hat for a moment. Then he grabbed his bag and headed out to the front porch of the bunkhouse.

He grabbed a chair on the tiny front porch and sat back in it, his bag next to him. He had no idea when the bumpkin attorney friend of Big Dave's would arrive. He could wait. When the attorney did show up, he would be on his way home and back to his normal life among civilized people. And his mother.

After almost an hour, Woody drove up in his father's big Lincoln. He got out, reintroduced himself, grabbed Lee's bag, and put it in the trunk of the Lincoln.

"Hop in," said Woody and he then slid into the driver's seat of the big car. Lee got in the passenger seat and made himself comfortable.

Woody started the engine and then looked over at Lee. "You all right, boy?" he asked.

"Yep," replied Lee. "Let's get out of here."

"All right," replied Woody and he put the car in gear. He drove out of the ranch yard, down the entrance road and was soon on the highway headed south to the main highway that led to the airport in Salt Lake City.

As soon as the car had disappeared from sight, Big Dave emerged from his cabin. He stood on the porch, looked in the direction the car had disappeared and sighed. Then he saw Cookie headed for the bunk house carrying a couple of cloth bags.

Big Dave swung off the porch and headed for the bunkhouse as well. When he got there, Cookie was standing in the middle of the room looking at the mess that Lee had left on his bed and the floor next to it.

"Not very tidy was he," said Big Dave.

"Nope. He wasn't," responded Cookie.

Big Dave walked over to Lee's old bunk. He looked at the dirty clothes and cowboy boots on the floor. Then he looked at the pile of clean work clothes on the bed. Then his eyes caught something. He walked over to the bed and reached behind the pile of clean clothes Lee had dumped on the bed.

There on the bed, hidden behind the pile of clothes, was Lee's cowboy hat. The hat rested on its brim, not placed on its top with the brim up. Cowboy lore required real cowboys to always place their hats with the brim up whenever they took their hats off their head. According to legend, the cowboy's luck and knowledge safely tucked into the hat. Placed with the brim side down meant it all drained out.

Big Dave pointed to the hat. "See how he left the hat," said Big Dave.

Cookie looked at the hat on the bed and he sighed. "Not a good sign for the boy's future," said Cookie.

Then Cookie began putting Lee's clean clothes into one bag and the dirty items in the second bag along with the boots. He went to grab the cowboy hat, and Big Dave stopped him.

"Leave it," said Big Dave. "It'll make a good reminder to the other two boys about makin' bad decisions in your life."

Cookie nodded and Big Dave left the bunkhouse.

When Cookie had filled his two bags, he walked to the door of the bunkhouse. At the door he stopped and turned to look back at Lee's empty bunk. The lone cowboy hat sat improperly on the bed. It reminded Cookie of Lee's choices while at the ranch. Leaving his cowboy hat on the bed and leaving it wrong side up said a lot about Lee.

Cookie turned out the lights, closed the door, and headed back to the cook shack with his load of Lee's clothes and boots.

CHAPTER FORTY-THREE

It was about a three-hour drive to the airport in Salt Lake City in good weather. Today was a sunny day at the end of July and traffic on the highway was light except for the big eighteen wheelers that seemed to be in a never-ending line from east to west and then from west to east.

When they reached the end of the road and it fed into the main highway, Woody turned to head west toward Salt Lake City. When they passed the exit to Evanston, Wyoming, Woody broke the silence by asking Lee if he had learned anything by his two months working as a cowboy on the ranch.

Lee stared at Woody for a minute. Then he replied. "I hated every minute of it. All it was good for was to remind me of what I didn't want to do with my life. I plan to hire people to shovel shit, not have to do it myself."

Woody nodded, he understood and kept silent for the rest of the drive. When he reached the airport, Woody drove to the departure section and pulled over to the curb. Both got out of the car and Woody pulled Lee's bag from the car's trunk and set it on the curb next to the boy.

Woody reached inside his coat pocket and pulled out a manilla business envelope. "This is your check for fifteen thousand dollars, son," said Woody and handed the envelope to Lee.

Lee took the envelope and put it in his back pocket. He started to turn away from Woody, but then paused and turned back to face him. "Why did you think I learned anything from working like a hayseed on a ranch with guys who probably never made it through high school?" asked Lee.

"Because sometimes we learn things and don't realize it until later in life when those things pop up in our heads," said Woody with a slight smile on his face. "Good luck, son," said Woody and he turned to get back in his car. When he was behind the wheel with the doors to the car closed, he muttered to himself. "I think you're gonna' need all the luck you can muster up and then some with your attitude toward people and life."

Woody started the engine and pulled away from Lee standing on the curb with his travel bag. That image got smaller and smaller until it disappeared entirely.

• • •

Steve and Travis thought supper that evening might be pretty somber with the events of the day and Lee's empty chair at the long table. They couldn't have been more wrong. Not only was the conversation lively and often funny, but Lee's name wasn't brought up even once. After supper, as they were walking back to the bunkhouse, Travis mentioned it to Steve. Steve smiled.

"I don't think Lee did anything memorable while he was here other than complain. I think the message from the other cowboys was good riddance," said Steve.

The rest of the week seemed to fly by. Steve rode the fence with Wes and Travis rode with Shorty. Suddenly it was Friday, and they were all gathered in the cook shack for supper.

They were finished with their meals and piling up the dirty dishes on the countertop for Cookie when Big Dave asked them to grab a cup of coffee and have a seat at the table. When everyone was seated and quiet, Big Dave pulled out a small notebook from his shirt pocket. He flipped up several pages, then found the page he wanted and looked up at his ranch crew.

"Get your chores done tomorrow morning and as soon as you're done with them, you're free for the rest of the weekend. I got a small surprise for all of you," he said. He got up and walked to where his jacket was hanging on a wall peg. He pulled out seven white envelopes. Then he returned to the table and returned to his seat.

"The owner has decided that he is pleased with the progress of the new ranch set up and he asked me to give each of you a little bonus. Here it is," he said as he passed out the envelopes to each of the four cowboys, Cookie, and the two boys.

Preacher was the first to rip open his envelope and pull out a green one- hundred-dollar bill. "Woo wee," yelled Preacher. He was soon joined a happy chorus of "Hot Damn, Holy Shit," and other expletives.

"Just in time for Saturday," yelled out Shorty.

"Damn straight," said Wes. Steve and Travor just grinned at each other.

Five minutes later, the cook shack was empty except for Cookie and Big Dave. Big Dave was smiling. Cookie paused in putting dirty dishes in the sink of hot soapy water. "What's so funny, David?" he asked.

"It just struck me how much people appreciate even a small token of gratitude when they get one that is not expected. Them two boys are excited over a hundred-dollar bill when in less than a month they're gonna be gettin' a check for a lot more for finishing out the three months of work they signed up for," said Big Dave.

Cookie just smiled and went back to washing dishes in the sink.

CHAPTER FORTY-FOUR

The next morning the four cowboys and the two brothers wolfed down their breakfast and were out the door of the cook shack like they had been shot out of a cannon. By the time Big Dave drove his pickup truck up to the bunkhouse, both Steve and Travis had already showered and put on the best looking of their clean work clothes.

Steve got into the passenger side of the pickup truck and Travis put one boot on the rear bumper of the pickup truck and vaulted into the bed. He discovered Big Dave had placed a bale of hay up against the cab. He gleefully sat on the bale with his back to the cab and used his fist to thump on the roof of the truck's cab. "Let's roll!" said Travis. Big Dave smiled and let out the clutch and the truck rolled forward, picking up speed as they headed to Kemmerer.

The sky was almost clear of clouds. The sun shone hot and bright on the pickup truck as it sped into Kemmerer. Big Dave parked the truck in the hardware store lot and he and the two boys exited the truck.

Big Dave pulled out the familiar red ice chest and handed it to Steve. "I'll see you boys at 5:30 this afternoon by the park," he said. Then he paused, trying to hide a grin on his face. "Don't do anything I wouldn't do," he said. Then he paused. "Forget that crap. Just stay out of trouble."

The two brothers grinned and then took off in the direction of the old livery stable with Steve toting the ice chest. When they got to the old stable, nothing seemed to have changed. The big old door was still lying on the ground, and they could neither see nor hear any sounds or evidence of anyone else in the stable. The only evidence of occupation was about two dozen empty beer cans and a few empty beer bottles lying about on the dirt floor of the old building.

Steve set the cooler on the dirt floor and then he and Travis scrounged around and found two old wooden barrels suitable for substitute chairs. Once properly seated, Steve grabbed the ice chest and pulled it next to him. He opened the chest and pulled out two cold bottles of Coors beer.

"What did Big Dave leave us?" asked Travis.

"Looks like two six packs to me," said Steve.

"Two? For just two of us?" asked a surprised Travis.

"Two is what I see," said Steve. "Maybe Big Dave thinks we might get some company and need more beer to provide proper entertainment."

"Just so they are sociable and friendly," said Travis. "I've had enough of local assholes to last me for the rest of the summer."

Steve laughed and took a swig of cold beer. Travis quickly followed suit. They were on their third beer when they heard sounds from outside the stable. Soon two young men entered the old stable. One was carrying a small blue cooler. They looked to be about Travis' age. They were dressed like cowboys in denim shirts, jeans, cowboy boots, and cowboy hats.

"Sorry," said the one young man. "We thought this place would be empty. We'll leave you two fellers be."

"No need to leave. Place is big enough for a hell of lot more than two of us," said a smiling Steve. "Find something suitable to sit on and join us."

"Thanks," said the taller of the two. "That's mighty neighborly of you."

The two boys searched the old stable and produced an old barrel and a beat-up wooden box. They dragged their prizes over to where Steve and Travis were seated.

The two boys introduced themselves as Will and Trent Hutchins. The two were brothers and they lived with their parents on a sheep ranch located between Kemmerer and Cokeville. The four boys shook hands and got seated.

"What's in the blue cooler?" asked Travis.

"Just some beer we snuck out of our old man's stock at the ranch," said Will. "He drinks Falstaff, which I ain't real fond of, but a beer is a beer, I guess."

"This is your lucky day, Will," said Steve. "We've got Coors and plenty of it." He reached in the red cooler and grabbed two bottles of beer and tossed one to each of the Hutchins brothers.

"Thanks," said Will.

"Thanks, is right," said his brother Trent. "Coors beats the crap out of Falstaff."

All four of the boys laughed. Then they began asking questions about each other and sharing the ups and downs of rural life in Wyoming. They finished the day about the same time they finished off all the Coors beer. Then they shook hands, said goodbye, and Steve and Travis walked to Triangle Park and sat under a tree in the shade.

It wasn't long before Big Dave pulled up in his pickup truck. The boys put the cooler in the bed of the pickup truck and Steve and Travis piled into their respective seats.

"You boys do all right today?" asked Big Dave.

"We had a good day," said Steve. Big Dave smiled and put the truck in gear.

A few minutes later they were leaving the outskirts of Kemmerer and headed back to the ranch.

CHAPTER FORTY-FIVE

Sunday breakfast was a familiar scene. The four regular cowboys straggled in, one at a time. They were looking a bit worse for wear from their Saturday excursion into Kemmerer.

The two brothers had light headaches from their Saturday alcohol consumption, but they both felt pretty good. They both listened as the four cowboys bemoaned their latest experiences in Kemmerer Saturday night life. As they listened, they grinned at each other.

After breakfast, they loaded up a pack mule with gear and headed out to ride and repair fencing on the ranch. The August sun was hot in the sky and soon both brothers had taken off their shirts. The shirts were soaked with sweat and the shirts rubbed their skin unmercifully.

A little past noon, they stopped for lunch. The only shade they could find was against a large rock at the base of a small hill. Steve broke out the lunch Cookie had packed for them. It consisted of ham and cheese sandwiches on sourdough bread with mustard and a large dill pickle for each of them. They wolfed down the lunch and washed it down with lukewarm water from their canteens. They were just finishing their lunch when Big Dave rode up on his horse.

He pulled up in front of the two boys. Then he leaned over the saddle and studied them like they were insects under a microscope.

"You boys are taking a pretty big chance," he said.

"What chance?" asked a puzzled Steve.

"Both of you look to have a good start on a painful sunburn," said Big Dave. "That shirt may be wet and uncomfortable, but it ain't nothin' compared to a bad sunburn. Get them shirts back on and keep 'em on," he ordered.

Both boys quickly got to their feet, unrolled their shirts, and struggled to get the wet shirts back on. Big Dave tried to hide his grin as he watched them twist and turn as they tried to get control over the sweat soaked shirts. Finally, they succeeded and Big Dave rode away, shaking his head as he rode.

The rest of the day was just like the morning. Lots of riding. Lots of fence. And lots of repair work. Later in the afternoon the sky gathered up some clouds and it gave the boys some much needed relief. Their shirts managed to dry out and some of it was due to the fact they had exhausted their water supply early in the afternoon. Both boys were very thirsty. When they headed back to the ranch, Steve took care of the gear, and the horses, and the mule, and Travis ran to refill their canteens from the ranch well pump.

When he returned to the barn, he helped his big brother finish up with the animals and then both sat on a bale of straw in the shade and drank the cool water from their canteens until both canteens were bone dry.

When Cookie rang the dinner bell, both brothers were sore and tired, but no longer thirsty. They washed their heads and upper bodies using the well pump. And then put their sweat stained shirts on over their still wet upper torsos.

Supper time was devoid of much conversation as the cowboys, Big Dave, and the two brothers were intent on eating everything they could put on their plates and drinking cold lemonade until they could take no more.

When they hit the bunkhouse, the brothers took turns using the shower and changed clothes. Then they sat on the porch of the bunkhouse and listened to the four cowboys trade lies about their hot Saturday night in Kemmerer.

About fifteen minutes later a late model black Ford F-250 pulled into the ranch yard and parked in front of Big Dave's cabin. Two men in cowboy hats got out and walked up to the door and one knocked. Big Dave opened the door, and the two men stepped inside. The door closed behind them. Then there was no motion and no noise. Just silence except for a few crickets chirping.

The arrival of the truck acted like a wet blanket had been thrown over the cowboys and the two brothers sitting on the bunkhouse porch. All conversation stopped and six pairs of ears were tuned in to try to catch any snatch of a conversation originating from Big Dave's cabin.

They heard nothing. So, they sat and waited. No one spoke. Finally, Travis said, "What's goin' on?"

Shorty looked over at the boy. "We don't get no visitors late in the day and if we do, it's damn sure they ain't bringin' no good news," he said.

The silence returned and the crickets took up their strange music.

Half an hour passed and then the door to Big Dave's cabin opened and the two strangers walked out, followed by

Big Dave. The two men got in the Ford and drove out of the ranch yard. Big Dave stood and watched them go. Then he headed for the porch of the bunkhouse.

"Get ready for God knows what," said Shorty with apprehension in his voice.

Big Dave walked up to the front of the porch and then stepped up on it and leaned back against the railing.

"I just got some disturbing news," he said.

The four cowboys and the two brothers sat there in rapt attention. Even the crickets shut up.

Big Dave paused and looked around like he was expecting to find someone eavesdropping on what he was about to say.

Satisfied, he turned back to the group. "Them two jaspers were from the Triple T ranch over by Cokeville," said Big Dave. "They came here to warn us of a new problem of rustlers in their area and probably working their way toward our spread," he said.

"How much trouble?" asked Shorty.

"Apparently they aint' rustlin' herds of cattle, but they are grabbin' small batches of around six to eight head at a time," said Big Dave. "The boys from the Triple T said they didn't notice the loss of cattle at first, but after about two weeks, they found a calf and no mama cow. They were searching for the mama, and they found tracks that led to their fence. There they found the fence had been cut and then restapled to allow a truck and a long horse trailer into the ranch. The crooks loaded cows into the trailer and then drove out and repaired the fence behind them. No one seemed to notice until they went lookin' for the lost cow," said Big Dave.

"Did they ever see the varmints?" asked Shorty.

"Apparently not," said Big Dave. "They started patrolling at night by horseback and the thieves must have spotted them and they didn't come back for more cows."

"Damn," said Shorty.

"Starting tomorrow, two of you will function as night herders and sleep during the day. I don't intend to lose any of our beef to some damn rustlers," said Big Dave.

"What do we do if we see something or some riders on our ranch?" asked Slim.

"You ride like hell to the ranch and sound the alarm," said Big Dave.

"We got an alarm?" asked Preacher with a puzzled look on his face.

"Fire off your damn pistol," said Big Dave. "The sound of a gun oughta work just fine."

"Won't that scare them off?" asked Wes.

"That's the idea, Wes. I want them scared and off our land and afraid to ever return," said Big Dave.

"What about license plates and descriptions of the truck?" asked Travis.

"What?" asked Big Dave.

"If our fence rider can see them, he should try to get the license plate of the truck or the trailer and a description of the truck so we can give it to the sheriff," said Travis.

"That's a damn good idea, son. The rest of you try to remember that if you should spot these bastards on our ground," said Big Dave.

"When do we start this fence patrol?" said Shorty.

"We start tonight," said Big Dave. "Rocky and Slim will work tonight from sundown to sunup. I'll make a schedule up and have it posted in the cook house by tomorrow at noon. I want the night guards to always have pistols and Winchesters with them. Is that clear?"

The four cowboys and the two brothers nodded their heads. Big Dave headed back to his cabin and Rocky and Slim went into the bunkhouse to grab any gear they felt they might need, including their weapons. Then they headed to the barn to saddle their horses.

The remaining two cowboys and the two brothers stood on the bunkhouse porch and watched the duo ride out of the ranch yard and away toward the nearest pasture.

CHAPTER FORTY-SIX

The first night was uneventful. Slim and Rocky joined the others for breakfast in the cook shack. When asked what happened that night during their watch, Slim smiled and said it was hard work.

"Hard work?" asked Steve.

"Staying awake with nothin' but grasshoppers and cows and calves to keep you company is damned hard work," said Slim.

Everyone laughed, even Big Dave.

When things quieted down, Big Dave looked over at Slim and Rocky. "Just how did you two patrol the ranch last night?" he asked.

The two cowboys looked at each other and then over at Big Dave. They both had frowns on their faces.

"What do you mean how did we patrol?" asked Rocky.

"I mean did you ride together or separately. Did you ride in a pattern or just rode around the pasture areas of the ranch," said Big Dave.

"We rode together, and we just started out at one spot on the boundary fence and followed it till we got back where we started. Then we did it again," replied Rocky.

Big Dave paused and tilted his cowboy hat back on his head and scratched himself just above his right ear. Then he tilted the hat back down and looked up at the two cowboys.

"I think we need to work a pattern," said Big Dave.

"A pattern?" asked Rocky.

"Yep, a pattern. Tonight, I want the two guards to start at the same spot, but each goes in the opposite direction and ride until you meet up. Then continue until you meet again until your shift is over," said Big Dave. "That way you cover more ground faster and up the odds of running into these jaspers," said Big Dave.

"Whatever you say, Big Dave. You're the boss," said Rocky.

Big Dave grabbed his coffee cup and had it halfway to his mouth when he noticed Travis was sitting across from him with his hand in the air.

"You got a problem with that arrangement, Travis?" asked Big Dave with a frown on his face.

"No, sir," said Travis. "I think it's a good plan."

"So why is your hand in the air. This ain't no school room, son," said Big Dave.

"It's just that I got an idea about that," said Travis.

"Well hells bells, why didn't you say so," said Big Dave.

"I was trying to, but I was waiting until you called on me so I could speak up," said Travis.

"Well, you got it, son. Spit it out," said Big Dave.

"I think we should vary the pattern during the shift of the guards," said Travis.

"What do you mean, vary the pattern?" asked Big Dave.

"Well, I read where smart crooks watch for patterns of folks guarding something and use the breaks in those patterns to sneak in and steal stuff," said Travis.

Big Dave scratched his chin. Then he spoke. "The kid's got a good idea. Let's make a change in the pattern."

"What change?" asked Slim.

"After one circuit of the ranch, we'll have one of the riders slip over to the ridge at the south end of the ranch and go to the top and spend half an hour scopin' out the land below him to the north," said Big Dave.

"But it'll be dark. What the hell can he see in the dark?" asked Preacher.

"If it's dark the damn rustlers gotta use lights or they can't drive a truck and long horse trailer over rough ground and they gotta use lights to find and cut the fence," said Big Dave.

"Sounds like a plan to me," said Wes.

"Wes, you and Preacher are on tonight," said Big Dave. "Make sure you got both a pistol and a rifle and a box of ammo for each of you."

"We will," said Wes and Preacher almost in unison. Big Dave smiled and finally took a long drink of his coffee.

Afterwards, when Travis and Steve were walking to the barn to saddle horses for the day's chores, Travis looked over at his older brother.

"I got a strong feeling that any rustlers that try to steal cattle from this ranch are gonna regret it for the rest of their life."

Steve just smiled.

CHAPTER FORTY-SEVEN

For the next four nights, the men took turns patrolling the ranch at night and other than a coyote or two, they saw nothing to be concerned about. They didn't see any trucks on the old roads near the ranch, let alone rustlers in a pickup truck pulling a long horse trailer.

That morning at breakfast, the report was the same. Lots of time spent in the saddle and nothing to see but cows, calves, and the occasional coyote.

"That's all you saw?" asked Big Dave.

"Well, that ain't quite all," said Rocky. "We did see two jackrabbits, but they was headed for the Red Desert."

"How the hell did you know they were headed for the Red Desert?" asked Big Dave.

"Both of them were totin' canteens," said Rocky with a big grin on his face.

The ensuing laughter was mixed with catcalls, and other cowboy insults.

After breakfast was finished, Big Dave went to his truck and headed to Kemmerer. He stopped near Triangle Park and parked his truck. Then he made his way to Irma's Café. He entered the crowded café and after taking a quick look around, he joined five other ranchers at a big round table in the center of the café.

A waitress appeared out of nowhere and took his order for hot coffee, black. By the time she returned with his coffee, he was chatting with the other five ranchers.

"Any of you boys been hit by these night rustlers using a truck and horse trailer?" asked Big Dave.

The five ranchers looked around the room, like they were about to share a top-secret military analysis and didn't want to be overheard. Then a short, slim rancher named Will Giese finally spoke.

"I ain't been hit, but my neighbor, Tim Farnsworth, got hit twice in one week," he said.

"How bad did he get hit?" asked Big Dave.

"He says they got five cows each time. Left the damn calves bawlin' for their mamas. That's what alerted him somethin' was wrong," said Will.

Silence covered the table, until a heavy-set rancher with a long droopy mustache broke it.

"I got hit a week ago," he said. The rancher was Leroy Townsend, and he had a small spread just north of Kemmerer. "Damn bastards musta come three nights in a row. They took fifteen head from my herd. I reported it to the sheriff, but that's about as helpful as pissin' into the wind."

"They didn't come back?" asked Big Dave.

"Nope. After I got hit, I had a hand on night guard and he ain't seen anything bigger than a jackrabbit in the last week," said Leroy.

There was a little more discussion about the rustlers and their tactics and the uselessness of the sheriff's office to do anything about it. Then Big Dave finished his coffee, got up and slipped out the door of the café.

Ten minutes later he was stepping through the front door of the law office of Woody and his old man.

Woody was surprised to see him. "To what do I owe this great honor?" he asked.

"Cut the bullshit. I'm here on serious business," said Big Dave.

"Did something happen to one of the boys?" asked Woody with worry in his voice.

"Nope, nothing like that," replied Big Dave. "I got me a new problem and it ain't got nothin' to do with them two boys."

"What's the problem?" asked Woody in a concerned voice.

"Rustlers. That's the new problem," said Big Dave. "Bastards hit the ranch and tried to get away with about a half dozen head of prime beef."

"Tried?" said Woody.

"The kid Travis scared them off," replied Big Dave.

"Rustlers. I heard a few ranch herds had been hit," said Woody. "Any idea who they are?"

"If I knew who they were, I wouldn't be wasting my time here jawin' with you. I'd be burying the bastards," said Big Dave.

"That's the sheriff's job, Big Dave. Don't be doin' nothing that can blow back on you," said Woody.

Big Dave looked over at his long-time friend. His face was hard, and his eyes looked like cold blue ice. "If I find these bastards, no one, including you or any of the sheriff's people will ever know about it or ever find a trace of them ever again," said Big Dave with firm conviction in his voice.

Woody hesitated, but then spoke. "Just be careful, Big Dave. You ain't the only rancher these polecats have tried to steal cattle from," he said.

"Maybe so," said Big Dave. "But them yahoos are gonna learn that stealing anything from me is one of the biggest mistakes they'll ever make in the rest of their miserable lives."

Woody waited until he was sure Big Dave was done venting. Then he spoke. "How can I help you?" he asked.

"Tell me what you've heard and what you might know about these rustlers," said Big Dave.

"Let's go in my office," said Woody. Then he led the way to his private office and closed the door behind them. He sat behind his desk and Big Dave took one of the two chairs in front of the desk.

Woody then opened a drawer and pulled out a thick file folder. He placed the folder on the desk and opened it. Then he pulled out a half dozen pieces of paper and set them on the desk.

"I don't work for the sheriff, but I do have my sources in his office. I heard you got hit by the rustlers, so I managed to get copies of each of the theft reports," said Woody.

"Are those the reports?" asked Big Dave.

"Yes, they are. There ain't much in them because so far no one has actually seen them, their truck, or their trailer. All the sheriff's office has is photos of tire tracks and boot prints in the dirt," said Woody.

Then he pulled out a map of Lincoln County. The map contained several small red circles with dates next to them, also printed in red.

"These are the reported sites of cattle being rustled. The dates indicate when the crimes may have occurred. I say may, because not all the thefts were reported promptly, but the dates have to be close. I made this map because I knew you'd be coming in to talk about the rustlers and it does show somewhat of a pattern," said Woody.

"I knew you'd be on top of this," said Big Dave with a smile on his face. "What's this here map tell you?"

"The pattern is a bit irregular," said Woody. The rustlers are not just going from ranch to ranch in a set pattern. Judging from the dates of the crimes and the locations, I'd say two things are evident."

"What are they?" asked Big Dave.

"First of all, they are picking spots that are remote, but next to decent roads. I figure that's because of the horse trailers they are using," said Woody. "Secondly they appear to be hitting the ranches on just two nights."

"What two nights?" asked Big Dave.

"Almost all the thefts have occurred on Saturday night or Sunday night. I think that's because most cowboys are in town getting drunk on Saturday night and they are still sleeping it off on Sunday night," said Woody.

"You could be right," said Big Dave. "Those are the two nights when there is less chance of being seen."

"Plus, those two nights are likely to have more vehicles driving around than during the week," said Woody.

"Right again, counselor," said Big Dave. "Have you passed this on to the sheriff's office?"

"Not yet," said Woody.

"Why not?" asked Big Dave.

"They ain't asked me," said Woody.

"That's not a big surprise," said Big Dave. He got to his feet, shook hands with Woody and headed to the door.

When he got to the door, he stopped, turned, and looked back at his good friend. "Thanks," he said. "I'll keep you posted on what I learn."

Then he turned and went out the door. Minutes later he was headed back to the ranch. He made a detour and stopped at his home to retrieve a few items, talked with his wife, Connie, got back in his truck and headed to the ranch.

CHAPTER FORTY-EIGHT

Once he arrived at the ranch, he removed the items from the truck and carried them into the cabin. There he carefully checked each of them and placed them in a small closet. Satisfied, he headed outside and back to his truck.

Soon Big Dave pulled up next to the barn. He got out of the truck and entered the barn. Minutes later he exited the barn leading a bay mare he had saddled. He grabbed the saddle horn and swung his body over the saddle and settled in with both boots in the stirrups. He checked his shirt pocket for the small spiral notebook he always carried along with a small mechanical pencil. Satisfied, he touched his spurs to the mare and guided her out of the ranch yard and down along the fence line that constituted the eastern border of the ranch.

As he rode the fence line, he kept his eyes on the fence and the ground beneath it. The highway ran along the eastern border of the fence and occasionally his peaceful study was interrupted by a car, truck, or big semi. After almost an hour of plodding along the fence, he brought the mare to a halt and sat back in the saddle and carefully studied his surroundings. Access to the ranch and its cattle was the easiest from this part of the ranch with its proximity to the highway. But the highway was a double-edged sword. It provided good access, but it had a reasonable amount of traffic, even at night. That wouldn't work for most careful cattle thieves.

He pulled the little notebook out of his pocket, made a notation, replaced the notebook, and urged the mare forward along the long fence line. He rode slowly, taking his time and his eyes constantly looking for what didn't belong. It was the oldest tracking trick in the book, and he had learned it as a young boy. As a result, his eyes were always moving.

By the time he had reached the northern end of the fence line it was late afternoon. He turned the mare to follow along the inside of the fence that now was running east to west and plodded along. After about twenty minutes, he halted the mare. He had seen nothing suspicious so far and any interloper would have to trespass on his neighbor's ranch to get to this section of fence. He touched his spurs to the mare's flank and trotted down the fence line until he reached the Ham's Fork River. The river was shallow at this point, so he eased the mare into the water, and they slowly made their way to the west bank of the river. The fence extended across the river using the strong posts on either side to serve as anchors.

He followed the fence to the western border of the ranch and then made another entry in his little notebook. Then he looked up at the sky, turned the mare, and had her head back to the ranch, the barn, and the horse's supper. The mare quickly caught on and picked up the pace.

Big Dave rode to the barn, dismounted, and proceeded to unsaddle and wipe down the mare. When he was finished, he gave the mare grain and water. Finished with the mare, he headed to his small cabin that served as the ranch foreman's quarters. When he was inside, he pulled a bottle of good bourbon, Buffalo Trace was his drink of choice, and poured a stiff drink. Then he went outside, sat on the old chair on his small porch and slowly sipped his whiskey. He savored the taste and the whiskey's bite as he thought though his still raw and unfinished plan to nail the cattle rustlers.

At supper that evening, after everyone finished eating, he asked all the hands to stay for a bit. Then he outlined his plan. Everyone, the four veteran cowboys, the two young greenhorns, and the grizzled cook paid close attention to what Big Dave had to stay.

Then he reached into an old feed sack he had placed by the wall of the cook shack and took out two odd looking pistols.

"These here guns ain't really guns," said Big Dave. "They're called flare guns, and they are used a lot at sea and on land by the military and the coast guard. I'll show you fellas how the darn thing works."

He pulled out a large awkward looking pistol, pushed a lever and the gun broke open like a hinge. Then he took out a large fat cartridge and inserted it into the pistol. Then he snapped the gun back together.

"That's how you load the gun. To fire it, you pull the hammer back with your thumb until it locks. Now it's cocked. Then you point the gun with the end of the barrel up in the air and away from your body and pull the trigger. The gun shoots a red flare that will explode and be damn bright in the night sky."

Big Dave paused and looked around at his captive audience. "Any questions?"

"Can we handle it?" asked Preacher. Preacher loved guns. He loved any kind of gun.

"Sure," said Big Dave and he unloaded the flare gun and handed the bulky weapon to Preacher. Preacher turned the gun over in his hands, pulled the hammer back to cock it, and then uncocked the gun and handed it to Rocky. Rocky went through the same motions and then handed the gun off. The flare gun traveled around the table until it finally rested on the table in front of Big Dave.

"Each of the two men on guard duty will be carrying one of these here flare guns. You will take the gun and three of these red flares with you every time you are out on guard duty. Is that clear?" asked Big Dave.

Everyone at the table nodded their assent or said "Yep," or "Yeah."

"All right then, let's get some work done today," said Big Dave.

All the hands filed out of the cook shack except Big Dave and Cookie.

Big Dave picked up the flare gun. He looked over at Cookie. "Ever fire one of these things, Cookie?" he asked.

"Yep, couple times when I was in the Navy," replied Cookie.

Big Dave looked surprised at Cookie's mention of service in the Navy. "Ever had any trouble with one?" asked Big Dave.

"Nope. Worked fine every time," replied Cookie. Then he rose from his seat and began collecting empty coffee mugs.

Big Dave put the flare gun back into the sack and then got to his feet, hoisted the sack, and headed out the door of the old cook shack.

Two weeks passed without any sign of rustlers near the ranch. The patrols got more boring by the day. Long nights of patrol interrupted only by coyotes and jackrabbits were restful, except for the possible threat of danger from unknown sources.

Steve and Travis felt it more than the older, more experienced cowboys. They missed the Saturday trips to Kemmerer and the private outings at the old stable.

It was a Monday and Big Dave, and all the hands were just finishing up breakfast when a big white Ford F-250 pickup roared into the parking area in front of the cook shack and slammed to a sudden dust scattering stop.

In an instant, Big Dave, the four cowboys, the two boys, and Cookie were running out the door of the cook shack to discover what in the world was going on.

The dust was still settling to the ground when the doors of the truck were thrown open and two old, grizzled cowboys dressed entirely in denim and old cowboy hats decorated with dust and sweat stains emerged.

"Jesus Christ, Amos, what the hell is the matter with you?" bellowed Big Dave.

The shorter and older of the two men turned to face Big Dave. He had a high voice for a man, and it seemed to pierce even the dust that still hung in the air.

"Goddammit, Big Dave. Them sonsofbitches hit my ranch early this morning. They was loading some of my stock into a long horse trailer when they got surprised by one of my hands who was doin' night patrol. It appears he was as surprised as the rustlers. He rode in on them and they opened fire. They shot him twice. Once in the shoulder and once in the leg. Then they hightailed it out of there, but not before those assholes shot and killed my man's horse. Who the hell shoots a man's horse after they done shot the cowboy who was riding it?" said Merv Thomas.

Merv was an old-time rancher who had a spread east of the Crooked L ranch. He was breathing hard and was staring off into space. Big Dave could see he was both excited and exhausted at the same time.

"How's your hand?" he asked.

Merv seemed to return to the real world with Big Dave's question.

"He's gonna be ok," said Merv with a sigh. Old Tucker was headin' out to relieve him and couldn't find him until he came onto the dead horse. Then he found Whitey on the ground about thirty yards away. He gave Whitey his bandana to plug the hole in his shoulder. He used Whitey's bandana to wrap the leg wound and then high tailed it back to the ranch. We got Whitey to the hospital in Kemmerer and then rousted the sheriff's office," said Merv.

"So, the Sheriff's on this case?" asked Big Dave.

"Sheriff, my ass," said Merv. "All they had on duty was some snot-nosed kid who'd probably shit his drawers if someone even pulled a gun on him."

"Shit," said Big Dave.

"I hightailed it here when the kid deputy said he'd try to find the Sheriff. You're the only hombre I know who is tougher and meaner than any stupid rustler," said Merv. "What should we do?"

Big Dave paused, as if to think for a minute. Then he barked out orders to his crew. "You boys get your chores done and then wait for me to get back here." Then he turned to Merv. "Let's go back to town and let me see what I can get done with the sheriff's office. I'll ride with you, but maybe I better drive that truck of yours. You seem a touch unsettled to be driving," said Big Dave.

Merv nodded his agreement. Minutes later, Merv's pickup truck roared out of the ranch yard and headed north on the highway to Kemmerer with Big Dave driving, Merv in the passenger seat and his ranch hand back in the bed of the truck.

CHAPTER FORTY-NINE

Big Dave was out of the truck before the engine died. As Merv got out of the passenger seat, Big Dave was already in the alcove of the Sheriff's office in Kemmerer.

When Merv got inside the Sheriff's office, Big Dave was leaning over a desk and telling a young deputy what for. The deputy was obviously scared to death of the angry big rancher leaning over him.

"What's he sayin'?" asked Merv.

"He says ain't no one here but him," said an angry Big Dave.

Big Dave turned to the frightened young deputy and looked him in the eye from a distance of less than twelve inches.

"You get someone with some real authority in here and you get it done pronto! Do you understand me, boy?" said Big Dave.

"Yes, sir," blurted out the deputy. He picked up the phone and was relieved when Big Dave stepped back, increasing the space between him and the deputy to about three feet. The deputy had to dial the phone twice as he hit the wrong numbers on the phone the first time he tried.

After a few seconds on the phone, the deputy finally got someone to answer, and he began to blurt out a story that made no sense to either Big Dave or Merv who were standing there with puzzled looks on their face.

Then the deputy spoke again. "Yes, sir. Yes, sir," he said. "I'll slow down. I'm sorry. I got two really pissed off ranchers here in the office and I need someone with authority here damn fast," he said nervously. After a few more seconds with the deputy nervously nodding his head up and down, he said, "Yes, sir," and hung up the phone.

He turned his head and looked hesitantly at Big Dave. "The Sheriff said he'll be here at the office tomorrow morning at ten," said the deputy, carefully choosing his words.

"I'll be here," said Big Dave. Then he turned on his heel and quickly got out the door of the office. Merv was right behind him. When they got to Merv's truck, both men paused and looked around as if to make sure they were out of earshot of anyone else. Satisfied, Big Dave spoke.

"Can you git hold of some of the ranchers who've lost livestock, Merv?" he asked.

"Yep," said Merv.

"Have them all be here at nine thirty tomorrow morning. Tell them to come armed. We need to have a reception committee for the damn sheriff and force him to tell us what the hell is going on in Lincoln County," said Big Dave.

"Amen to that," said Merv. Both men got in the truck and headed back to the ranch.

After they arrived at the ranch, Big Dave shook hands with Merv and watched as the rancher drove his truck out of the ranch yard and down the gravel road to the highway. Then he turned and strode into his small cabin.

Once inside, he grabbed a coffee cup out of the cupboard. Then he opened an old wooden box by the counter and pulled out a bottle of Buffalo Trace bourbon. He poured half a cup and then put the bottle back in the crate.

Then he went to the small table next to the tiny kitchen after grabbing a pad of paper and a pencil. He set the tablet and the pencil on the table, went over, and grabbed his cup and returned to the sturdiest of the old wooden chairs around his small table.

Once seated, he began to write on the tablet. On the first page he printed the names of all the ranchers he knew had suffered rustling losses. Then he did a quick estimate of just how many cows had been stolen. When he was finished, he looked at the total livestock thefts and let out a low whistle. Even though the rustlers seemed small time and only managed to steal four to six head at a time, the total came to almost a hundred head of cattle.

He was unsure of the exact dates of each theft, but he had a good idea of when it started and that gave him a total of thefts per week since the rustling had started. He looked at the numbers and let out a long sigh. "Them boys have been averaging about eight head of cattle a week. That's about two successful trips to steal cattle every week. He realized the thefts seemed small, but they quickly added up to a sizable amount of stolen beef and a good-sized loss to each rancher affected.

Big Dave sat at the table and thought about what he had just written. Then he got to his feet and walked into the kitchen. He picked up the wall phone and used the rotary dial phone to call his home. His wife answered and he explained to her what he needed, and she said she'd take care of it and hung up.

Big Dave returned to the table and made a list of ranchers and their men he knew he could count on when the chips were down. He was on his way to the cook shack when his wife drove into the ranch yard and came to a stop next to the cook shack. He walked over to the truck and smiled at his wife. She smiled back. She reached to the passenger seat and handed a long canvas gun case to her husband. He thanked her and leaned into the truck window for a kiss.

"Thanks Connie," he said. "Did you include three boxes of shells?"

"Of course. I didn't think you were gonna use it to beat someone to death," she said, grinning.

Big Dave grinned back.

"I'm not gonna ask you why you want this, because I don't think I want to know," she said.

"You're probably right," said a smiling Big Dave.

"I'll be glad when this three-month deal is over and you're back home safe and sound," she said.

"Safe and sound is a state of mind, honey," said Big Dave with a grin on his face. He turned away and Connie put the truck in gear and roared off down the dirt road to the highway.

Big Dave continued into the cook shack and once inside he placed the canvas gun case in a corner out of sight.

After dinner was over and all the hands had headed for the bunkhouse, Big Dave looked at the closed door. Then he looked over the kitchen counter where Cookie was busy washing dishes and cleaning up his kitchen. When Cookie's back was turned, Big Dave got to his feet, quickly retrieved his gun case and was out the door without making a sound.

He walked carefully to his cabin and once inside, he locked the door and set the case on the small kitchen table. He grabbed a small case containing his gun cleaning tools and materials and sat down at the table. Then he carefully opened the end of the case and slowly slid the rifle out and into the lamplight of the kitchen. The gun was thick and black. It looked nothing like a typical Winchester saddle gun. Its black finish gleamed with malice. He carefully turned it over in his hands. Then he opened the bolt and set the rifle on the table. He carefully cleaned the rifle, even though it had not been fired since he last put a brush, gun oil, and a rag to the weapon. Then he sat the gleaming black rifle down on the table. The rifle was both unique and unusual. Developed only a few years before, the rifle was a military weapon capable of both semi-automatic and fully automatic fire.

Big Dave had ended up with the gun a year before after helping the ageing father of a Marine infantry officer go on a successful elk hunt and coming home with a prize bull elk. The Marine officer managed to thank him by providing him with a military weapon not allowed to civilians. The rifle, an XM-21 or M-14, had just been replaced with the new lighter M-16. The M-14 fired a .308 round with extreme accuracy. The Marine officer had included an Unertl 8X sniper scope. Big Dave had zeroed the rifle in and was amazed at its accuracy at up to nine hundred yards. The rifle was deemed too heavy by the army, and they had transitioned to the much smaller and lighter M-16 rifle.

Big Dave loved the rifle. It had arrived with the standard army Unertl 8X scope mounted on it. He had yet to take it hunting, but he felt he just might be just the ticket when he went hunting for rustlers who were capable of shooting back.

He slid the rifle back in its canvas cover and then placed it and three boxes of .308 ammunition in the cabin's small closet, carefully placing it behind some coats. He put the gun cleaning supplies away and knew the rifle was ready if he needed it. Tomorrow was going to be an interesting day.

CHAPTER FIFTY

By five in the morning, Big Dave was in Kemmerer, having coffee at Irma's Café. The air in the place smelled of hot coffee and cooking bacon. Half an hour later, Merv walked into the café with five other cattle ranchers in his wake. He spotted Big Dave and soon the six men were seated around a large round table drinking coffee and complaining about rustlers.

After listening to all their complaints, Big Dave produced the paper he had made the night before so they could all see just how much damage the rustlers had caused in Lincoln County. Angry as they were, the ranchers were shocked by the total number of cattle that had been stolen. When their hubbub finally died down, Big Dave spoke.

"We're gettin' robbed by some slick crooks who know what the hell they're doin'," he said. "I want to find out if the damned Sheriff knows what we know and if so, then what the hell he is doin' to find these bastards and toss their asses in jail."

"So, how do you want to handle this meetin' with the sheriff?" asked Merv.

"I plan to get his ass out in front of all of us, either inside the office or out on the street. It don't matter none to me.

Then ask him to explain what the hell is going on with these rustlers and what he plans to do about them," said Big Dave.

His words were met with strong approval from the other ranchers seated at the table. Big Dave looked them over. They were mostly older men in their fifties and sixties. Their faces were hardened by the Wyoming wind and weather and a lifetime of making a living on top of a horse.

"They'll do," thought Big Dave. He let them continue talking and he sat back and enjoyed his morning coffee. For what he had in mind for their meeting with the sheriff, he could have used a shot of good whiskey in it, but strong black coffee would have to do.

At a quarter after nine, Big Dave got to his feet. "Let's go boys. We got us an important meetin' at ten this mornin'."

The other ranchers got to their feet, their chairs scraping on the old wooden floor of the café. When the group of ranchers reached the sheriff's office at nine thirty, they were forced to park their trucks about two blocks away. Every parking spot near the office was full. When they reached the front of the sheriff's office, they were greeted by a large crowd of very pissed off ranchers.

As Big Dave surveyed the crowd he was surprised to see a handful of his fellow sheep ranchers among the large crowd of cattlemen. The sight caused him to smile.

"Hell, even the sheepmen are pissed at the sheriff doing nothing about livestock being stolen," he thought to himself.

The crowd of ranchers parted like the Red Sea when Big Dave walked toward the front of the Sheriff's office. When he reached the front door, he stopped. He turned to face the crowd which had become suddenly quiet.

He scanned the faces of men he had known most of his life in Wyoming. The faces of men tall and short, thin, and thick, hairy, and bald looked back at him. He saw one thing in common. They were pissed and they were there to demand results from a sheriff who supposedly worked for them as citizens of Lincoln County. He saw the expressions on their faces. He understood they needed no words of encouragement from him. They were ready.

Big Dave turned and faced the front door of the sheriff's office. He glanced down at his battered wristwatch. It was five minutes until ten. He waited.

At exactly ten o'clock, the front door of the office opened, and the sheriff stepped out followed by three armed deputies. The sheriff, Orville Swanson, was a Mormon from Star Valley and he was short, heavyset, and balding. He looked uneasy and nervous. His face seemed paler than usual.

He took a step forward and faced the crowd spread before him.

"Citizens. I am happy to hear what you have to say, but not outside in the street with a mob of people. If you choose three of you to come inside and meet with me in my office, I will be happy to accommodate you," said the Sheriff.

A low murmur spread throughout the crowd. The sheriff shifted from one foot to the other as he nervously waited for a response. Finally, he got one.

Big Dave took a step toward the sheriff. He stared hard at the nervous, overweight, and out-of-shape elected official.

"That ain't gonna work for us, Sheriff," said Big Dave in no uncertain terms.

"Why not?" the sheriff managed to say.

"Whatever you got to say, you need to say it to all of us, not just a couple," said Big Dave. "We all are citizens of Lincoln County. You work for all of us. You need to talk to all of us and you need to do it now."

Sheriff Swanson looked to his side at his three deputies. All three of them appeared to be scared out of their wits. He realized he was not in charge of this meeting. The crowd was, and in particular Big Dave, who appeared to be the obvious spokesman for the ranchers.

He knew he was out of options. He nervously pulled up on the waistband of his pants and took a deep breath. "All right," said the sheriff. "Let's hear what you boys have to say. Who's first?"

"We want those goddamned rustlers caught and hung," came a loud voice from the back of the crowd. The remark was immediately joined by voices saying, "Damn right," "You bet," "Git it done now, and do your job."

Sheriff Swanson put up his hands in a plea for silence and the voices faded away until it was quiet on the street in front of the office.

"Could you just raise your hand, and I'll call on you," pleaded the sheriff.

"We ain't schoolboys," said Big Dave. "We're men and we're damned pissed off men, not boys. I'll go first and then anybody else can join in when I'm done. That work for you, Sheriff?"

"Yes, of course," muttered the sheriff. He turned to look at his deputies, but they had retreated through the door into the possible safety of the confines of the sheriff's office. Sheriff Swanson stood alone in front of a mob of angry ranchers, and it scared the crap out of him.

"Our complaint is pretty damn simple," said Big Dave. "An organized gang of rustlers are using a pickup truck with a long horse trailer to sneak around the county and cut fences and then rustle up to a half dozen head of prime beef and then disappear. The facts back up they are doin' this about twice a week and they have hit at least fifteen ranches in this county in the past three months."

Big Dave paused and scanned the crowd of ranchers next to him. He had their full attention. He looked back at Sheriff Swanson.

"Your office has no suspects, no leads, and sure as hell no arrests. Each report shows about five to six heads of cattle stolen. But when you bother to add them reports up it amounts to over a hundred head of cattle rustled in Lincoln County in the past three months. We want action. We want arrests. We want results," said Big Dave.

"I only got six deputies for the whole county," pleaded Sheriff Swanson. "We got other crimes to solve as well as this here rustling."

"That's your problem," said Big Dave. "You wanted to be a sheriff. It's time to start acting like one." Big Dave paused and stared at the pitiful face of the frightened Sheriff Swanson.

"Here's a suggestion. Do you need deputies? The law in Wyoming allows you to deputize any or all of us for this emergency," said Big Dave.

He turned to face the crowd. "How many of you are willin' to volunteer to be temporary deputies for Lincoln County? Raise your right hand," he said.

Almost every man in the crowd raised their right hand.

Big Dave turned to face the sheriff. "Get one of them deputies out here with a pad and pen. Have these ranchers get in a line and have them sign up on that pad of paper and then choose however many ranchers you need to help you patrol the county and nail these thievin' bastards."

The sheriff looked both relieved at Big Dave's suggestion and confused about how to implement it.

"You heard me. Get one of them deputies out here and start takin' names," said Big Dave.

"Yes, yes of course," said the sheriff. He retreated inside the office and soon two deputies came out with a card table and two chairs and a pad of paper and some pens.

"Line up and sign up," said Big Dave to the crowd of ranchers. "I'll go first," he said. Then he signed the pad and turned to pass the pen to Merv who was standing right behind him. Merv signed and the line began to form.

Big Dave stepped to the side and Merv joined him. "That was a good move," said Merv.

"Maybe," said Big Dave. "At least we got the sheriff off his fat ass and got something in motion."

"That you did," said Merv.

"I hope he does something smart with this list of good volunteers, but my fear is he'll just file it away and do nothing," said Big Dave.

"You also got yourself with the power of a deputy of the sheriff's office in Lincoln County," said Merv.

"Yes, I did," said Big Dave with a big smile on his face. Then he turned and headed back to his truck. He had work to do and plans to get in motion.

CHAPTER FIFTY-ONE

By the time he reached the ranch, Big Dave had come up with a plan. He sat down at the small table in his cabin and pulled out his paper tablet and a pen. Then he wrote down a few key items. When he was finished, he sat back and stared at the list he had just made. Then he leaned forward and made a few corrections and additions. Again, he sat back at looked at his rude list. Satisfied, he tore off the paper, folded it, and stuck it in his wallet. Then he looked at his watch. It was almost lunch time. He stood up, grabbed his cowboy hat, and headed out the door for the cook shack.

He was just a few minutes early for lunch, so he poured himself a cup of coffee and watched Cookie as he was finishing his cooking in the rough kitchen. When Cookie was finished, he came over to sit next to Big Dave, bringing a mug of hot coffee with him.

"You're here early," he said to Big Dave.

"Early bird gets the worm," said a smiling Big Dave.

"Don't care much for worms," muttered Cookie. "Piss poor source of protein if you ask me."

Big Dave laughed.

The cook shack door swung open and in trooped the four regular cowboys of the ranch.

"Notice who arrived first," remarked Cookie to Big Dave.

"I noticed," replied Big Dave.

The four hands each grabbed a mug and filled it with hot coffee and grabbed a seat at the long table. Ten minutes passed and the men chatted. Then the door swung open again and in strode the two young brothers.

"Hell, we can eat now," said Preacher. "The damn greenhorns finally got here."

The two boys blushed at the unwanted attention. and each grabbed a mug, filled it with coffee, and took a seat at the table.

Big Dave waited until the two were seated. Then he cleared his throat. The room became very quiet.

"Just to be clear to all you gents," said Big Dave. "As far as I'm concerned, Steve and Travis are cowboys. They passed up bein' greenhorns weeks ago. They deserve to be treated as such."

Then he looked slowly around the room. "Any of you old hands get in a jam, you'd be damn lucky to have one of them show up to help you out," said Big Dave. "Anybody got anything else to add?"

He was met with absolute silence.

"In that case, Cookie, bring out the food. I'm starvin'," said Big Dave.

Cookie rose and soon brought a hot lunch in containers to the table. The men began to pass the containers around the table and fill their plates. Normal conversation soon reestablished itself and the cook shack was filled once again with the chatter of working men enjoying a hot meal. Both Cookie and Big Dave sat back and smiled.

When lunch was over and the table had been cleared, Big Dave motioned for the hands to stay for a bit. They refilled their coffee cups and sat at the table, quietly waiting for Big Dave to speak.

"Me and some of the ranchers had a meetin' with the sheriff this morning. We demanded he do somethin' about these damn rustlers. He ended up making temporary deputies out of all of us, including me. That don't mean shit to you, but it gives me the power to arrest any rustler I can find," said Big Dave.

He waited a minute for that new fact to sink into the brains of his hands. Then he continued.

"When you men are out patrolling the ranch and you see anything suspicious, your job is to do two things," said Big Dave. "One is to let me know as soon as you can. The other is to delay or prevent them thievin' assholes from leaving. That means stoppin' them from gettin' away. Is that clear?"

All four hands and the two brothers nodded their heads acknowledgement.

"I don't want you boys doin' anything stupid. I don't want any of you getting' hurt or killed. But I do want you to do anything you can to detain any jokers you run across that look like or are doin' anything suspicious. Is that clear?" said Big Dave.

"Yes, sir," said Rocky and the other hands and the brothers echoed his statement.

"Remember, if you're on patrol at night and you see something suspicious, fire them damn flare guns into the air. I'll come a runnin' and so will everyone else here on the ranch. Don't forget to take them damn flare guns with you every time you go out on patrol," said Big Dave.

All six hands nodded their heads in agreement.

"Enough of this crap," said Big Dave. "Let's get movin' and get some work done. There's still half a day of daylight left."

Seconds later the cook shack was empty except for Big Dave and Cookie.

Big Dave looked over at Cookie. "You got a question?" he asked.

"Nope. But your little talk was impressive," said Cookie. "I'm pretty sure they got the message."

"I sure as hell hope so. I want them damn rustlers caught, but I don't want none of our men gettin' hurt doin' it," said Big Dave.

"Me either," said Cookie.

CHAPTER FIFTY-TWO

All of the hands were pretty tense after Big Dave's talk, but after a couple of days and having nothing happen, things fell back into their normal routine and work got done fixing the fence, tending to cattle, and then putting up the last stand of wild hay.

The two brothers found themselves stacking hay bales and in August, it was hot, dirty work. Not to mention hard work. The two boys had just finished unloading a hay wagon and as Wes drove away on the tractor towing the now empty hay wagon, the two boys moved to the water jug with a tin cup hanging on it. They took turns downing at least two full cups of the cool water. Then they sat on bales of hay in the shade of the barn, waiting for the next wagon load of hay.

Travis looked over at his older brother. Steve was leaning back against the hay bales, smiling.

"What are you smilin' about?" asked Travis. "We still got a couple of loads of hay to go."

"I'm smilin' because when we finish today we're done with the second hay crop and we got just twenty days left," said Steve.

"What?" asked Travis.

"It's August 11th," said Steve. "In twenty more days, we will have finished up our three months as cowboys and go home as rich young men."

"I forgot it ended with the month of August," said a surprised Travis. "I wonder what old Lee is up to?"

"He's probably out buying a Slurpee at the 7-11 store," said a grinning Steve.

"A Slurpee sounds really good to me about now," replied Travis.

"Hell, little brother. When we get home, I just might decide to buy the 7-11 store," said Steve.

"I'd settle for two Slurpee's," said Travis.

Both boys laughed.

The long, hot day finally ended with the last bale of hay being pulled off the hay wagon and the haying season officially ended at the ranch. The boys made their way back to the bunk house and stripped off their sweaty, dirty clothes and took showers. Then they put on clean clothes and headed for the cook shack.

Arriving at the front porch, they found Rocky and Preacher already there. Both cowboys were sitting on old rickety chairs and had their cowboy hats tilted down over their faces.

"What are you too looking so happy about?" asked Steve.

"Well, sonny, it's kinda like this," said Preacher. "We're finally done with hayin' for this year. It's Friday night. And tomorrow is Saturday, and I plan to go to town and get drunk as a skunk."

Steve's face featured a grimace.

"What's wrong?" asked Travis.

"We start midnight patrol work tomorrow for two days," answered Steve.

"At least it'll be cooler at night," said Travis wistfully.

"That's about all that's good about it," replied Steve.

Cookie stepped out of the cook shack, looked at the hungry cowboys and rang the dinner bell.

No sooner were the four ranch hands seated at the table than the door opened and in walked Slim and Wes. A few minutes later Big Dave slipped in the door.

Cookie served beef stew and roasted potatoes and almost everyone had two helpings. Afterwards, Steve and Travis stayed behind to help Cookie clear the table and clean up the kitchen. Then they headed back to the bunk house. The hot August sun had taken the starch out of all six of the hands and it wasn't long before all six were in their bunks and sound asleep.

CHAPTER FIFTY-THREE

Saturday morning found breakfast over and the chores done and Rocky, Slim, Wes and Preacher piled into two pickup trucks and headed for Kemmerer.

Big Dave walked over to the bunk house where the two brothers were sitting on the front porch. "You two have lunch at the cook shack and then get some shuteye. You got a long night ahead of you," he said.

"Yes, sir," they responded, almost in unison.

After lunch, the boys walked to the bunk house and went inside. Steve stripped to his underwear and climbed into his bunk. Travis took off his boots and his shirt and just lay down on top of the blanket that covered his bunk. Soon both boys were sound asleep.

• • •

About seven that night, Big Dave entered the bunk house and shook each of the boys awake. "Let's move it," he said. "Time to get dressed, get saddled and get out there on patrol."

Minutes later the two now fully dressed boys were walking to the barn to collect and saddle their horses. When they were finished, they led the saddled horses out of the barn and next to the main corral. There Big Dave and Cookie awaited them.

As each brother mounted his horse, Big Dave handed each of them a lever action Winchester rifle. "Stick this in the saddle scabbard," he commanded. Both brothers complied with his command.

Then Cookie stepped forward. He handed Big Dave two old, battered leather saddle bags. Big Dave placed a saddle bag behind each boy's saddle and tied it on.

"There's sandwiches and a thermos of hot coffee in each of them bags," said Cookie. "The coffee will help keep you boys awake and alert," he said with a smile.

Then Big Dave stepped forward and put a flare pistol in each boy's saddlebag. "Don't use these damn things unless you really need to," he admonished the two brothers.

"Yes, sir," they both said in unison.

The two brothers turned their horses' heads and put spurs lightly to their flanks and the horses moved out of the ranch yard.

Once the duo was over the first rise and out of sight of the ranch buildings, Steve brought his horse to a halt and Travis pulled his horse up next to him.

"I think we should split up and head in opposite directions until we meet up on the other side of the ranch," said Steve.

"Works for me," said Travis.

Steve headed north and after he watched his older brother ride out of sight, Travis turned his horse and headed south along the fence line. He knew from previous experience it would likely be almost three hours before he saw his brother again.

As he rode, Travis kept moving his eyes back and forth. He remembered the advice he had received from Big Dave when he was teaching him to hunt. "Look for what don't belong," Big Dave had advised him. It was good advice.

About ten o'clock that evening he heard his brother's horse before he saw it. They met on the far side of the ranch, away from the highway and across the Ham's Fork River.

Steve brought his horse to a halt. Then he dismounted and tied the horse to a sagebrush. Travis swung his leg over his horse and slid to the ground. Then he tied off his horse to the same sagebrush plant and the two boys walked awkwardly around to loosen the cramping muscles in their legs. After Steve found a pair of rocks to use as chairs, Travis brough the sandwiches and coffee thermoses from the saddle bags.

The two brothers sat, ate the thick ham sandwiches, and washed them down with hot, black coffee. When they had finished, Travis collected the wrappings from the sandwiches and the two thermoses and returned them to the saddlebags. Then he came back to where Steve sat and lowered himself gingerly to his rock.

"Tired butt?" Steve inquired.

"You guessed it," said Travis.

"Me too," replied Steve.

"You'd think my butt would be used to that saddle by now," said Travis.

"I think that might take some time to get used to and we've only been riding for about two and a half months. Rocky, Preacher and the others have been riding for years," said Steve.

"I think even they get tired butts," said Travis.

"Maybe, but in a little over two weeks we'll be done getting saddle sores and I don't plan to ever sit in a saddle again unless it's on a merry-go-round horse," said Steve.

"I can't argue with that, but I have to admit, I do like riding a horse and I do like the cowboy work we've been doing," said Travis.

"Suit yourself," replied Steve. "I've enjoyed this summer a lot more than I thought I would, but I won't be sorry to see this job come to an end."

"We should be heading out," said Travis as he stood and scanned the night sky. Hopefully, the rest of the night will be as quiet as the first part," said Travis.

"You're right. Let's mount up. See you in about three hours," said Steve.

The two boys mounted their horses, touched their fingers to the brim of their cowboy hats and headed in opposite directions.

The next time they met it was about one o'clock in the morning. They stopped for about ten minutes and drank hot black coffee and then continued their lonely patrols of the ranch.

By five o'clock that next morning, they had returned to the ranch and unsaddled their horses. Both boys then wiped the horses down and then watered and grained them. By the time they got to the cook shack it was nearing six in the morning.

When they walked into the cookhouse Big Dave and Cookie greeted them. Cookie had made fresh donuts and he and Big Dave were sampling them, washing down the sweet delights with hot coffee. The two boys quickly joined them.

Fifteen minutes later the four regular cowboys entered the cook shack. Within minutes there was no trace of a single donut.

CHAPTER FIFTY-FOUR

Sunday was a repeat of Saturday. The two brothers slept most of the day and were roused from their bunks by Big Dave shortly after six that evening. They ate supper with the other hands and then headed out on patrol after saddling their mounts and adding the obligatory saddlebags.

When they reached the starting point, they turned their horses in opposite directions, touched their finger to the brim of their cowboy hats and urged their mounts on. Within a few minutes they were out of sight of each other.

As each of the brothers rode, they worked to keep scanning their surroundings. Travis in particular remembered Big Dave's admonition to him. "Look for what don't belong."

During his ride, Travis saw jackrabbits, a few quail, and lots of wild birds. Cows and calves were the exception to the rule. He saw plenty of them.

By the time the two brothers finally met up on the far side of the ranch, it was almost nine in the evening and getting dark. Both brothers reined in their horses and sat in the saddle and gazed over the expanse of the ranch in from of them. They were on the west side of the ranch and could neither see nor hear any traffic on the highway that bordered the east side of the ranch.

"See anything interesting?" asked Travis.

"Not unless you consider a dead rattlesnake interesting," replied his brother Steve.

"Did it die of old age?" asked Travis.

"Looked more like lead poisoning to me," said Steve. "The dang thing had been blown in half."

"Musta happened since last night. I don't recollect seein' any dead snakes yesterday," said Travis.

"Somebody shot it," replied Travis.

"I wonder who?" said Travis. "It had to have happened earlier today and the four hands were all in town havin' fun."

"Maybe it was Big Dave," suggested Steve.

"Yeah. That sounds more likely," said Travis.

Steve scanned the lower part of the horizon surrounding them. "Looks like we'll have a full moon tonight," he said.

"That'll help seein' what's goin' on," said Travis.

"Yep. It sure will," said Steve. "Well, time to make another circuit."

"Wait," said Travis.

"Wait for what?" asked Steve.

"How about we do something different," said Travis.

"Different like how?" asked Steve.

"Instead of continuing on the way we have been, let's each turn around and retrace our steps back the way we just came from," said Travis.

"Why?" asked a curious Steve.

"See things from a different angle. Maybe see something we missed the first time," said Travis.

"I got no objection," said Steve.

"O.K," said Travis. He turned his mount's head back towards the direction he had come from and touched his spurs to the mare's flanks. In minutes he was out of Steve's sight.

"And I thought I was bored," thought Steve. He turned his horse and began to retrace his route backwards.

As Travis rode, he kept scanning his surroundings. It had turned dark, and it was harder to see much. The full moon helped as it provided a lot of illumination. He slowed the pace of his mare and paused about every fifteen minutes. During each pause, he would use his nose to sniff the air and then listen carefully for any odd or unusual sounds. There was a slight breeze, but no real wind to speak of. He kept up this method for the next hour and a half but found nothing to alarm him.

Ten minutes later he brought the mare to a halt and then slid out of the saddle and while holding the reins, he walked and led the horse for the next ten minutes to stretch his legs.

After ten minutes had passed, he brought the mare to a stop and then put his foot in the stirrup and swung up onto the saddle. He was about to urge the horse forward when his eyes caught a flash of light. The light had appeared below him and to the east. He sat quietly in the saddle, gently stroking the mare's neck. Then he saw the light again. The light was moving from east to west. As it passed by low hills the light disappeared and then reappeared again when the object passed a hill.

Travis sat quietly in the saddle and watched and listened. He sniffed the air. At first all he sensed was the cool night air. Then he got a whiff of something different. His brain tried to identify the smell. Finally, he smelled it again and this time the scent was stronger.

"Diesel." He realized he was smelling the exhaust of a diesel engine. As he sat and watched, he could see the outline of a large dark truck pulling a long, white horse trailer. From the size of the trailer, it looked like a four-horse trailer. Then he remembered the rustlers were using a long horse trailer to load their stolen cattle.

As Travis watched, the truck and trailer made their way over the prairie, the truck and trailer slowly moving up and down as they went over uneven ground.

Travis turned and looked back to where the truck and trailer had come from. He could barely make out the gravel road and the fence line of the ranch in the dim light of the moon. He was glad the sky was almost cloudless.

Looking back to the headlights of the truck, he realized the rustlers were almost a mile inside the ranch fence line. Then he remembered the only cattle he had seen were watering at a small old pond about a quarter mile from where the truck and trailer were currently located. He was sure they were headed for the cattle at the pond.

He turned the mare's head and had her head down the side of the small ridge he was on and then moved parallel to the ridge line to stay close to the rustlers. By keeping himself and his horse below the top of the ridge, he would be invisible to them.

When he thought he was close to the small pond, he stopped the mare, dismounted, and tied her to a big sagebrush. Then he made his way on foot up to the top of the ridge line, moving as quietly as he could. Just before he got there, he dropped to his knees and crawled the rest of the way. He did not want the rustlers to see his silhouette against the night sky.

When he reached close to the top of the ridge, he removed his cowboy hat and laid it on the ground. Then he slowly raised his head so he could see down the side of the ridge to the pond. He saw what he expected and then worked hard to keep his excitement under control.

There were four men in dark clothing outside the truck and trailer. Two men walked to the rear of the trailer and let down the back gate. Then they led two saddled horses down the ramp and onto the prairie.

Quickly two of the men mounted their horses and slowly rode toward the pond and the small herd of cattle that were grazing near the water.

Travis could see they were going to try to cut some cows out of the herd and move them toward the trailer. He watched the other two men pull what looked like wooden gates out of the trailer and put them along the sides to make a temporary kind of chute to direct the cattle into the trailer.

Travis slowly crawled backwards down the ridge until he was sure the rustlers could not see him. He grabbed his cowboy hat, slapped it on his head, and slid on his butt down the slope to his tied off mount. Once there he got to his feet, opened his saddlebag, and pulled out the flare gun. He checked to make sure the flare gun was loaded and then he pulled the safety, pointed the gun up into the night sky, and pulled the trigger.

The gun let out a sound like a swoosh and bucked in his hand. Seconds later the flare erupted into a bright red flash of light, almost like a cheap firework on the Fourth of July. Travis returned the gun to the saddlebag and then vaulted into the saddle. He grabbed the reins and then rode hard back up to the top of the ridge. When he reached the top, he reined in the mare. He looked down towards the pond.

He could see the four men had panicked at the sight of the flare. The two men on foot, had tossed the wooden gates on the ground and were trying to lift the tailgate and fasten it to the trailer. The two men on horseback were racing toward the truck and trailer.

Travis immediately dismounted and tied the mare to a rock. Then he grabbed the Winchester rifle from its scabbard and moved about ten yards in front of the tied off mare. The truck had made a wide U-turn and was now facing the way they had come. The two mounted rustlers were racing to the east ahead of the truck.

Travis moved to the far edge of the ridge. Then he went to one knee and tried to steady his nerves and calm himself down. He brought the rifle up and used the iron sight to aim and then fired. The noise was loud and what appeared to be a small spurt of flame appeared at the barrel of the rifle against the black of the night sky.

Travis reacquired his aim and shot again. Then he looked to assess the results of his two shots. He had hit the two tires on his side of the trailer, and both had gone flat almost immediately. One of the men in the truck got out and ran back to the trailer. He hurriedly jacked up the tongue of the trailer, unhitched it, and then ran back to the truck's cab. He jumped in and the truck took off, leaving the trailer behind like so much prairie trash.

Travis brought the rifle back up, and aimed for the front tire of the truck which was now speeding away from the doomed trailer. The truck was bounding up and down over the uneven ground and moving past large clumps of sagebrush. He fired, but the truck kept going. He knew he had missed.

By the time he was ready to fire again, he did not have a clear shot, and he released the rifle's hammer and slowly got to his feet. He stood there and watched as the brake lights of the truck occasionally flashed red light in the dark night until the truck was gone and so was the light.

Travis returned to his mare. He replaced the rifle in the scabbard and mounted the horse. Then he slowly made his way down the ridge in the dark until he reached the now slightly lopsided abandoned horse trailer.

Once there, he dismounted, tied the reins of his mare to the trailer, and proceeded to search the trailer. It was empty. Not even any gear was evident. Ten minutes later, he heard horse hooves on the rocky prairie. Then Big Dave appeared out of the darkness on a big chestnut gelding.

He reined in his horse, dismounted, and walked up to Travis.

"Are you all right, son?" he asked.

"Yes, sir," he replied.

"What the hell happened here?" asked Big Dave.

Travis started to reply, but his words came out too fast and were too jumbled.

"It's all right, Travis. Slow down. Take your time. Just tell me what happened here," said Big Dave.

Travis took a deep breath and then slowly recounted the events of the last few minutes of his night patrol of the ranch. When he was finished, Big Dave handed him a canteen. "Take a drink, son. Then take another," said Big Dave.

Travis did. While he was getting some water in him, Big Dave took a flashlight out of his saddlebags and proceeded to thoroughly search the horse trailer, including the Wyoming license plate. Now calmer, Travis began to recount what had just happened to Big Dave. While he was talking, his brother Steve rode up and reined in his mount. He remained in the saddle as he leaned forward to listen to what Travis was saying.

"Do you recognize the trailer?" asked Travis.

"Nope. I seen lots of them just like this one. The plate is from Sweetwater County, though. My guess is when we get it checked, we'll find this here trailer was stolen," said Big Dave.

"Crap," said Travis.

"You didn't wing one of them, did you son?" asked Big Dave.

"No, sir. I was trying to hit the tires. I hit the two on my side of the trailer, but I missed trying to hit the front tire of the truck," said Travis.

Both men stood there, staring out into the blackness of the night. Looking in the direction the rustler's truck had disappeared.

"Should I continue my patrol?' asked Travis.

"Don't see no need," said Big Dave. "Them rustler's ain't coming back here tonight. You surely scared the shit out of them. We'll head back to the ranch and call this into the sheriff's office." He turned to face Steve. "Can you fix the fence break, son?"

"Yes, sir," replied Steve and then urged his mount down the slope to where the fence line lay.

Big Dave and Travis mounted their horses and began a slow walk back to the ranch house.

CHAPTER FIFTY-FIVE

Monday morning in the cook shack, Travis found himself peppered with questions from the four ranch cowboys as well as his brother. Cookie and Big Dave just sat there and listened.

When Travis finally finished his recounting of the previous night's adventure, every one of the hands was on their feet, shaking his hand and slapping him on the back.

"Take it easy, boys," said Big Dave. "Young Travis had himself one hell of a night and I doubt he got a whole lot of sleep. Don't beat the poor kid to death."

Everyone laughed. Even Travis.

Shorty broke the silence. "Who owns the trailer?" he asked.

"I called this into the sheriff's office last night," said Big Dave. "They looked up the license plate and it seems the trailer was stolen from a lot down in Green River about six weeks ago. They're sendin' up a deputy to dust the trailer for fingerprints sometime today."

"Fingerprints? On a horse trailer? What good will that do," said Wes.

"What do you mean?" asked Steve.

"Any cowboy, even a rustler would be wearin' gloves when he was workin' with cattle," said Wes.

"Maybe they'll get lucky," said Steve.

"Not likely," said Shorty. "Wes is right about the gloves.

● ● ●

Travis and Steve were awakened from a hard-earned sleep by the front door of the bunkhouse banging open. Both brothers sat up on their bunks as they found themselves faced with a young deputy and Big Dave.

"You boys up for a few questions from the deputy?" asked Big Dave.

"Yes, sir," replied the two brothers, almost in unison.

"This here is Jacob Thompson," said Big Dave.

"Howdy, boys," said the young deputy.

The two brothers returned the greeting and slid from their bunks. After they pulled on their britches and shirts, they padded barefoot over to the small round table in the bunkhouse the cow hands often used to play cards. They took chairs as did the deputy and Big Dave.

"Which one of you boys saw the rustlers?" asked Jacob.

"That'd be me," said Travis.

"How old are you, son?" asked Jacob.

"I'm eighteen," replied Travis.

"Well, son, I got to hand it to you. You handled yourself like a full-grown man last night," said Jacob. "Shooting the flare gun off was one thing, but takin' out your rifle and shootin' out two tires on the horse trailer was damn impressive."

"I just tried to stop them," replied Travis.

"You damn near did," said Jacob. "Did you get a good look at the truck?" he asked.

"It was dark out and the truck was a dark color. Maybe black. Maybe brown. I just can't say," said Travis.

"I see," said Jacob who had taken out a small notebook and was writing in it as they chatted.

"You say there were four men?" asked Jacob.

"Yes," said Travis.

"Did you notice anything about them. The clothes they were wearin', the hats they wore. Were any of them short, tall, fat, skinny?" asked Jacob.

"I was a good distance from them, and I was lookin' down from the top of the ridge. They all looked about the same size and their clothes were dark colored. I think two of them were wearing cowboy hats. Now that I think about it, the two on horseback were wearing cowboy hats. The two in the truck were wearing what looked like ball caps," said Travis.

"Did you notice anything about them that was different or noticeable?" asked Jacob.

Travis thought for a moment. Then he responded. "It was dark, and I was not close. Plus, I was scared to death," said Travis.

Jacob closed his notebook and slid it into his pocket. "You may have been scared, son, but you did damn well last night. I'm pretty sure them rustlers were pissin' their pants when you shot out them two trailer tires."

The deputy shook hands with Travis and Steve and then he was out the door, and the two brothers were left sitting at the bunk house table with Big Dave.

"He's right, you know," said Big Dave.

"About what?" asked Steve.

"Travis done a damn good job last night. He got close to them rustlers without them seein' him. He shot off the flare gun to alert me. Then he had the sense to pull his rifle and get into a good firing position. He didn't rush himself. He got that trailer in his sights and then he shot out two tires. I know experienced, old cowboys who wouldn't have done as well as he did," said Big Dave.

Big Dave rose from his chair and walked out of the bunkhouse.

"What just happened?" asked a confused Travis.

"You just got a big compliment from Big Dave. That's what happened and it's the first time I can remember him approving of anything we've done," said an admiring Steve.

Travis got up and pulled off his shirt and britches.

"What're you doin'?' asked Steve.

"I'm still tired," said Travis. "I'm headed back to bed."

"Sounds like a good idea to me," said Steve. He shed his shirt and britches and within minutes the two brothers were fast asleep in their bunks.

CHAPTER FIFTY-SIX

When the brothers awoke, it was almost one thirty in the afternoon. They showered and dressed and headed to the cook shack. They stepped inside to find Cookie and Big Dave waiting for them.

"What'll it be?" asked a smiling Cookie.

"What do you mean?" asked Steve.

"I got orders to give you two anything you want to eat," replied Cookie. "Sounds to me like you boys earned it after last night."

The boys settled for pancakes, sausage and fried eggs plus orange juice and coffee. While they waited for Cookie to work his magic in the kitchen, they sat and looked around as if this was some kind of dream.

"I talked to the sheriff's office a bit ago," said Big Dave.

"What's happened?" asked Steve.

"The trailer was stolen. The owner will be coming up to reclaim his trailer and get it off the ranch tomorrow," said Big Dave.

"That's it?" asked a surprised Travis.

"And someone called the sheriff's office to report a speeding black pickup truck that almost drove them off the road last night. The caller said the truck was a late model black Chevy ¾ ton with two guys wearing ball caps in the cab and two other scalawags sittin' in the bed of the truck wearing cowboy hats," said Big Dave.

"Did they get the license plate on the truck?" asked Steve.

"They did. The sheriff's office checked the license plate out. It was also a Sweetwater County plate. And it too came off a stolen truck," said Big Dave.

"So, the Chevy was also stolen?" asked Travis.

"No. The plate was off a Ford ½ ton pickup that was parked in front of a bar in Rock Springs about a week ago. When the owner came out the truck was there, but someone had lifted his license plates," said Big Dave.

"So almost everything the rustlers were using was stolen?" asked Steve.

"Not quite," said Big Dave.

"What do you mean?" asked Travis.

"You forgot the two horses," said Big Dave.

"Horses?" asked Travis.

"A state trooper found them along the highway about four miles south of the ranch. Turns out their brand belongs to a rather shady rancher who owns a spread just east of Rock Springs. The sheriff's boys will be payin' him a visit sometime today," said Big Dave.

"So, he's likely the head of the rustlers?" asked Travis.

"We don't know. We do know the horses the rustlers were usin' had this guy's brand on 'em," said Big Dave.

"What's his name?" asked Travis.

"They can't tell me until they have proof he's involved in this rustling," said Big Dave.

"When will that be?" asked Travis.

"I got no idea," replied Big Dave. "Our sheriff seems to have his own peculiar calendar and clock."

The boys finished their meal and headed out to do their chores. No matter the time of day or how tired one might be, the chores always came first.

• • •

After a day of chores and doing their laundry, the two brothers headed for the cook shack for dinner. When they got there, they found the four ranch cowboys had already arrived and were seated, drinking coffee.

Cookie started bringing out the dishes of hot food and placing them on the long table. Food dishes were passed, and men forked meat and potatoes onto their plates. About halfway through the meal, the door to the cook shack opened and in stepped a young, uniformed deputy. He cautiously looked around and said, "I'm here to see Mr. Olson."

Big Dave turned in his seat and said, "You found him, son. What can I do for you?"

"Can I ask you to step outside where we can talk in private, Mr. Nelson," asked the nervous young deputy.

"Sure thing," said Big Dave. He rose from his seat and followed the young deputy out the cook shack door. Inside the cook shack, everyone had stopped eating, and no one spoke a word. It was obvious they were trying to hear what the deputy was telling Big Dave. But the voices were so low all they could make out was muttering and mumbles. Still, nobody spoke, and nobody moved, not even to steal a bite of hot food, or a swig of hot coffee. Even Cookie seemed frozen in place.

Finally, the cook shack door opened, and Big Dave stepped in. The waiting men could hear the deputy's truck start up and then pull out. Big Dave walked to his seat. His face was grim.

"Eat up, boys. The damn food is gettin' cold," he said.

Everyone immediately grabbed a knife or a fork and returned to devouring their supper. They noticed that Big Dave did not pick up a single utensil and ate nothing nor drank any coffee. They did not take that as a good sign.

When the men were finishing eating, they gathered up their plates and stacked them by the sink in the cook shack kitchen. They each refilled their coffee mugs from the big coffee pot and then returned to their seats. Then they sat there and waited for Big Dave to tell them what was going on.

Big Dave looked up from his untouched plate and glanced around the room. Then he pushed back his chair from the table and tilted it back on the hind two legs. Again, he scanned the room and then brought the chair back on all four legs. The noise it made was a loud "clack."

"That damned sheriff is the biggest coward we ever elected to the office in the history of Lincoln County," said Big Dave. "He's too scared to come and give me bad news so he sends the greenest deputy he's got to come tell me."

"Tell you what?" asked Rocky, taking a risk of being the first one to speak since the deputy departed.

"The brand on them two horses were from the Triple T ranch, which is located southeast of Rock Springs, just north of the Colorado border. The two state troopers who went there to ask about them horses got a bit of a surprise," said Big Dave.

"A surprise?" asked Rocky.

"Turns out the Triple T ranch changed hands about nine months ago," said Big Dave. "The crooked jasper who owned it sold out and moved to Mexico."

"Who owns it?" asked Rocky.

"Some corporation bought it," said Big Dave. "According to the state cops the owner of the ranch is QRQ Corporation. It's one of them sub-S corporations folks use to hide the identity of the real owners."

"Who's runnin' the ranch?" asked Shorty.

"Some dude from back east," said Big Dave. The cops said he was a tall, well-dressed tenderfoot with a snotty attitude. They didn't much care for him. They asked him about the horses, and he said he had no idea what they were talking about. He finally brought his foreman up to the house and the cops questioned him."

"Who's the foreman of the Triple T?" asked Shorty.

"Some guy I never heard of," said Big Dave. "Said his name was Snuffy Likes. He told the cops he had drifted up here from Texas. He still had a Texas driver's license according to the cops. He told them they had a few horses disappear about a month ago. They asked him why there was no record of the theft being reported to the Sweetwater County Sheriff's office. He said he thought it was reported. The cops took his statement and the theft report and left. They called our sheriff, and he had his deputy come out and report it to me. What a chicken shit he is."

"So, what do we do?" asked Shorty.

"You boys do your jobs. You also keep on patrolling at night. I aim to get to the bottom of the Triple T crap. Something here sure don't smell right," said Big Dave.

No one at the table disagreed with him.

CHAPTER FIFTY-SEVEN

The next morning, Big Dave was leaning against the law office building when Woody showed up to unlock and open up the place.

"You're meetin' me here at the office and not at coffee?" asked a surprised Woody. "That can't be good."

"We need to talk," said Big Dave.

Woody unlocked the door, and the two men stepped inside. Woody switched on the lights and turned to face Big Dave.

"Should I put the coffee on?" he asked.

"Fine by me," said Big Dave.

Woody led the way to his office, switched on the lights and motioned for Big Dave to have a seat. Then he disappeared out the office door.

Seven minutes later he was back with two mugs of steaming hot black coffee. He handed one to Big Dave and then took his big chair behind his desk. He took a swig of his coffee and then set the mug down on his desk.

"Who died?" He asked.

"Nobody," replied Big Dave. "I need you to do some snoopin' around for me."

"That sounds right up my alley,' said Woody. "What do you need?"

"You know anything about the Triple T ranch down in Sweetwater County?" asked Big Dave.

"I heard it got sold a few months ago," said Woody. "I never cared for the asshole who owned it so good riddance to bad rubbish as far as I'm concerned."

"Seems the new owner is some corporation. QRQ Corporation to be exact. They got some smart-ass manager from back east and a foreman I never heard of named Snuffy Likes," said Big Dave.

"That I didn't know," said Woody.

"I need you to find out all you can about this QRQ Corporation and anything you can dig up about this ranch manager and the foreman named Snuffy Likes," said Big Dave.

"How soon do you need this information?" asked Woody.

"Yesterday," said Big Dave.

"Might be tough to make that deadline," said Woody with a grin.

"Soon as you can get it," responded Big Dave.

Woody took a few notes on a legal pad and then looked up at Big Dave. "I'm on it," he said.

"Works for me," said Big Dave. He got to his feet, shook hands with Woody and was out the door and gone.

Big Dave had looked up the address for the Triple T ranch and it looked to be about eighteen miles southeast of Rock Springs. Rock Springs was about ninety miles from Kemmerer, so he estimated a trip of about almost two hours. He started the engine to his truck and headed out of Kemmerer towards Rock Springs.

He drove south from Kemmerer and after passing through Rock Springs, he made his way on a series of county roads until he found the entrance to the Triple T ranch. He drove into the ranch and soon reached the main ranch house. The ranch was fairly large for Wyoming and in addition to the main ranch house, there were about three small cottage like houses and several outbuildings and barns. All of the buildings looked in need of a coat of paint and some repair. Big Dave knew neglect when he saw it.

He got out of his truck and was greeted at the front of the ranch house by a tall, well-dressed man who appeared to be in his early forties.

"What's your business here?" said the man in a less than friendly greeting.

Big Dave pulled out his wallet with the new deputy sheriff badge and showed it to the man.

"I'm looking for the manager of this ranch," said Big Dave.

"That would be me," replied the man. "I'm Oliver Hastings, manager of the Triple T ranch."

The man did not offer a hand to shake so Big Dave ignored it. "I'm investigating some rustling up in Lincoln County and I have some questions for you."

"Why me?" asked Oliver. "I have no idea where this Lincoln County is located."

Big Dave smiled. It was not a friendly smile.

"Two of the rustlers were ridin' horses with the Triple T brand," he said grimly.

"Our horses? Impossible," snorted Oliver. "I had two state officers here before asking about stolen horses and I referred them to my foreman. He told them we are not missing any horses."

"I've seen the horses. They have your brand on them," replied Big Dave.

Oliver seemed about to make a snarky reply, then he paused, as if he were rethinking his response. Then he spoke. "I have no knowledge of what you are inquiring about. I suggest you talk to my ranch foreman, Mr. Likes."

"Where do I find Mr. Likes," said Big Dave.

"He should be down at the big barn located over there to your left," responded Oliver, who was pointing with his right arm.

"Thanks," said Big Dave. Then he turned, walked toward the largest of the two barns on the spread.

As he walked, Big Dave could almost feel the ranch manager's eyes boring into his back. He was obviously not happy with Big Dave's visit.

When he reached the largest barn, he found two cowboys working on repairing some tack in a small area in the front of the barn. Both of them looked up at him with suspicion when he stood in front of them. Big Dave introduced himself and told them he was looking for Mr. Likes.

The one cowboy laughed and pointed to his shorter companion. "You done found him, mister," he said.

The smaller cowboy was about five and a half feet tall with a broad, husky build. He wore worn blue jeans and a dull colored denim shirt. His cowboy hat was once pearl grey, but now was stained with sweat, dirt, and grease.

"What the hell you want from me?" asked Snuffy.

"I have some questions for you," said Big Dave. "You want to talk here or go somewhere private?"

"Here's fine," replied Snuffy. He motioned to two wooden barrels sitting side by side a few feet away. Both men took a seat. The other cowboy decided to slip out the door of the barn and leave them to chat.

"I'm here about the two horses with the Triple T brand the two state policemen asked you about," said Big Dave.

Snuffy looked surprised. "I told them fellers all I knew about some horses," said Snuffy in a defensive tone of voice.

"Maybe you did, but sometimes our memories play tricks on us," said Big Dave.

Snuffy looked down at the straw covered floor for a bit. Then he looked up at Big Dave. There was anger on his face.

"Ain't nothin' wrong with my memory," said Snuffy defiantly.

"Maybe. Maybe not," replied Big Dave.

Snuffy shrugged. "What's your question, mister?" he asked.

"How can you be sure those two horses with the Triple T brand ain't from this ranch?" asked Big Dave.

"I checked all our stock and we ain't got no missing horses," retorted Snuffy.

"How many saddle horses does the Triple T have?" asked Big Dave.

Snuffy looked startled by the question.

Then he looked up and said, "I ain't sure."

"If you ain't sure, how come you told state cops you had no saddle horses missing from the ranch?" asked Big Dave.

Snuffy's face was getting red. "I already told them state cops all I knew. You ain't got no right to keep asking me about them horses."

"Look Mr. Likes. I asked you a question. You have refused to give me a straight answer. I want an answer. You can give it to me here or we can ride up to the sheriff's office in Kemmerer and do it there. Which will it be?" asked Big Dave.

Snuffy looked around the barn as if looking for an escape route. Finally, he stopped looking and said, "I aint sure how many horses we got. I'd have to check with Mr. Hastings. He's the one who got all the records and information on how much stock we got here on the ranch," said Snuffy.

Snuffy looked like he wanted to say more, a lot more, but he had had enough run-ins with the law to know when to shut up.

"Thank you for your time, Mr. Likes," said Big Dave. Then he rose from his barrel and walked out the door of the barn. He got in his truck and then drove off the Triple T ranch in the direction of Rock Springs.

CHAPTER FIFTY-EIGHT

All the way back to Kemmerer, Big Dave thought about his meeting with both Hastings and Likes. Hastings was arrogant and Likes had all the reactions of an experienced thief.

When he reached Kemmerer, he drove straight to the law office. Once there, he stepped inside and told the receptionist he was there to see Woody.

Woody came out of his office and shook hands with his old friend. Then he led him into Woody's office. As Big Dave entered the room, he carefully closed the door behind him.

"That's not a good sign," said Woody glancing at the now closed door. "What's goin' on?"

Big Dave sat down in front of Woody's desk and then proceeded to tell him about all the events he had just experienced, including his opinion of manager and foreman of the Triple T ranch.

Woody listened carefully and when Big Dave was finished, he leaned back in his leather office chair and stared up at the ceiling for a minute. Then he dropped his gaze to Big Dave in front of him.

"So, you think the new owners of the Triple T are behind this new bout of rustling here in Lincoln County?" he asked.

"Does a bear shit in the woods?" replied Big Dave.

Woody laughed.

"Think about it," said Big Dave. "The rustling started right after the Triple T ranch got sold to some corporation. The timing is too close to be a coincidence."

"You know I don't believe in coincidences," replied Woody.

"Neither do I," said Big Dave.

"What other evidence do you have?" asked Woody.

"Did you get a full accounting from the sheriff's office about just how many cattle have been stolen and when and where?" asked Big Dave.

"I did," said Woody. Then he turned his chair and reached behind him to grab a thin file from his credenza.

"Take a look at this," said Woody. "I had my secretary reorganize the reports from the sheriff's office and type them up."

Woody handed the file to Big Dave. He opened the file and pulled out four pages of typed paper. Then he started to read the pages.

"I can save you some time," said Woody. "I did summaries on the last page."

Big Dave pulled out the last of the four pages and stared intently at it.

"What you see is that just in Lincoln County in the past six months, over four hundred and twenty head of cattle have been rustled. Each theft was at night and each theft was from four to five head of cattle. Where the rustlers were seen, which was seldom, they were using a pickup truck and a long, four horse trailer," said Woody.

Big Dave put down the file and thought for a minute. "Have there been any cattle stolen in Sweetwater County in the past five months?"

"None that was reported to the sheriff's office in Rock Springs," replied Woody.

"So, the rustlers are smart enough to do their thievin' away from where they are located," said Big Dave.

"Looks that way and that tells me the rustlers are not stupid," said Woody.

"Damn," said Big Dave.

"I agree," said Woody. "If the folks at the Triple T are holding cattle to resell, they are doing it in small lots. That way it takes longer for a rancher to realize he's had stock stolen and then report it. In addition, by taking only a few head at a time it's harder for a rancher to know he's had stock rustled. In addition, when they go to sell the cattle, they have a lot of mixed brands and no large lot of cattle from any one brand."

"They'd need a bill of sale to sell them cattle," said Big Dave.

"Forging a bill of sale ain't that hard, especially with small numbers of cattle," said Woody.

"We need to get on that ranch and inspect the herds," said Big Dave.

"Good luck with that," said Woody.

"Why?" asked Big Dave.

"You have no probable cause to get a warrant," replied Woody. "No judge around here is gonna give you a warrant when you have no tangible proof that the Triple T has anything to do with cattle stolen in Lincoln County."

"Shit," said Big Dave. "There's gotta be a way to get on that ranch and check the herds."

"Not legally, there isn't," replied Woody. "Let me do some research today and see if there is a loophole in the law we can use. I'll call you tomorrow with what I find."

"Thanks," said Big Dave. "I appreciate you helpin' me with this mess."

"Anytime," replied Woody.

Big Dave who folded the sheets of paper and slipped it in his shirt pocket.

The two friends stood, shook hands, and Big Dave was out the door. Minutes later he was headed south to the ranch. He was not happy.

CHAPTER FIFTY-NINE

When he got back to the ranch, Big Dave sat in a chair in his small cabin and stewed. He was frustrated. He was sure he knew who the rustlers were or at least who was running the cattle rustling operation, but he was powerless to legally get on the ranch in Sweetwater County and inspect the cattle herds there.

Finally, he got up and headed to the cook shack. It was supper time. He had not eaten much all day, and his stomach was complaining.

After dinner had been served and consumed, the men sat around the kitchen table drinking coffee. Big Dave knew they were hanging around because they hoped to hear some news from him about the pursuit of the rustlers.

After a couple of sips of coffee, Big Dave proceeded to tell them what he had learned on his trip to the Triple T Ranch. When he was finished, he looked around the men at the table and could see the disappointment in their faces.

Except for one. Travis had a different look on his face. It was one of excitement. Why he was excited made no sense to Big Dave.

He pointed at Travis. "You got somethin' to say, son?" he asked.

Travis looked a bit embarrassed at being called on like a kid in school who had not done his homework. But he soon got over it and then he spoke.

"Why don't we turn the tables on the rustlers?" he asked.

"What do you mean?" asked a puzzled Big Dave.

"You said we can't legally go on the ranch and look for stolen cattle," said Travis.

"That's right," replied Big Dave.

"What if we snuck on the ranch and took the cattle from there and herded them to a place where you have friends and we could hold them for a brand inspection," said Travis.

"Steal the cattle?" asked an astonished Big Dave.

"Think about it," said Travis. "What are they gonna do? If the cattle are stolen, how are they gonna prove the cattle belong to them? The brands on the cattle would keep them from going to the sheriff. They can't prove ownership so they would be admitting holding rustled cattle. Even they can't be that stupid," said Travis.

Big Dave was struck silent. Then he hit his fist on the table so hard several empty cups of coffee seemed to lift off the table briefly.

"That just might work," said Big Dave. "Let me make a couple of phone calls and get some folks together and work out a plan."

With that, Big Dave rose to his feet, clapped Travis on the shoulder and said, "Good work, son." Then he was out the door, headed for his small cabin.

• • •

While the men were having breakfast the next morning, pickup trucks began pulling into the ranch yard. By the time breakfast was over, a dozen trucks were parked haphazardly around the cook shack.

Big Dave soon had a crowd of almost twenty ranchers standing around him. He led them to his cabin, and they sat on chairs, the steps, and the small porch railing. The four ranch cowboys and the two brothers, along with Cookie, stood a ways back from the group, but they could hear every word spoken.

After a short meeting of about thirty minutes, most of the ranchers left in their trucks, leaving Big Dave and two other ranchers who retreated into Big Dave's small cabin. Two hours later, Big Dave and the two ranchers emerged, and the ranchers got in their trucks and drove off the ranch. Big Dave returned to his cabin. The cowboys looked at each other and then left to do their assigned chores for the day, including the two brothers. Cookie returned to the cook shack.

CHAPTER SIXTY

Two days had passed since the ranchers had gathered at Big Dave's cabin. During that time, he had put together a plan and had managed to gather the resources he felt he would need. He made a few phone calls to make sure everyone was on the same page and ready to go. Then he did something very uncharacteristic of him. He took a nap.

Immediately after supper, he, Shorty, Wes, and Travis climbed into two pickup trucks, each towing a two-horse trailer. Then they drove south towards Rock Springs. Just southeast of Rock Springs, they met up with ten other trucks, each towing a two-horse trailer. The trucks formed a caravan and headed southeast toward the Colorado border.

They ended their journey at the Mau sheep ranch, a large spread that lay just east of the Triple T ranch property. There they were greeted by Windy Mau, the owner of the ranch. He directed the trucks to park in a small pasture and the ranchers quickly unloaded and then saddled the horses they had brought. Each rider quickly slid a lever action rifle into a leather scabbard on the side of each horse.

The ranchers tied off their horses and headed to the big barn on the sheep ranch. Once inside they took seats on bales of hay that had been placed on the dirt floor of the old barn. Big Dave and Windy Mau were standing in front of the closed large rear door to the barn. Kerosene lanterns were hung on posts and standing on the tops of the sides of several wooden stalls to add light to the dark interior of the old barn. Two of Mau's sons stood by the sides of the barn's rear door.

When everyone was seated, Big Dave strode up in front of the assembly of armed ranchers. He looked out over the group and smiled.

"I know all of you are here tonight to reclaim your stolen stock and maybe get a bit of revenge. Our objective is to get back the stolen beef and any form of revenge ain't on the program. We need to do this fast. We need to do this clean with no slipups. If the plan works, you will all be headed home tomorrow with your stolen beef and hopefully no injuries or problems," said Big Dave.

"The plan is simple. At dark, we send in six men on horseback from different points onto the Triple T ranch. Mr. Mau's ranch borders the Triple T, so we launch from his spread," said Big Dave.

"The six men will use the night as cover and carefully patrol the Triple T and locate any herds of cattle and mark them on the little map each of them has been given," said Big Dave.

Then he turned to the barn door behind him. Mau's two sons took a large piece of white butcher paper and thumbtacked it to the barn door. Big Dave stepped up to the paper with a black magic marker. He drew a crude outline of the Triple T ranch and then Mau's ranch. He marked each point of entry to be used by the six scouts with a big X.

"Their scout will last two hours at the most. Then they will return to the Mau ranch and meet at this point," said Big

Dave as he pointed to a spot on the crude map and marked it with a large X.

"Once we have a good idea of where the cattle are located, we will enter the Triple T ranch and split up into groups and proceed to herd cattle to this point in the fence between the two ranches," said Big Dave, again pointing to the large X he had just made on the crude wall map.

"Me and Travis along with Mr. Mau and his two sons will remain here at the "X" on the map. We will cut the fence and make a good opening for you boys to drive the cattle through. Then we herd them back to the Mau ranch and put them in four temporary corrals the other ranchers will be erecting in the next few hours. Once we get the cattle in the corrals, we will run them through chutes and separate them by brand. Then each rancher will load up his cattle and head for home," said Big Dave.

Then he turned and faced the seated ranchers. "Any questions?" he asked.

One rancher stood up. "What if we get shot at?" he asked.

"Shoot back," replied Big Dave.

Another rancher stood. "What if they chase us onto the Mau ranch?" he asked.

"I don't think that will happen," said Big Dave. "First of all, it's Saturday night. I doubt there will be many Triple T hands on the ranch tonight. Secondly, they are stuck in a bit of a pickle."

"Pickle?" asked one rancher.

"Them cattle are all stolen. They got brands that ain't Triple T. They can't go to the sheriff and claim we're cattle thieves if the cattle don't belong to them. Even them dumb bastards will be able to figure out they been snookered and there ain't nothin' they can do about it," said Big Dave. "We're just stealin' back cattle that got stolen from us." Then he grinned.

Laughter rolled through the small crowd of ranchers,

"But be careful. I don't want nobody to get shot or hurt. If you get confronted, you run for it. Do not get caught in some stupid shootout. Understand?" said Big Dave.

All the ranchers nodded their understanding of Big Dave's instructions.

Big Dave looked at his watch. Then he looked up at the group of seated ranchers. "You six scouts need to mount up and move out. We'll be waitin' for you at the spot on the boundary fence I showed you on the map," he said.

Six of the ranchers, including Wes, got to their feet, and headed out to the front of the old barn. They mounted their horses and moved out of the barn area, the sound of their horse's hooves on the hard dirt the only sound that punctuated the silence of the darkening night sky.

Big Dave watched them disappear into the darkening sky. Then he turned to the rest of the group of ranchers. "Make sure your saddles are tight, and your guns are loaded," he said. "We meet back here in an hour."

CHAPTER SIXTY-ONE

The sky was cloudy and there was little if any moonlight. The riders split up and headed for different points on the fence line that separated the two ranches.

In slightly over half an hour each of the six riders had reached their destination point on the fence line and they cut the fence and entered the Triple T ranch.

Each rider carried a small notebook with a rough map of the ranch and his assigned area to inspect. The riders rode slowly, using handheld compasses to direct them. They moved slowly and occasionally stopped to look, listen, and smell their surroundings. When they found grazing or sleeping cattle, they noted the location and number of cows in their notebooks.

After they had been out for one and a half hours none of them had encountered anyone from the Triple T. With a half hour left, they turned and made their way back to the fence line where they had entered the ranch. All of them reached the fence line without being detected. Once there they followed the fence to the location Big Dave had given them.

As each of the six scouts reached the collection point, they could see a large group of saddled horses held by the figures of silent men in dark clothing, while standing silently and immobile like statues in the night.

Each scout rode up and dismounted, and then, one at a time, they gave their reports and maps to Big Dave. He talked quietly to each of the scouts and handed the notebooks to Travis, who made a tally of all the cows the scouts had seen.

When Big Dave finished talking with the last scout, he turned to Travis. "How many?" he asked.

"My total came to about six hundred and forty head," replied Travis.

"Hmmm. That's about two hundred and twenty head more than I thought," said Big Dave.

"We don't know how many of those cattle really belong to the Triple T," said Travis. "The count was of cattle, and it was in the dark."

"It don't matter none," said Big Dave. "We'll take all we can find and when we get to Mau's place, we'll sort them out. Any Triple T cattle we'll drive back to the fence and push them back onto the Triple T."

Big Dave then walked over to where the men and their horses were gathered in the darkness. He divided the group into four groups of six riders each. He handed one man in each group a small handmade map.

"Each of you men take your group to your assigned area and start moving them cattle back to this point on the fence line. If you get jumped by any Triple T men, fire three shots in the air and the rest of us will come runnin'" said Big Dave.

Big Dave walked over to his horse. He paused to look around him, then swung up onto the saddle. "Let's move out. We're burning time."

He then turned his horse's head towards the break in the fence and touched his spurs to her flank. The mare surged forward, and the rest of the men followed her into the black night in front of them.

Once past the fence, the four groups of riders separated and then disappeared into the dark of the night.

Travis and four other riders followed Big Dave. They rode for about twenty minutes and then found a sizeable herd of cattle gathered around a water tank at the base of an old windmill. Two of the riders rounded up the herd and headed back to where they had started on the fence line. Big Dave, Travis, and two other hands moved further into the section of the ranch they had been assigned.

They found six more groups of cattle and after an hour and a half they decided they had as many cattle as they could handle and turned the herd back toward the break in the fence line. The going was slow, but steady and other than a lone coyote, they saw nothing but cattle during their drive.

Big Dave and Travis were riding drag on the herd, when Big Dave saw something he didn't like.

"Shit!" he said in a low voice.

Travis pulled his horse to a stop and turned in the saddle to try to see what Big Dave had noticed.

There on the horizon, coming over a small rise, was a lone cowboy on horseback. He was moving slow and headed in no particular direction, but sooner or later he was bound to notice the herd.

Before Big Dave could decide what to do about this new threat, Travis dismounted, handed his reins to Big Dave, and then grabbed something out of his saddlebag. Then he began to run swiftly towards the unknown rider. When he got about thirty yards away, he came to a stop and pulled both his hands up. He pulled one hand back and then dropped it. No sound had been made, but suddenly the unknown rider fell from his horse like he had been poleaxed. The horse came to a stop and just stood there.

Travis ran back to where Big Dave was still holding the reins to Travis' horse. He took the reins and vaulted up onto the saddle.

"What the hell was that?" asked a still astonished Big Dave.

Travis grinned in the darkness. Then he held up his right hand with a small object in it.

"Slingshot," said Travis.

"Slingshot?" responded Big Dave. "What did you hit that feller with?"

"A ball bearing. Got a sack of them in my saddlebag," replied Travis.

"I'll be damned," snorted Big Dave. He looked over where the lone rider still lay motionless on the prairie. "He gonna be all right?"

"He'll be bruised and sore, but he should be fine," replied a confident looking Travis.

"Let's get these cattle off this ranch before more of them sumbitches show up," said Big Dave.

"Yes, sir," replied Travis.

They resumed their positions on the flanks of the herd of cattle and kept them moving toward the Mau ranch.

By five o'clock that morning, Big Dave's crew had moved five hundred and forty-two head of cattle off the Triple T ranch into a large fenced in area on the Mau ranch. Then, as daylight began to creep up over the eastern edge of the plains, cowboys began separating the cattle after running them through a livestock chute. The ranchers' men had set up separate pens for each ranch and the cattle were then herded into the correct pen depending on their brand.

Eight large semi-tractor trucks with long livestock trailers patiently waited side by side near the pens where they had been parked since they arrived during the night. Once the cattle were separated by brand, they were counted and then loaded onto the trucks.

It was almost noon before the sorting process was complete. Mau had his cook busy making a pancake breakfast and serving it to hungry cowboys.

Big Dave sat with Travis and five ranchers at a makeshift table with old barrels for seats. All of them were devouring pancakes and washing them down with hot coffee like it was their last meal.

Big Dave looked up as Windy Mau strode over to their table and squatted down on the ground next to him. Big Dave saw the tally book in Windy's hand.

"How many?" asked Big Dave.

"Your ranchers claimed four hundred twenty head stolen. We got five hundred forty-two in the pens. Four hundred and eleven head have your folks' brands. We also got one hundred thirty-one head with the Triple T brand, "said Windy.

"What do we do with the Triple T stock?" asked Windy.

Big Dave thought for a moment. Then he turned to the five ranchers at the table. "Can you get some of your boys to herd the Triple T stock back to their ranch?" he asked.

The five ranchers all grinned and Slim Tolliver said, "It'll be our damn pleasure, Dave."

"Well, that settles that," said Big Dave. "Any more of them pancakes left?"

The man at the table roared with laughter.

Big Dave just grinned.

CHAPTER SIXTY-TWO

Travis and his brother Steve sat nervously in the big leather chair in the large walnut paneled conference room of the law offices of Nate Chandler in Salt Lake City, Utah. They were dressed in the same knit golf shirts they had worn when they flew into the tiny airport in Kemmerer, Wyoming three months before. But instead of khaki pants, both of them wore faded blue jeans and cowboy boots.

Across from them sat Big Dave and Woody. Big Dave wore his everyday blue jeans and denim shirt. Woody wore a new looking linen summer suit complete with a University of Wyoming necktie.

Placed on the long gleaming mahogany conference table in front of Travis and Steve were their Stetson cowboy hats, crown-side down. Big Dave had kept his on his head.

Each of them had a cup of coffee in a fancy cup in front of them. Woody and Big Dave had emptied theirs. The two boys' coffee remained untouched.

The door to the conference room opened and in walked Nate Chandler. He wore an expensive silk suit of dark blue with a contrasting red silk necktie on a white silk shirt.

In his hand he held a small folder. He moved to the head of the table and took a seat. Then he looked up and welcomed all of them to the meeting,

"I have two items to complete this morning," he said.

"First, I need to thank Woody and Big Dave for all their assistance and hard work." Then he reached into the folder and withdrew a long white envelope.

"This is for you, Mr. Olson," said the attorney.

He handed the envelope to Big Dave, who took it and placed it in front of him without opening it.

Then Nate placed the folder on the table in front of him and looked directly at the two brothers.

"I have a bit of a surprise for your two young men," said Nate. "I know you are expecting a check for your three months of hard work, but it will not be coming from me."

With that he rose from his chair and walked over to the closed door to the conference room. He opened the door, and a man dressed in an expensive suit entered the room.

The man had a tanned face, a short stylish haircut, and no facial hair. He walked into the room and took a seat across from the two brothers.

"Do you boys recognize me?" he asked. Until he spoke, they had no idea who he was. His voice gave him away.

"Cookie?" asked a surprised Steve. Trevor found himself speechless.

"You have known me as Cookie for the past three months. I am a pretty accomplished trail cook, but my name is not Cookie. My name is Wayne Mann. I'm your father."

The room became instantly silent. Both sons, along with Woody and Big Dave had faces frozen with surprise,

Finally, Trevor broke the silence. "But our father is dead!" he said in a choked -up voice.

Mr. Mann smiled. "I am sorry for deceiving you, son, but I was forced to stay away from you for years and I decided I wanted to see what kind of men my sons were becoming. I determined a good test would be to work on a ranch for a summer as regular hired hands would tell me all I wanted to know. I made myself the cook so I could observe firsthand just who you were and what you were made of. I have to tell you that I am both pleased and proud of who both of you have become and I apologize for the deception, but I felt it was the only way for me to really know what kind of young men you had become."

Travis leapt out of his chair and rushed over to his father. Mr. Mann rose out of his chair, and both wrapped each other in a firm embrace. Steve quickly followed and the two sons and their father joined together in a three-way embrace.

When the three men, the father and his two sons finally broke the embrace, Mr. Mann reached inside his suitcoat pocket and pulled out two white envelopes. "I believe this is what you were promised if you fulfilled your end of the bargain and in my mind you most certainly did and earned every dollar of it." He then handed the envelopes to his surprised sons.

Still seated at the table, both Big Dave and Woody were grinning from ear to ear.

Big Dave rose to his feet and touched Woody on the shoulder. "Let's go, Woody. Our work here is done and now we are as out of place as two old whores in church."

Woody got out of his chair. Then he and Big Dave shook hands with Mr. Mann and his two sons and slipped out of the conference room.

On the drive back to Kemmerer, Big Dave was silent, but he had a smile on his face.

"What are you thinking about?" asked Woody.

"That young boy, Travis. He'll be back. He's a natural born cowboy," said a smiling Big Dave.

"I doubt it," replied Woody.

"I got a hundred bucks says he comes back to work on the ranch," said Big Dave.

"You got a bet," replied Woody.

Big Dave smiled.

THE END

ACKNOWLEDGEMENTS

This is the first story I ever wrote where I started out with an idea for a beginning, but I had no real idea of an ending. All I had was an idea for a story. When I felt I was almost done with the story, I realized I had no ending in mind. I had to sit down and think about it, but I still came up empty. That night I lay in bed and then it just came to me. It was so simple, so obvious, it was ridiculous.

I hope you enjoyed the story. As a father of three sons, none of whom take after any of their brothers, it was both fun and challenging.

I started this story over a year ago, but during December of 2023, my daughter, Christine, texted me to consider putting all of the short stories I had written each Christmas and put them together in a book. I stopped working on this novel and spent two months on the book of short stories. Then I resumed writing.

Writing this book was difficult for me. My wonderful wife, Nancy, had stage four cancer. My new job was to be a caregiver for her. It was a hard job for me. I had to learn to do things she did easily, but now could not perform those tasks. Some things I did better than others, but I was no match for what she had always done, seemingly effortlessly.

When she passed away on April 16, 2024, it hit me hard. I took several weeks to grieve, adjust, and try to move on. Then I discovered that when I was writing, my mind was focused on the novel, and not my situation.

I enjoyed writing and creating this story. There are bits and pieces of my life as a father in this story, but almost all of it is pure fiction.

As a father, you want the best for your children. Sometimes you get it. Sometimes you don't. But, no matter what happens, you are still their father.

I would like to acknowledge the amazing assistance and support I get from my small group of proofreaders and self-styled literary critics. They were particularly supportive during the creation of this novel.

I would like to recognize them. My oldest son, Steve Tibaldo from Athens, Alabama. My dear friend, Mary Marlin from Longmont, Colorado. My good friend and fellow fire department board member, Marcia McHaffie. My fraternity brother from Bethel, Connecticut, Craig Morrison. And my classmate from Galva, Illinois schools since the seventh grade, who now lives in Surprise, Arizona, Shirley Nordstrom Roth.

Last, but by no means least, is my loving wife, Nancy Lee Callis. She was my best critic, my best friend, and the love of my life. I will miss her forever.

This group of friends have given me incredible help and support in my efforts as a writer. A good friend is one who is not afraid to tell you the truth, even if you don't really want to hear it.

Lastly, I want to thank you, my reader, for buying my books and traveling with me into a world of fiction, where anything is possible.

If you would like me to know how you felt about the book, feel free to email me at <u>rwcallis@aol.com</u>.

Robert W. Callis

BOOKS BY ROBERT W. CALLIS

Kit Andrews Series:

Kemmerer	2010
Hanging Rock	2011
Buckskin Crossing	2013
The Ghosts of Skeleton Canyon	2015
The Night Hawk	2017
Above The Timberline	2018
The Reunion	2019
Swifty	2020
Doc Charlie	2021
The Reluctant Tracker	2022

Other Books:

The Horse Holder	2016
Big Dave	2023
Footprints	2024
The Test	2024